THE DRAGON AND THE
SERPENT-GODS

The attacking monster suddenly halted. The gaping mouth closed and the talons relaxed. Incredulous silence fell as the dragon slowly backed away, staring at the form taking shape before it.

Materializing from nothingness appeared a great, coiled serpent, with scales of burnished gold, its head rising majestically until its jewelled eyes were level with those of the dragon. Then, slowly solidifying, on the serpent's head there appeared a lovely woman, with raven hair, deep, dark eyes, and skin of rose-tinted ivory. She was dressed in a cobweb robe of palest blue, through which gem-encrusted gold breastplates were visible. A sparkling silver crown was on her head and jewels of lapis lazuli about her neck.

Alan MacDougall recognized her now. She was the Goddess Inanna as he had seen her walking toward the Great Below—and toward her death!

Also by Lloyd Arthur Eshbach
Published by Ballantine Books:

THE LAND BEYOND THE GATE

The Armlet of The Gods

Lloyd Arthur Eshbach

A Del Rey Book

BALLANTINE BOOKS • NEW YORK

For Don and Dan,
my sons

CONTENTS

Background:
Beyond the First Portal

When Malcolm MacDougall's archeological search led him to an abandoned tower in the Scottish Highlands, he found a tiny bronze sword—and, incredibly, remembered it as his own. Moments later, he was attacked by Caermarthen, an ancient Druid. He killed the Druid, thereby freeing the last of the Little People—the Sidhe—from their ensorcellment. Then Malcolm suddenly found his essence fusing with Cinel Loarn, leader of the band, while his abandoned body fell to the ground.

Several years later, Alan MacDougall came to the tower, searching for his lost brother. He found Malcolm's remains and those of the Druid—and also an ancient scroll, the Druid's sword, and a golden armlet in the shape of a two-headed serpent. These he picked up, slipping the armlet on.

When he looked around, he found everything changed. The previously bare walls now bore four bronze Portals. He opened one, to see a land totally unfamiliar and a road leading to a distant, beautiful city. On the road, in a caravan, was a lovely woman.

Alan stepped through to the road in the mysterious land. There he was attacked by a band of Outcasts, but saved by Taliesin—the ancient Bard of Celtic mythology!

The Bard took Alan to his home in the city and explained that this was Tartarus, a land created by Lucifer for the Daughters of Lilith. They were gone, and now those who dwelt there were Celtic gods and groups of men who had all died on Earth fourteen hundred years ago, but had been recreated here, to live in eternal boredom.

That night, half-asleep, Alan suddenly began to hear telepathically the council of Danu, Nuada, and the other gods. They spoke of him, greatly excited; since he had come from the Other World without first dying, he must know the location of the Gate, which they had sought for centuries for their escape back to the real Earth! Some advised forcing Alan to reveal the secret immediately, but Danu, the mother of the gods, quelled that idea for the moment.

Next morning, Alan was visited by a group of Druids, obviously sent by the evil gods to pry the secret from him. Taliesin helped to thwart them and send them away. But later, returning from a visit to Darthula, the woman he had seen on the road, Alan was attacked. He fled to the Hall of the Dead, a Forbidden Area to all others, where he saw stored bodies reanimated and leaving to replace any who were killed in accidents or fighting.

When he returned to the Bard, he learned that Darthula had been kidnapped to use in blackmailing him. To free her, he went with Taliesin to Murias, home of the twisted Fomorians. There the Bard went to seek news of her, leaving Alan, cloaked in invisibility, behind. But Alan was forced to flee, pursued by the evil gods and a band of the Fomorians changed into wolves.

He was rescued by Danu and Dagda. But they left him when he went to explore a golden tower which they could not see and which was in a Forbidden Area. He was welcomed into the tower by Ahriman, who claimed to be Lucifer's lieutenant, and was shown the model with which Ahriman could control everyone and everything in Tartarus.

Soon after he left the tower, he was rejoined by Taliesin, who told him Darthula had been restored to her city. They went there, where Alan found a few days of peace. But already, the gods were fomenting war over who should force the secret from Alan. It was all pointless, since the Bard had learned from the scroll that any from Tartarus who went through the Gate would wither to dust. But they could not believe that.

Caught up in the war, Alan managed to escape and fled toward the Gate, using the invisibility which he had mastered. But he was spotted. Mad Dalua and Balor of the Evil Eye pursued him. Then, as he neared the Gate, Ahriman turned off the aurora that was the only light source for Tartarus.

Alan managed to find the Gate in the dark and plunge through, but Balor came right behind, and the Evil Eye could kill before the god disintegrated. Then Alan saw that Cinel Loarn, and the Sidhe were there to help him. They drove their swords into Balor as he came through, driving him back, mortally wounded.

Alan went out into the Highlands, thankful to be back and determined to forget the tower and the Gates forever...

CHAPTER 1

The Call From Beyond

West of Ballydhu, the rutted gray road entered a dark and lonely glen, peat-covered slopes rising to right and left, ending in craggy outcroppings of dull red sandstone that seemed to gash the lowering gray of the sky. Moorland, three or four hundred yards wide, made up the floor of the narrow valley. Stunted and thinly growing grass along the roadsides, merging into the black of peat, was the only sign of life in the bleak spectacle, except for the tussocks of green rising here and there from the blacker waters of the bog.

The valley walls seemed to meet on the western horizon, where, for a moment, a crimson sliver of setting sun slashed through the clouds, then vanished.

Scowling, Alan MacDougall stared through the lone window in his scantily furnished room in *The Red Bull of Ballydhu,* barely aware of the sound of voices and the clink of glasses rising from the public room on the lower level. As he watched, coils of fog crept silently down the slopes to settle on the floor of the glen, to thicken and grow as though to hide the sullen scene from his sight.

By all that's holy, he thought, why build an inn at a spot like this? Without intending to, he spoke aloud. "More to the point, why are *you* here?"

As MacDougall turned away from the window, he caught a glimpse of himself in the small mirror over the shabby dresser. He halted, frowning at his image. The well-groomed blond hair and beard scarcely registered on his consciousness; rather, he looked squarely into the slightly narrowed blue eyes.

"Why *are* you here?" he continued. "Not just in Ballydhu—but in Scotland. Why aren't you home in the States? Be honest with yourself, MacDougall. Five weeks of driving around Scotland, just to see the country? You know that's bilge. You're waiting for something to happen."

And he knew what that something was. Five weeks ago he had escaped from an unbelievable world and an incredible experience—and he could not rid himself of the conviction that the adventure had not ended. He glanced toward the long, narrow, black leather case standing in a shadowed corner—a case he'd had made to hold his sword, the weapon he had borne in that Other World. It was an awkward thing to carry about Scotland unconcealed, and somehow he knew he'd be wearing it again.

There was more; reluctantly he admitted it. Four weeks ago he had phoned Heathrow Airport in London to book flight to New York and, even as he talked, he had felt a strong mental influence negating the very thought of his leaving. He had rationalized, had convinced himself that he must take advantage of the chance really to see the country of his ancestors—he needed the vacation; he could afford to do as he pleased. That was when he had bought the used Austin-Morris and had set out on his aimless wandering. And here he was—waiting.

He looked squarely into the eyes of his reflection. Time for complete honesty, MacDougall. That rejection of his thought of leaving—what was its source? Certainly it was not his own idea—which left only Ahriman, the self-styled lieutenant of Lucifer and the controlling power in that Other World. If it was Ahriman, that meant not only that the Persian could influence his thoughts outside of Tartarus, but that he had Alan under observation! It was a disturbing idea, to say the least. Alan saw in memory the impressive and forbidding figure in his conical tower, invisible to all in the Other World, seen only by himself through the power of the armlet. He felt a sudden surge of anger; he also felt a stab of fear.

Again the armlet! Why had he ever touched the accursed thing?

He caught up his suitcase, dropped it on the bed, then switched on the overhead light, a weak shadeless bulb centered and suspended from the ceiling. He hesitated, then bolted the door. So far as he knew, he was the only guest in the inn, but there were patrons in the pub, plus a maid—and he did not want unexpected company.

Unlocking the suitcase, he extracted an object, half-buried under soiled clothes and wrapped in several thicknesses of heavy woolen cloth. His pulse quickened as he brought it to light. This was at the root of everything that had happened.

It was a massive red-gold armlet; slowly he turned it in his fingers, examining it intently, as if seeking with sight and touch to fathom its mysteries. Only twice since leaving the Highlands had he handled it. The first time had been to pack it in the suitcase. The second was when, awakening from an unusually troublesome nightmare in which the armlet figured strongly, he had decided to get rid of it. He'd sought out a pawnshop and had entered with the jewel in his jacket pocket. When he had grasped it to offer it to the pawnbroker, the same negation which had prevented his booking flight had poured into his mind. He had thought of the powers it had given him and of the mystery surrounding it. He had left the shop after making a lame inquiry about a watch displayed in the window.

The armlet, nearly four inches across and about two inches wide, was a four-coiled, two-headed serpent, both jaws gaping and its pointed tail curving upward to end within a half inch of the lower head. It was a masterpiece of the goldsmith's art, minute triangular scales, perfectly formed, covering each cylindrical coil, as if an actual snake had been placed in position, reduced in size, then magically changed into solid gold.

The twin heads—there lay its almost hypnotic fascination. The jaws spread wide in lifelike fashion with laidback fangs; the forked tongues were carved of crystalline ruby; and the strangely mismatched eyes were oval cabochons of identical size. One head held a coldly blue aquamarine and a four-rayed moonstone; the other a flawless emerald and a blood-red ruby.

He thought of his first experience with the jewel and the tricks it had played with his sight. When he had put it on his arm, it had clung as if it were part of him, defying removal, and had opened his sight to a Gateway into the Other World—four Gateways, actually, though he had opened and gone through only one.

He had pictured his finding the jewel, lying amid mouldering brown bones on the floor of an ancient round stone tower in the Highlands, where he had also found his sword, a very old vellum scroll—or maybe that should be Scroll, considering its later importance—and the long-dead body of his brother Malcolm—Malcolm who, he later learned, had become by some inexplicable transformation one of the Sidhe, the Little People. He shook his head in doubt he could never completely dispel, though he *knew* the impossible had happened; then he thrust aside all thought of the traumatic and mystifying events.

Of one thing he was certain—he was *not* going to put the armlet on again!

Why not? The question struck him solidly. If he wanted something to happen, why not make it happen? For that matter, there was no certainty that anything *would* happen; after his return from Tartarus it had become—just a jewel. Alan's jaws tightened stubbornly. He was taking no chances. He didn't *want* things to happen; he just felt they would. But there was no point in hurrying the matter.

Carefully, he laid the armlet on the dresser beside three stacked books. Deliberately, he turned his thoughts from the jewel, picking up the top volume, *The Magic Arts in Celtic Britain*; the second was *Mythology of the British Islands*; and the third was a Bible. The three volumes had filled his evenings ever since he had found them in a used book shop in Edinburgh. It was fascinating to read about people whom he had met in the Other World, dead for fourteen centuries, yet alive in a land—and in bodies—created by Lucifer. He'd found Lucifer in the Bible with the help of the concordance and marginal notes. And in the other two books he found Taliesin, as well as Danu, Nuada, and others of the ancient Celtic gods, the *Tuatha de Danann*, but all were pale shadows of the gods and goddesses he had met.

Strange, he thought; there was no slightest hint about the armlet nor, for that matter, about the golden tower and its occupant, the self-named Ahriman.

Suddenly Alan MacDougall stiffened.

He was being watched! Some inner sense was acutely aware of eyes fixed upon him. It was an uncomfortable feeling, something he had experienced in days gone by. He recalled the time in the Other World when he was being followed by the invisible Dalua, the Witless One, and had felt the god's gaze upon him.

He turned toward the window, then flicked off the light and looked out into a darkening world gray with velvety fog. No one could be peering through that veil. Feeling foolish, he glanced around the room, concentrating on the door. Light from the hallway marked the space beneath it and outlined its sides and top, but nowhere could it permit spying; there was not even a keyhole. It was only imagination, probably, though momentarily the feeling had been so intense.

The armlet caught his eye, the polished gold reflecting

a vagrant gleam from the hallway. The gem-eyes were watching! He felt a fleeting chill, then grimaced with annoyance. For an instant those eyes had seemed to glow.

Startlingly, there came a burst of raucous laughter, rising from the pub. MacDougall shook himself; he'd better snap out of this; it was getting on his nerves. A visit to the lower floor might be a good idea. He'd had an early dinner—food no better than it needed to be—but a bit of wine might clear his head, though it usually worked in reverse.

There came another burst of laughter from below; and Alan suddenly decided he was not in the mood for hilarity. He crossed to the window to look into the wall of gray. The men of Ballydhu would have trouble finding their ways home tonight, especially after they'd had a "wee drap" more than they should have had. He thought of another fog, magically created in the Other World, and the recollection was dreamlike, unreal.

The room was in semidarkness now, with the only illumination the light filtering in from the hallway. Alan dropped onto the lone chair and looked steadily at the armlet, its twinned heads still dimly visible. He relaxed and closed his eyes.

He thought of the land he had called Tartarus, of Taliesin the Bard of Bards, of Darthula the lovely, of the gods, the *Tuatha de Danann*, so very human, and of the Four Cities, strange and beautiful, out of myth. One image merged with another and became a phantasmagoria of magic and dancing aurora above armored Norsemen and pastel-robed Ch'in; and hazily superimposed over all was the coldly mocking face of Ahriman. Then everything was suddenly swept aside by a single startling vision.

The serpent armlet—incredibly, it had begun to glow, emitting a soft golden light! As suddenly, it was twice, thrice its original size, still growing—now as thick as a strong man's arm! And as it grew, losing none of its solidity or details, it slowly uncoiled, the twin heads rising, turning, and facing each other, gaping mouths closing.

Golden ripples ran up the scaled forms as sinews moved; and the eyes—the strangely mismatched eyes—were subtly aflame. Gaze met gaze and held; and Alan thought from pallid moonstone and icy aquamarine came sly mockery, and from fiery ruby and verdant emerald, haughty arrogance. Both gave the impression of dark wisdom and power as ancient as the dawn of time.

Alan MacDougall was afraid.

He felt his scalp tighten, muscles tense, jaws clench, and the blood drain from his face. He had felt fear under the hard eyes of Ahriman, but nothing like the dread that held him now. Ahriman was a man, at least in outward form, but nothing as alien as this jewel come to life. And that serpent—he had worn it, had gained from it unearthly powers!

A voice formed in his mind; and he knew without knowing how he knew that the words came from the serpent head with the haughty eyes.

"So at long last, my Lord Enki, you have decided the time has come for us to reveal ourselves to the mortal. As always I bow to your wisdom. Perhaps now he will learn more quickly. But as you know, such revelation was forbidden—"

"Forbidden?" There was derision in the reply. "Not, my Lady Inanna, by the Lord of Light. Only by the one who dares to call himself Ahriman . . . But we are neglecting our—master!" MacDougall sensed a vast amusement in the thought as the four gem-eyes fixed themselves on him.

The head of the Lord Enki addressed him silently. "We are two who have become one. I am the Lord of Wisdom, the Lord of the Waters of the Abyss, the God Enki. I have been before the worlds were formed." White and blue eyes flamed with frigid fire. "I have been Muchalinda who dwelt under the Tree of Trees, who sheltered the great Buddha; I who knew the food of life and the water of life. I have been Kaliya with breath of fire who frightened Krishna on the banks of the River Yamuna. I have been Shesha the Mighty. And I—" Bitterness freighted the words. "—I am imprisoned in this band of gold."

The thought changed, coming from the mind of the one whom Enki had called my Lady Inanna. "Goddess am I, older than time. The Queen Inanna was I called when Ur of the Chaldees was young. In Egypt I was Neveb-Kau and Uazit. I was—no, I *am* Durga the Creatrix, Chandra the Fierce, Kali the Destroyer; aye, and Nintu and Kandalini and Bhanjangi." Ruby and emerald eyes burned with fierce intensity. "And I am bound, enslaved!"

"You claim over much, my Lady Inanna," the Lord Enki commented mockingly. "Where were you when I was in the Garden of Yahweh where grows the Tree of Wisdom and the Tree of Life? Where—"

"Where was I?" Queen Inanna interrupted indignantly. "I was in that Garden reasoning as woman to woman with that silly Eve. As for my boasting—jealousy moves your tongue because you know my worshipers were ten thousand to one of yours. And had it not been—"

A question hastily asked halted the tirade; and Alan MacDougall realized incredulously that he had somehow had the temerity to interrupt. "How did you get where you are now—together in this jewel?"

After a brief pause, the Lord Enki answered, reluctantly, it seemed, "You ask, and we must answer. Inanna, will you tell the tale?"

Communication came that was startlingly new to the mind of Alan MacDougall—as if he were drawing from wells of memory scenes long forgotten, now recalled with total fidelity. Mingled with the visions were verbal comments, narration; together they formed imagery as real as life.

"In the long and long ago when Sumer rose to greatness, I was goddess of the seven cities. Goddess was I of Uruk and Badtibara, of Zabalam and Adab, of Nippur and Kish and Akkad."

MacDougall saw sharp against a deep blue sky, cloudless and aflame with sunlight, the walls and palm-shaded

terraces, the towers and ziggurats of ancient cities. Wide
rivers flowed by, crowded with exotic vessels. Wide streets
were thronged with bright-robed men and women. All was
seen as from high above. And over all hovered a vision
of dark beauty, with skin of rose-tinted ivory, long, arrow-
straight hair, shimmering ebon-black, and eyes as dark—
Inanna!

"From the Great Above, I set my mind toward the
Great Below. I, the Queen Inanna, set my mind from the
Great Above to the Great Below, where dwelt my sister-
self Ereshkigal and the Lord Gugulanna, her husband,
whom death had claimed."

With the words came a vision of a realm wrought of
the stuff of rainbows, ephemeral as a nightingale's song,
of castles built of clouds, of mountains formed of dreams,
crumbling as they formed, and of scintillating sapphire
seas and emerald woodlands—all vanishing even as they
appeared. The Great Above.

"Although it was forbidden by the Bringer of Light for
one in the Great Above to visit the Great Below, I purposed to do so. There would be danger, for there was
anger and jealousy in the hearts of those in the nether
realm; but Ereshkigal was my sister-self, image of my
image, and surely she would bid me welcome. Yet because
I could not see what lay ahead, in prudence I did what
could be done.

"I called Ninshubur, the messenger of favorable winds,
the warrior who fought by my side, and Ilabrat the winged
one, and told them that if I did not return, it would be
because I had been treated evilly and had my life taken
from me. Then should they weep before Enlil, god of the
air, and weep before Nanna, the moon-god, and if these
did naught, to weep before Enki, the Lord of Wisdom,
who knows the food of life and the water of life. He, I
said, would surely bring me to life.

"I prepared to descend to the nether world."

MacDougall sensed the lovely Queen Inanna in her
night-blue and gold-flecked bath of paneled lapis lazuli;

attending her was a score of short-kirtled maidens, bare above the waist, with shoulder-length hair squarely shorn. Bathed and anointed with rare creams and unguents, Inanna was then adorned.

"The seven divine decrees which could not be seen I fastened to my side; the *shugurra*, the crown of the plain, my maidens placed upon my head. The ointment of radiance they applied to my countenance. The rod of lapis lazuli I held in my hand. A necklace of skillfully wrought lapis lazuli they placed about my neck; then a breastplate of fine gold they bound around my breast; upon it they placed many chains of sparkling stones. A golden ring they put upon my finger and the blue robe of royalty upon my body.

"And I, the Goddess Inanna, walked toward the nether world."

MacDougall seemed to be in a dark, cylindrical well and was aware of an endless descent with the Goddess, down and down on a spiral stone stairway, smooth when it began, but growing steadily rougher as it progressed until, at its end, it scuffed Inanna's sandaled feet.

"I came at last to the Great Below, to the palace where ruled my self-sister; to the first Gate of the palace of the nether world I came. And there was I greeted by Neti, Chief Keeper of the Palace Gate. All alone, I came to the first Gate of the palace of Ereshkigal."

Stark and forbidding, the blue-and-gold walls loomed out of the darkness, more fortress than castle. Behind it, remotely distant, dimly perceived, rose the smoldering red of burning, shot through with sulphurous yellow and gray-black smoke. Before the Great Gate towered Neti, barring entrance. He asked, "Who are you who come unbidden to the house of the Queen Ereshkigal?"

Inanna answered, "The Queen of the Great Above, the place of eternal dawn."

Neti asked, "If you are Queen of the Great Above, why have you come to the land where none return? You know it is forbidden."

Inanna answered, "Ereshkigal my sister grieves for her husband, the Lord Gugulanna. I have come to grieve with her."

Inanna picked up the tale again in her own words. "Neti, after telling me to tarry while he spoke with his Queen, left me there, waiting like a suppliant outside the Gate. Then Neti returned and I followed him into the castle. Inside the first Gate there were those who guarded; and one of them removed my *shugurra*, the crown of the plain. When I objected, Neti told me I should not question the perfected decrees of the nether world or its rites."

As the narrative continued, MacDougall saw a vision of Neti the Gatekeeper leading the Queen Inanna through one dark corridor after another and through portal after portal.

"At the second Gate, my rod of lapis lazuli was taken; and again Neti said I should not question the perfected decrees of the nether world. Upon my passing through the third Gate, the necklace of lapis lazuli was removed; and again, when I protested, Neti spoke as before.

"At the fourth Gate, the sparkling stones were removed from my breast; at the fifth, the ring was taken from my finger; at the sixth, I lost my golden breastplate; and at the seventh, all the raiment of my body was removed. When I asked why, again I was told not to question the perfected decrees of the nether world.

"Naked as a slave came I before my sister Ereshkigal and the seven judges of the nether world, the Anunnaki."

The throne that Alan saw was of polished black stone, inlaid with gold and gems in great profusion, standing high on a dais in the center of a great vaulted chamber. Below it, forming a wide half circle, were seven lesser thrones, holding seven judges. The Queen Ereshkigal sat resplendent in cloth-of-gold; on her night-black hair rested a high, glittering crown. The face of the queen was as the face of Inanna, but there was malice in her eyes and unholy joy in the smile on her scarlet mouth. She uttered no greeting as the Lady Inanna was led before her; nor did the red-robed judges speak. Inanna attempted greeting, but Ereshkigal motioned her to silence; and the Anunnaki bade her kneel.

"Then Neti made accusation concerning my trespass," Inanna continued, "and the judges stared at me in my nakedness. Their eyes were as the eyes of death. They judged without word, looking one to the other; and my self-sister continued smiling, with no word uttered in my defense. By a look, the Anunnaki brought death to me— to me, the Goddess Inanna. And they hung my body in a dark place alone from a stake."

MacDougall felt the repressed fury in the thought of the Queen Inanna. A grim picture formed. A wide, bleak plain with a high and shadowed ceiling as in a vast cavern, with the limply hanging body of Inanna suspended from the arm of an inverted L . Behind it, tinting the sad form of the Queen of the Dawn like a baleful sunrise, rose the somber glow of yellow-red fires; in the flickering shadows, there seemed to be skulking figures, slightly darker than the shadows.

"For three days and three nights, my body hung there. Then, in the Great Above, my messenger Ninshubur raised cries of distress to all who would hear. She wept before Enlil, god of the air; and she wept before Nanna, moon god of Ur; but they gave no heed. Then she cried to Enki, Lord of Wisdom—and he heard."

The thought of the serpent-mind of Enki continued the tale. "I heard and I cried out, 'What has Inanna done? I am troubled. What now has the Queen of all the lands done—the Queen of the Great Above—what has she done? I am troubled.' So I searched and from afar I saw her. Then of clay I fashioned two beings, one a *kurgarra*, the other a *galatur*, and gave them of my life. I prepared them to do my bidding. To the *kurgarra* I gave the food of life; to the *galatur*, the water of life.

"I gave them my instructions and sent them into the Great Below. From the life within them, they were to direct the warmth of fire upon the body taken down from the stake. Sixty times were they to sprinkle it with the food of life, and sixty times with the water of life. They did so, and Inanna arose.

"When Inanna arose, her self-sister Ereshkigal fled; and with her fled the seven judges, the Anunnaki, into the dark of the nether world."

The Queen Inanna continued the tale: "When I came again to life and walked toward the castle of Ereshkigal, out of the shadows poured the dead, the demons from the nether world. From the pit came the thousands and the thousand thousands to run behind and before me. And my self-sister Ereshkigal, knowing, fled in terror into the deeper dark, and the Anunnaki and all in the castle with her. It was in my mind to tell her not to question the perfected decrees of the Great Above as I slew her, but she had fled."

In disordered profusion, the pictures passed before Alan MacDougall's perception. A vast unnumbered multitude swept up from dark and shadowed places. The Queen Inanna stalked with regal tread toward the castle of lapis lazuli. He saw the flight of Ereshkigal and the seven judges, of Neti the Gatekeeper and all the guards, and the rising tide of the released dead going round and round through the endless spiraling stairway from the nether world to the Great Above.

The Queen Inanna continued, "When I ascended from the nether world, the small demons and the large demons followed; into the land of the sunrise they came dancing and shouting; with wild rejoicing they came. Long and long they poured up the stairs, the thousand thousands.

"And I, the Queen of the Dawn, sought the Lord Enki, the Lord of All Knowledge—"

Enki interrupted. "In her serpent form came my Lady Inanna. And in our joy we became as one—we merged into one—"

Inanna spoke, her thought filled with sorrow. "And the Great One, the Anointed One, the Lord of Light, Lucifer himself, watching, was not pleased. He was not pleased with what we had done. The separation he had made had been undone and he was not pleased. And judgment was passed."

Enki continued. "And his judgment—we who were as one would remain so, in the shape he chose, serving until we had accomplished his purpose. And the golden armlet came into being—"

A loud crash shattered the stillness, and a deep voice bellowed, "I'll ha' nae fechtin' i' the Red Bull! Robbie, ye're drunk, an' ye're a daft fule. An' Angus, ye'll be payin' for yon chair. Oot—oot, the baith o' ye!" There was a rumble of other voices and the slamming of a door.

At the first jarring noise, Alan MacDougall sprang to his feet, his eyes staring wide and unseeing in the semi-dark. Disoriented and with heart thudding, he tried to remember where he was. His thoughts were a hodgepodge of wild questioning, of recollection of a fantastic tale of a god and goddess, and of a great two-headed serpent, male and female—the Lord Enki and the Lady Inanna—

He must have fallen asleep, and the crash from the pub below had jarred him awake. What a dream! Memory returned. He had been staring at the golden armlet—had closed his eyes . . .

Automatically, his gaze turned toward the dresser top where he had placed the serpent-jewel. With a gasp he leaped to the light switch and flicked it.

The armlet was not there! It was gone! But that could not be. He checked the door—the bolt was still in place. Yet the armlet was gone.

No!

As if paralyzed, he froze at a sudden thought. He felt a familiar weight on his upper right arm. His left hand groped, touching the coiled serpent beneath his sleeve.

MacDougall slumped onto his chair, trying to bring order to his reeling thoughts. Somehow, while he dozed and dreamed that unparalleled dream, he must have gotten up and slid the armlet into place, prodded, probably, by his subconscious, his thinking about his waiting for something to happen. Even the mental suggestion that he put it on was logical enough.

But what was logical about that dream? Every detail was etched in his memory. Doubt began to awaken. Dream? If dream, whence had come those strange names? None had been mentioned in any of the books he had just read—of that he was certain—nor in anything he had read in the past. And certainly he had heard nothing of them in Tartarus. Were they names and incidents born of his imagination? Absurd! His mind didn't work that way.

Restlessly MacDougall paced about the small room. He became aware of the creaking of the floorboards and crossed to the window, staring out into the world of gray. There was nothing to be seen; the fog was like a moist blanket, touching the pane inches from his face. On impulse, he raised the window and took a deep breath of the damp, dank air. He could see the tendrils of fog writhing and twisting, and figures seemed to be forming. They were the ghostly echo of the visions appearing in his dream.

"Dream, hell!" MacDougall exclaimed, slamming shut the window and crossing to the door. He shot the bolt, descended the stairway, and entered the pub.

The landlord, Jamie MacKenna, was just vanishing into a back room, carrying pieces of a broken chair. A handful of villagers still lingered; they seemed to do their best to appear unaware of Alan's arrival. Returning to the bar, MacKenna greeted MacDougall.

"I troost th' wee bit tribble didna disturb ye, Meester M'Dougall. Twa o' th' lads let the dreenk get th' upper hand; they sud be able tae tak their drappie cannily an' no' mak fules o' themsel'. But Angus an' Robbie, noo— a gless or twa o' speerits turned their heads. There's nae denyin'—"

"Think nothing of it," Alan hastily interrupted. "I've come down for a nightcap. A glass of your best red wine, please."

He was served briskly by the rotund landlord. "A deil o' a nicht," the latter commented. "It'll be rain afore the morn, I doot. Aye, it's gaun tae be an oncome, I'm thinkin'."

Several hours—and glasses of wine—later, when Alan made his way to his room, he had almost convinced himself that he had indeed been dreaming, despite the jewel on his arm. For some reason, the details of his dream were a bit confused now. He was quite relaxed when he slid under the covers, his eyelids heavy. By morning, his thinking would be clearer.

"Alan—Alan MacDougall! Taliesin!" The words formed clearly in his mind. *"Can you hear me? This is the bard Taliesin. I don't want to ask this, Alan—but if you can, return through the Gate. Your world and mine require it. I would not ask, were it not of greatest importance. The Scroll—"*

As suddenly as it came the thought was cut off.

Taliesin! Dazedly, he repeated the name of his first and best friend in that other realm, whose deciphering of the vellum Scroll had ultimately made possible Alan's return to his own world. Taliesin had revealed some of the mysteries of Tartarus—and now he was calling for Alan to come back.

Wide awake now, all the wine-induced tranquility gone, Alan MacDougall lay in the silent dark, staring into nothingness.

CHAPTER 2

The Four Gates

The narrow road, little traveled, meandered on its course for mile upon mile through the lonely Scottish country-side. Alan MacDougall drove mechanically, with scarcely a thought given to the austere scenery flowing by. He was driving now with a definite destination, no longer wandering aimlessly. Somewhere ahead lay the village of Kilmona, from which he hoped to find his way back to an ancient stone tower in an oak grove.

The decision to return to the Other World had not been arrived at easily. Indeed, though he knew he was going back, he was still beset with misgivings—and that was totally unlike him. Normally, when he decided a matter, he carried it out without second thoughts.

What did he expect to accomplish by his return? The obvious answer was release from the armlet. And, he added grimly, the chance to get a night of undisturbed sleep. A chilling thought came. Would he be permitted to shed the twin-headed serpent? Or would he have to play out the game, whatever it was, to its conclusion? He had been given one chance to get away—or had he really? Even that was not a certainty.

He had gone through the Gateway the first time on impulse, accepting the challenge to see what was there, to solve an intriguing mystery. Going back, knowing what he faced—at least *something* of what he faced—was another matter entirely. That island he called Tartarus was a land of the dead! Everyone in that realm had died, including Taliesin. But they were alive and had bodies. They were not phantoms or ghosts. They were living— in bodies created by Lucifer!

What was death? A transition from one plane of existence to another, or so it appeared. The great leveler, it was called; but in Tartarus there were high and low, master and serf, even as here in this life. Shakespeare, he believed it was, had written, "A man can die but once." How wrong he was.

Cut it out, MacDougall, Alan told himself. You're getting morbid.

The road led up a steady rise and curved around the shoulder of a ridge. Beyond lay a Highland loch, like a mirror held in the hands of green-cloaked hills. His course followed the shoreline, bearing to the left. Ahead, where the loch ended, Alan could see steeper hills rising ruggedly, like barriers against the world. He had been told to watch for this loch as a landmark; Kilmona had not appeared on any map he had been able to find. But it was evident now that he was approaching the village he sought.

And that meant he was getting closer to the stone *broch* and the bronze Gate—and Tartarus!

With the thought came the recollection never far from the surface—the story of the armlet and of the serpent-gods, the Lord Enki and the Queen Inanna. He had tried to avoid thinking about the fantastic tale; but despite every effort, the images recorded in his mind returned again and again.

The two gods were the source of the powers the armlet had given him! And with that thought came a recurring question. Would that magic power work here and now? Invisibility, telepathy, and, according to Ahriman, powers beyond any possessed by the ancient Celtic gods of Tartarus. That included—who knew what? The creation of illusions and perhaps even physical transference from place to place. He felt his pulse quicken. If the armlet's magic worked here, there was no limit to what he could do—not that he had any reason to think it would work outside Lucifer's domain.

But he wanted no part of such powers! He couldn't be trusted—nor could anyone else—with a working magic. Thoughts like these had troubled his slumbers; they were no less disturbing in broad daylight. Better get back into Tartarus before he was too greatly tempted to try.

He had thought of attempting to reach Taliesin to get more information, but had rejected the idea. It would be time enough to meddle with the serpents after he re-entered the Other World.

The blue waters fell away behind him, and the road wound deeper into the Highlands, passing through a narrow gorge of granite-gray rock; then before him opened a broad strath, in the heart of which lay the tiny hamlet of Kilmona. Alan recognized it immediately, recalling its whitewashed houses with their gray roofs and double chimneys, clustered around the white church, its slender, graceful steeple pointing heavenward, with a golden cross at its apex.

About a mile beyond Kilmona lay the farm of Duncan Cameron, the dwelling nearest the spot where Alan had come upon the road after his descent from the ancient stone tower. There he had eaten a belated and hearty breakfast before heading into the village. By good fortune, he had found a lorry delivering supplies to Kilmona's only store and had been able to secure a ride to the nearest rail station. It was at Cameron's that he hoped to leave the Austin-Morris during his stay in the Other World.

Slowly, Alan drove along the main street of Kilmona, the only street deserving the designation, and past the general store; beyond that, set back from the road on a carefully groomed lawn, was the white-steepled kirk. Behind it lay an ancient churchyard with its weathered gravestones; nearby, Alan caught a glimpse of a one-story school with a gray slate roof. Except for a few children, who stopped whatever they were doing to watch the passing car, and the clanging of a hammer on anvil rising from a hidden blacksmith's shop, the village appeared deserted.

In moments, Alan left Kilmona behind him, entering a wide expanse of rolling fields, dotted here and there with small farmhouses and their retinue of buildings, forming self-contained, square barnyards. He saw well-cared-for gardens, patches of oats and barley, and pastures in which black-and-white cows and black-faced sheep peacefully grazed. Irregular walls, formed of high-piled field stones, divided one field from another. Narrow lanes, leading from the road, gave access to the dwellings.

Ahead MacDougall saw two figures moving along the roadside. One was a young woman in a blue print dress, bright and crisp, walking with firm, swinging stride, her head crowned by a halo of honey-blond hair, glowing in the late afternoon sunlight. Beside her skipped a brown-haired boy of about eight. As Alan pulled abreast of the pair, he stopped the car and leaned through the window.

"Good day," he greeted. "Perhaps you can help me. All these lanes look alike to me. I'm trying to find the Cameron farm."

Excitedly, dark eyes wide, the boy exclaimed, "That's our home! Wha' can ye be wantin' there?"

"Mind your manners, David," the girl chided, the faintest trace of the Scottish influence in her words; then, to MacDougall, she said, "I'm Elspeth Cameron, and this is my brother David." As she spoke, recognition dawned, and her blue-gray eyes expressed sudden interest. "You must be the man who visited my father some weeks ago. Father spoke of—" She broke off. "You were walking—"

"Spoke of my yellow whiskers," Alan concluded,

laughing. "I must have been a sight to behold after months of unshorn growth. I am Alan MacDougall; and indeed I enjoyed a fine breakfast at your home that day. I had run out of food and I was famished."

Quickly, he stepped out of the car and held the rear door open. "Won't you ride with me and be my guide? I have business to discuss with your father."

Instantly, the boy David scrambled in, his sister following more sedately, a slight, puzzled frown on her face. On their way again, Alan commented, "Your father spoke of a daughter and son at school, but I thought—"

"Logically you thought we both were pupils. I'm the teacher."

Casual conversation continued, but Alan's thoughts were busily contrasting two feminine faces. There was the Dresden doll perfection of Darthula, whose loveliness had led him into Tartarus; and there was the strong, very human face of the girl in the rear seat—not perfect but greatly appealing, with wide-set, grave eyes, which nonetheless held a ready twinkle, and lips made for smiling, and—

"We turn here," Elspeth's low-pitched voice broke into his thoughts.

At the end of a narrow, grass-grown lane lay the farmhouse, white-walled, with a gray gabled roof and a chimney at each end of the gable, a tendril of smoke curling up from one of them. As he drove into the barnyard, Alan became aware of flowers in beds bordering slate walks and edging the sides of the house. As the three alighted, the mingled perfume of sweet peas, mint, and roses scented the lazy air, with just a hint of ever-present heather, borne on a vagrant breeze.

A door opened, and Duncan Cameron, standing straight and tall, appeared in the opening, surprise and question on his long, lean face.

"Wha's the trouble, lass—" he began; then as he recognized Alan, his rugged features broke into a broad smile.

"Well—'tis the MacDougall! Come into the house, lad, come in. I dinna expect to see ye so soon again."

As Cameron stepped out to extend his greetings, Alan noticed a massive plaster cast on his lower right leg. The Scotsman, seeing the direction of his gaze, shook his iron-gray head and scoffed, "'Tis nothing—a wee break i' the bone. But come into the house. We'll see wha' Norah has in her cupboard. Come wha' may, there'll always be a morsel for a wayfarer as long as Cameron's livin'."

MacDougall tried to protest; but the Scot paid no heed, calling, "Norah!" loudly, as he strode through a doorway into what Alan supposed must be a pantry or kitchen. Elspeth Cameron gestured helplessly and led him into a cheery living room, with David at their heels.

As they seated themselves, she said cordially, "It's too late for tea; and you *will* stay for dinner? Father will be offended if you refuse. You're truly welcome—and there's nowhere else to eat."

"Aye," her brother added eagerly, "an' you can tell us a' about America!"

"Thank you so much," Alan replied, "but I had no thought of imposing. I'm sorry I arrived so late in the day; my drive took longer than I expected—and your mother—"

Elspeth interrupted smoothly, "Norah is our house-keeper. Mother—"

"Mither went awa'," David concluded brightly, "when I was born. It was the good Lord's will."

At that moment Cameron rejoined them. After a brief period of general conversation, during which Elspeth, with a murmured apology, left the room, he asked, "An' wha' brings ye back to the Cameron farm?"

"I plan to make an extended hike through the Highlands," Alan explained, "starting where I left off on my last trip. While I'm gone—and I have no idea how long that will be, perhaps a month—I should like to leave my car here on your farm. I'll be happy to pay for the accommodation. It doesn't have to be under roof; I'm only concerned that it be available when I return."

Duncan Cameron shook his head in wonderment. "Leavin' it here is no problem—but wha' can ye do with a' that time i' yon hills?"

"Looking for old ruins—towers, forts, maybe remains of the Roman days—"

"Perchance the wee folk!" David chimed in. "The *Shee*—"

"Hush, lad," his father exclaimed. "I'll no' ha' Norah fillin' yer head wi' such heathen thoughts!"

Elspeth re-entered, having changed into a dark dress, even more becoming; and Alan added, "And while I'm gone, I'd be happy to have Miss Cameron use the car—perhaps for her daily trip to school—"

The girl's instant protest and her brother's excited approval led into a discussion that continued until the housekeeper announced dinner. There followed an evening more enjoyable than any Alan could recall in many years. He found Duncan Cameron's dry wit and seasoned wisdom, expressed in the broad Scots, most amusing; and David's spontaneous childish outbursts were a delight. Then there was Elspeth! In all his years of bachelorhood, he could not remember meeting another woman to whom he had been drawn so fully, with whom he had felt so—comfortable was the only word he could find to describe his feeling.

Norah, the housekeeper, was seventy-five if a day, with snow-white hair, tightly coiled at the nape of her neck, and a small wiry face, deeply wrinkled, but with eyes incredibly *alive*. Her pertinent comments, interjected when least expected, indicated her complete awareness of all that was said, even as she served.

As the meal progressed, conclusions were reached. Alan would leave his car, for which there would be "no' a shillin' paid"; and if Elspeth wished to drive, as on rainy days, she would do so. Of course Alan would "stay the nicht. It couldna' be said that a Cameron would turn out any mon to sleep on the ground when a warm bed was goin' to waste."

The end of the short evening lingered in Alan's memory for a long time afterward.

It began with Duncan Cameron announcing, "Dyvid'll be goin' to his bed, but before he goes we'll ha' a readin'. Ye'll join us, Alan?"

Of course MacDougall agreed, with no idea of what would follow. They were seated in the living room; and as Cameron crossed to a table on which lay a large family Bible, Norah slipped in quietly and sat in a corner. The Scot picked up the Bible and placed it on Elspeth's lap.

"Wi' ye read, Elspeth?"

Opening the book she said, "I'll read the one hundred twenty-first Psalm." In the quietness she began,

> "I to the hills will lift my eyes,
> From whence doth come mine aid—"

Reverently she continued reading through the majestic Scottish paraphrase of the classic Psalm. When she concluded, her father returned the Bible to the table, reseated himself, and said, "And now we'll pray." As all heads bowed Duncan Cameron began. "Almighty Father, we are a' Thy lost an' wayward bairns, an' we know no' which way to go. Forgive us our sins an' guide us i' the right road—"

As the earnest pleas continued, mingled with thanks for blessings past and future, Alan MacDougall thought wonderingly that to these people this was very real. It was not something that had to be done or that was expected of them. It was part of their life. And why shouldn't it be real? If Lucifer existed—why not his antithesis?

Through his wandering thoughts, a request of Cameron's caught his attention. "An', Father, we pray for the stranger who has come into our house. Be wi' him i' his travelin'. Keep a firm hold on him an' on a' of us.

Deliver us from evil. An' tak' a' the glory unto Thyself. Amen."

Softly from Norah's corner in her reedy voice came a fervent echo, "Amen."

Later as MacDougall sank into the soft comfort of a goose-down feather bed, his thoughts, rather than dwelling on the twinned serpents, relived the evening just past; and for the first time since his night in *The Red Bull of Ballydhu*, he enjoyed undisturbed slumber.

Briskly, Alan MacDougall strode along the road leading northward from the Cameron farm. It was midmorning and the sun had burned off the fog that had filled every hollow. He was dressed in the hiking suit that had served him during all his Highland wanderings and his adventure in Tartarus. His gear, ready before he had started his drive to Kilmona, was in his oversize backpack; the sword was in its long case, strapped to the outside. He had planned to make an earlier start, but a leisurely breakfast with the Scot and his family, followed by the necessary leave-taking, had delayed him. Norah had contributed to the delay by insisting on preparing a substantial lunch—slices of cold roast lamb, oatcakes, even "shortie," her delicious Scottish shortbread, and who knew what else? Probably all would be appreciated later on. As he thought ruefully about what might lie ahead, he didn't feel any enthusiasm for his self-assigned undertaking. Remaining with the Camerons—especially Elspeth—was a far more enticing prospect than going back into the Other World.

The road dipped into a hollow, then rose to crest on a little hill. Alan turned and looked back, seeing the distant gray roof of the Cameron farmhouse set against a field of gently waving green grain, just as he had caught sight of it upon reaching the road after making his descent from the stone tower. This was where he'd start his upward hike.

There was a gradual rise as he crossed a wide expanse of purple heather. This led to an undulating moor, tufted with clumps of golden gorse. It wasn't until he reached the edge of the stand of white-barked birches that he realized something was missing. The song of birds was something he expected to hear, but all was as silent as the woods in Tartarus. That might have no meaning, of course; at the moment the songsters were probably just not within earshot. But it seemed almost like an omen, a foretaste of his entry into a world where there were no birds.

The way grew steeper as he climbed through the copse of birches and entered the pine forest that grew at the higher elevation. He was listening now for the birds, recalling their presence when he had descended through these same trees; but a hush seemed to have fallen upon the world; not even a breath of air was stirring among the evergreens. He half expected to hear another sound, the chiming of singing blades; but that, he told himself, was illogical. How could the Sidhe know he was coming? Though, on the other hand, they had known of his entry into the forest on the other side of the mountain.

Ever steeper became his course, and the terrain grew more rugged; then he saw the oaks ahead. Conifers merged into the far older monarchs of the forest. Alan felt his heartbeat quicken. Soon he must see the tower.

The leveling of the forest floor told him he had reached the top of the mount and should be close to the tower. He glanced around; the *broch* was not in sight. Annoyed with himself, he looked more carefully, moving about, peering around trees that might be blocking his view. There was no sign of the stone tower. He thought of the mountain stream in which he had bathed and stood motionless, listening intently for its ceaseless sound.

Dimly he heard it, barely audible amid the rustle of the leaves overhead: the distant musical babble of the brook. He moved toward the sound and finally saw the gray stone tower looming ahead. He leaped across the rocky rivulet, made his way past the cairn he had erected over the body of his brother Malcolm, and halted at the narrow entrance to the *broch*. All appeared as he had left it.

He heard an unusual rustling sound behind him and turned. There, in a double row, stood the men of the *Shee*, with Cinel Loarn at their center, a foot or two to the fore. For the first time, Alan saw them clearly. They were about three feet tall, well muscled, with deeply tanned faces, handsome and keenly alert, their dark hair at shoulder length. Clad in leaf-green leather, waistcoat and kilts, shod in green moccasins, and armed with their round bronze shields and leaf-shaped swords, brightly polished, they stood motionless and silent. Thirty, MacDougall estimated.

"Malcolm—Cinel Loarn! I am so glad to see you. I hoped I would." Alan hesitated, then continued earnestly, "Are—were you really my brother Malcolm, as you said? I am not doubting your word—why would you say so, how would you know of Malcolm if it were not true? But it is so strange—"

Cinel Loarn smiled his understanding. "To me also it seems unreal. I feel I always was as I am now. Yet dimly, like a dream, I can remember that other life—the home in Brookville where we played as boys—father tall and blond like you, mother small, dainty, and dark—and the tales of the Highlands father told. Always, there was something drawing me to Scotland. So I came."

He told of his finding the oak grove, the puzzling "memory" of things he could not have known; and his finding the sword—*his* sword—hidden under a flat stone where he "remembered" having concealed it. Then there had been his seeking shelter from a storm in the *broch* and confronting Caermarthen the Druid, who had tried to claim his weapon—the swords and shields mounted on the wall, and within them, in enchanted bondage, the Sidhe and their mates. The duel had ended in Caermarthen's death and the freeing of the Sidhe, with their leader Cinel Loarn—whom, in some strange way, he had become, while his empty body collapsed and was forgotten.

As Alan tried to grasp what he had heard, Cinel Loarn concluded soberly, "I am sorry you returned, Alan, but not surprised. I was afraid you would have to come back. It seemed inevitable. Call when you need us. We will be here."

As suddenly as they had appeared, the little men vanished.

For timeless moments, MacDougall stood motionless, trying to adjust to what he had heard of what had happened. All of it had been so abrupt that nothing seemed real. One statement of Malcolm's lingered in his mind: "I was afraid you would have to come back." Afraid—the word held apprehension and concern.

Slowly, MacDougall faced the tower, moving toward the doorway without conscious volition. Stooping, his torch lighting the way, he passed through the tunnel-like entrance and straightened inside the tower, sweeping the circular space with the strong beam of light.

The four bronze Gates were there. Two were in the wall to the left of the entrance, and the other two in the facing wall. Quickly, he examined the rest of the room. There were changes. The floor had been swept clean. The brown bones of Caermarthen that had lain near the table were gone. And the table itself, which had been splintered by the same thunderbolt that had knocked him senseless during that last furious storm after his escape from Tartarus, had been beautifully repaired. It was the work of the Sidhe, of course. He checked the two narrow rooms whose entrances were at opposite ends of the fireplace; they, too, had been thoroughly cleaned.

Placing the torch on the table, he shucked off his backpack, then methodically set about following already-made plans.

The day after leaving Ballydhu, MacDougall, having decided that he had no choice but to return to the Highland tower and the Other World, had driven into a rather large town and had found a tailor shop. Here he had ordered an outfit made to his specifications—a design that raised the eyebrows of the normally imperturbable Scot. He had selected a heavy, rich, black woolen fabric—one which had been used but rarely over a score of years, the tailor confided, and that for garments of mourning—and sketched a shirt with full-cut, long sleeves and snap clasps at the wrists, an open collar, and over this a full-cut collarless jacket, zippers closing the fronts of both. Trousers, also full-cut, were gathered at the ankles and equipped with snap fasteners. Over everything was a great black cape, ending at mid-calf. Pockets were everywhere: four in the shirt, two inside, two outside; six in the jacket, four inside, two outside; and four in the cape, all inside. All were made of sturdy, canvaslike material, with zipper closures. To complete the outfit, he'd had a local bootmaker apply black dye to his hiking boots.

MacDougall had planned his clothing with a dual purpose in mind. He wanted something distinctive, though not *too* different from normal Tartarian dress; yet something which would eliminate the knapsack which had been a nuisance during his first stay in the Other World. And he wanted the usual conveniences—including a change of underwear!

He had debated about the delay entailed in having this tailoring done, in view of Taliesin's apparent urgency, but had decided that, with the variable time in Tartarus, it really wouldn't matter.

His new outfit was in his backpack, the pockets already containing what he planned to take with him, except for the flashlight. This included two of his books, the *Mythology* and the Bible, stowed in pockets in his cape. He had thought it wryly amusing to take the Bible into Tartarus. There might be time to read; and Taliesin might enjoy trying to decipher the books. To all of this he added the food Norah had prepared, stowing it wherever he found room.

Quickly, he changed into the black, leaving all the extra gear in one of the small rooms. He clipped a canteen to his belt; he had filled it at the Cameron farm. Over the cape he fastened his sword.

He trained his torch on the first Gate, the one through which he had entered the Other World. Briefly, he examined the shallow bas-relief design on the slightly convex disc, gaining an impression of an intertwined maze of serpentine swirls and angles, grotesque human figures, and writhing, twisting lines suggesting hieroglyphics—all, he supposed, with meaning, but not for him. He pointed his beam at the other Gates and saw a similar complex confusion of design.

With quickening pulse, he swung wide the first Portal.

The familiar landscape of Tartarus met his gaze—the dancing and constantly changing aurora coming out of a black and starless sky, the pallid turf like a well-clipped albino lawn that had never been exposed to the sun; the strange trees suggesting those on an old willow plate; and the undulating white road, dipping into valleys, climbing hills, tapering to a point on the horizon where he could see the gemlike suggestion of distant crystalline Falias, the City of the North. Significantly, the graduated stones and boulders that he had placed to mark the position of the Gateway, invisible from the other side, were still there, undisturbed. Tranquil and lovely in its own unique way, the landscape bore no trace of the violence that had marked his departure from the Other World. Nor was there sign of animated life.

He thought of the Four Cities of this island he called Tartarus, each a beautiful masterpiece of Lucifer's creative art, built for the Daughters of Lilith. Lucifer, who had purposed to "be like the Most High," had sought to show that he, too, was a Creator. Crystalline Falias was home of the Norsemen; Murias in the West, the city under the sea, held the grotesque and malformed Fomorians; Findias the torch-lighted, with its lance of light piercing the black sky, was the land of the Trolls; and Gorias in the East, quaintly Oriental, had as its people the Ch'in. In his mind's eye he saw them all.

The soft light of the aurora came through the opening, giving enough light to see by, so Alan switched off his torch and dropped it into a jacket pocket. Leaving the Gate wide open, he stepped to the second disc. With his hand gripping the cold metal, MacDougall hesitated for an instant, then shrugged. Why vacillate? He had to know what lay behind each of those openings.

He swung wide the second Gate.

He'd had no idea what to expect—certainly more of Lucifer's domain, but perhaps a world utterly alien. He saw at once that this was the same realm as that of Tartarus; the aurora proved it. But this was a timid aurora, its glimmering light misty and uncertain. It was somewhat lighter than the dark sky over Findias and the Desert of Gloom—a twilight world, all colors muted, gray dominating. The effect was somewhat like that of a night lighted by the moon.

There was little detail to be seen. Level, grayish turf filled the range of his vision. Noticeable was the complete absence of trees. From the left, curving past the Gateway, lay a narrow cobblestone road, ending about seventy yards directly ahead at a double metal gate set in a high stone wall. And far beyond the wall, jutting against the somber sky, he could barely discern the twin towers of a gray stone castle.

Whereas the view through the first Gate held a sort of elfin loveliness, this scene was the essence of gloom— murky, depressing, repellent, like something out of Dante. MacDougall grimaced. An apt comparison, he thought.

He reached for the bronze disk, then halted. He'd let it remain open for the present.

He crossed the room and opened the third Gate.

Trees! Gate two had not shown a single tree; in contrast he was gazing into a thicket as overgrown as a tropical rain forest! But it was like no forest he had ever seen or imagined. The massive trunks before him, pale and smooth as human skin, were twisted, writhing, tortured things that seemed to have fought through centuries for their very existence. They were not tall; the thick canopy of leaves was no more than twenty feet above the ground. And those leaves—not only was there no trace of green, but they were pale pink, tinged with crimson—long, fingerlike, fleshy things, dangling from thin stems, pointing toward the forest floor. And, like the leaves of an aspen, they were in ceaseless motion, fluttering and pointing.

As he stared, MacDougall realized that the crimson tints of the leaves came and went; they were reflections from the aurora which danced and shimmered with mingled red and white radiance!

Here there was undergrowth, vines, creepers, and thick-leaved cacti, all of them the pallid colors he had come to associate with the auroral world. Some were thorn-covered; others bore strangely formed flowers and fruit, their shape and colors equally grotesque. They were like Fomorians of the vegetable world!

About to turn away, Alan stared even more intently. He thought he had seen the movement of vines stirring, as if disturbed by a form wriggling through the barrier. The movement continued; for a brief moment, Alan was sure he saw a pale face peering furtively from under a great round leaf—a heavy-lipped, froglike mouth, a small, broad nose, widely spaced, puffy eyes, and great projecting ears, pointed at top and bottom, all crowned by long, stringy red hair. The face, if it existed, was gone in a breath.

Finally Alan turned away. Wondering what new grotesquerie he would see, he opened the fourth Gate.

MacDougall's eyes widened. He could scarcely believe what he beheld. The view was lightly veiled, as if seen through a breath of mist on a window, but it was none the less beautiful, not with an unearthly beauty, but with the loveliness of an immense formal garden or park. The slightly undulating pastel green lawn supplied an unusual setting for gracefully shaped and carefully placed flowering bushes, stately trees, and, here and there, round structures formed of delicately fluted marble pillars that supported domed silver roofs—what in England were called follies. There were white, branching walks, one leading to an alabaster castle-out-of-fantasy in the background, silhouetted against the aurora. And that aurora was a kaleidoscope of pastel colors, constantly changing, but so subtly that it was not obtrusive. He could see white-robed people moving about in the vicinity of the castle, but none were close to the Gateway.

Even as he studied the view through the fourth Gate, a vague thought persisted in nudging his memory. There was something he should recall, something having to do with the four Gates—and suddenly it came.

It had happened during his meeting with the Druids of the Four Cities after his first sleep in Taliesin's home, while they were trying to learn the location of the Gate through which he had come. Moirfhius, the garrulous and near-senile Druid of Falias, referring to Caermarthen during his centuries of guarding the Gateways, had volunteered, "He said he left all four Gates open for long periods and no one seemed to notice." Immediately Erus, Druid of Gorias, had interrupted and cut off any further revelation. Strange, Alan thought, that no one seemed to know anything about the lands beyond the other three Gates! Or, at least, they had not mentioned them. Perhaps this was another Forbidden Area, something one didn't even think about.

A brilliant flare of light behind him cut off speculation. He turned quickly and saw the radiance pouring out of the second Gate. He darted across to it—the scene that had been the somber gray of twilight.

Out of the black sky came a single tight beam, laserlike in its cohesion. But it was not the light that froze MacDougall's attention; it was the group of men it had caught in its beam. They were some distance from the Gateway, close to the stone wall, but he could see them quite clearly in the brilliant ray—ten men in the dress of ancient Roman soldiers—from the first century, he believed. Their armor dated them.

Most were bareheaded, but two wore iron pot helmets with brass cross-bands, a brass ring at the top, with curved neckguards and long, narrow cheek pieces. Their leather cuirasses were decorated with strips of metal; shoulder pieces were brass studded; the sleeves and skirts of their tunics were decorated with dangling strips; leather greaves guarded their shins; and heavy boots, ending at mid-calf, completed their dress. In short, they had stepped out of the pages of ancient Roman history.

With ready swords, they were moving menacingly toward a single, smaller man in a long blue cape. Suddenly MacDougall gasped. Taliesin! It *must* be Taliesin! Even at that distance, he could recognize the rounded figure and the thick white hair circling the base of the shining bald pate. But what was he doing here? The man turned, now facing Alan—and MacDougall was certain. It was the Bard!

The beam of light suddenly swung away, circled to the north, paused, then swung far to the east, and winked out. In the intensified darkness, MacDougall could see little. Impatiently, he closed his eyes, letting them adjust, his thoughts racing.

He had been uncertain about which Gate to pass through, though, of course, that into Tartarus would have been his probable choice. Now he had the answer. Taliesin had called him about new trouble; the Bard was inside the world of the second Gate—and that must be his destination.

He looked again into the twilight realm, just in time to see the double bronze gateway closing. That, evidently, was where Taliesin had been taken.

"Cinel Loarn!" he called out. "Malcolm!"

The *Shee* were there even as he spoke, suddenly visible, standing just inside the door of the tower. They must have been there all along. "We are ready."

"I'm going through the second Gate," Alan said. "Since

all of them lead, I am sure, to the same world. I'm leaving all Gates open, providing a better chance for me to return. Will you keep watch?"

As one, thirty stout bronze swords were drawn and struck thirty bronze shields. The tower rang with the bell tones. "We are your guard," Cinel Loarn said.

With a wave of his hand, MacDougall stepped through the second portal into the gray realm. He stood motionless to recover from the brief and now-familiar vertigo that marked his entry into the Other World.

He heard a shout behind him and spun around to face ten Roman soldiers with drawn swords.

CHAPTER 3

The Castle of King Arawn

Silence followed the single shout and no one stirred.
MacDougall's thoughts raced; his first impulse was to leap
back through the Portal. He had merely turned; the ghostly
tower and safety was a step away, the gaping soldiers
standing beyond it. But did he want to retreat? That
wouldn't help Taliesin. Invisibility through the armlet
would buy time. It seemed his best bet.

The first words of the Roman leader checked him.
"Master—we beg you—do not vanish!" The man sounded
urgent, his tones respectful. "If you do, we lose our heads.
We have been awaiting your coming."

"You—expected me?" Alan spoke haltingly, out of his
incredulity. The implications were staggering. "You were
waiting here—for me?"

Several heads nodded, and the spokesman answered
eagerly. "Yes, Master, though we knew not precisely when

nor exactly where—just this area. In a dream, Idwen the Seer foresaw your coming and told King Arawn—a man in black with yellow hair. It was Idwen who warned of your power to disappear. So here we have waited—long it has seemed—to escort you to the King."

MacDougall groped for understanding. "That light from the sky—did it not show soldiers taking a short, heavy man through the gate in the wall?"

The man shook his head in wonder, the others frowning blankly. Quickly the spokesman's face cleared. "You test us. The light came—but there was no one here beside the ten you see."

Never before had Alan felt so helpless, so like a marionette dancing on a string. He felt the chill of sudden dread. Ahriman, of course! The mocking, smiling Persian had kept him in Scotland; leading him to put on the armlet; sending a faked call from Taliesin; and creating the illusion inside the Second Gate. His coming—even his black garments—had been foreknown. His muscles stiffened. Get out of here, Mac, while you can! But the armlet? Maybe he could have it cut off! But that, he knew, would not be allowed—

Cold, raw Scots anger suddenly surged through him, sweeping away the fear and awakening a streak of implacable stubbornness. For the moment, he'd play Ahriman's game—but only as long as it suited him. He'd bested the Persian once. He'd do it again! He'd go to this King Arawn. But first came an important detail, the marking of the Gate.

"Your name?" he demanded of the soldier.

"Marcus Emilius, Master." The man drew himself up proudly. "In the olden times I was centurion in the Sixth Legion of Hadrian the Conqueror."

"Very well, Marcus." MacDougall spoke imperiously. "I will go with you and meet your King. But first I must offer thanks to my gods for safe journey from the Great Above." He liked that phrase; it sounded impressive. "You and your men turn your backs and walk ten paces. Then keep your backs turned, for none may see that which is sacred." As he saw a doubtful expression forming, he scowled and added brusquely, "Remember, I can vanish this very moment if I choose. I will not do so if you do as I command."

Marcus Emilius hesitated, then shrugged; following his example, the others sheathed their swords, turned, and began their pacing. At their move, Alan looked quickly around him, then grimaced in frustration. There was nothing he could use as a marker, not even a loose rock; there were only those in the road, too far away to consider. A possibility suggested itself, born of desperation. He thought into the armlet:

"Lord Enki and Lady Inanna, can you remember this spot for me if I need to return here?"

"Look in the four directions," came the mental command. Alan stared in what seemed to him to be a southerly direction, over the heads of the soldiers, to see a stretch of turf, with beyond it a narrow beach and then the open water, merging with the black of the sea and sky. He turned to the east; the road curved past, about twenty yards away, and beyond it a meadow blended into the darkness. To the north lay the view he had seen through the Portal: the grass, the road, and the wall with the bronze gate directly before him. And finally he looked to the west, seeing merely more pallid gray turf, certainly not a hopeful prospect.

"We will remember," came the thought. Fervently MacDougall hoped so, though he didn't see how.

"Marcus," he called out, "we go!"

Quickly the Romans joined him, and together they headed for the double gate. There was no conversation; and though the soldiers formed a guard around him, they remained at a respectful distance. Alan welcomed the silence. It gave him freedom to consider all that had happened, and to berate himself. What an idiot he had been!

That scene beyond the second Gate, Taliesin's capture by Roman soldiers under that brilliant beam of light, just at the moment when he was available to see it, and the wild coincidence of the Bard being there, together with that light, just when he had opened the Gates—he should have known it was illusion.

And this dream of Idwen the Seer was more of Ahriman's doing, moving another of his pawns.

That call from Taliesin back there in *The Red Bull*, obviously false, had been dependent on knowledge that the armlet was again active, else how could Alan receive the thought? This he could check by calling Taliesin— the *real* Taliesin—assuming he could reach him. But that could wait. Better now to keep his mind on what was happening.

They had passed through the gateway and were continuing along the cobblestone road toward the distant castle. About a hundred yards ahead lay a second curving wall; and to right and left of the road stretched a double row of barrackslike stone buildings, one story high, each about thirty feet in length, with infrequent narrow windows and regularly spaced doorways. Faint light filtering out of windows or doorways suggested candles burning within. A few soldiers sprawled on stone benches before some of the buildings. These barracks evidently were the living quarters of the army.

A more depressing place MacDougall couldn't imagine. Tartarus and its perpetual day was certainly to be preferred over this place and eternal dusk. He wondered if it had a name and asked Marcus Emilius.

The Roman looked at him curiously. "Surely you must know," he answered. "It is Ochren, and Arawn is its King."

As the walk continued, the gloom, the very air of the place, began to weigh on Alan's mind. He caught a glimpse of movement in the grass at the right of the road and saw a huge scorpion, tail arched, scurry away. So there was other than human life in this land. As they continued their march, he glanced about and saw other signs of darting, slithering things, quite in keeping with this ugly place. How dreadful, he thought, to be condemned to live forever in this dismal land. He thought again of Ahriman's deception and his own gullibility. How easily he had been deceived. What chance did he have in matching wits with the lieutenant of Lucifer? It was incredible that he'd even attempted it; better to have remained back there on the Cameron farm.

The thought stirred a memory, a request in the old Scot's prayer: "We pray for the stranger who has come into our home. Be wi' him i' his travelin'. Keep a firm hold on him..." Rather shamefacedly Alan thought, I hope his prayer is answered.

He sought for something positive, found it, and clung to it. Ahriman didn't have everything his way. In spite of all the extreme measures he had taken to prevent MacDougall's escape from the Other World—even to the turning off of the aurora—Alan had gotten away. There was another plus—the armlet with the two serpent-gods who didn't seem to think too highly of Ahriman; they had revealed themselves to Alan despite the Persian's orders not to do so and had said they were under his, Alan's, orders.

MacDougall's stride quickened. All he wanted was a fighting chance—and he believed he had it!

They reached the second wall to find a lone sentinel on duty; at their approach he opened the gates without a word spoken. MacDougall could see no reason for his being there, nor for the walls themselves, since there was nothing between the barriers except more of the endless, flat turf. Now their destination loomed ahead, a darker silhouette against the timorous aurora barely seen in the black sky.

For the first time Alan noticed the flame of redly burning torches set at regular intervals around the lower third of the castle—gas flames, he was sure. It would be good to get inside where there would be light other than this somber dusk.

Suddenly, as if in response to the thought, a pillar of brilliance leaped out of the darkness overhead. It fell to the east of them, lancing down without apparent target, then swinging in a slow arc as if searching—and, as suddenly as it had come, it vanished. The effect was disconcerting.

"What causes that?" MacDougall asked the centurion. "And what is its purpose?"

The Roman shrugged. "It comes and goes as it wills—and none know whence nor why."

Abruptly Alan halted. He'd better gain a bit more knowledge about this place; he wouldn't get a better opportunity.

"Tell me, Marcus, are there places in Ochren beside Arawn's castle where people live?"

The Roman looked at him oddly. "Surely, Master, you must know about Beli and Manannan." He hesitated. "And Titus."

"Tell me."

He shrugged resignedly. "There is also the castle of the god Beli, where he dwells with his Druids and Guards. And far to the north is the Castle of Manannan, who men say was god of the sea. And there is talk of an undersea city, now deserted. There are more of us here than at either castle."

"And what of Titus?" MacDougall inquired when the other gave no sign of continuing.

Marcus looked troubled. "Better I say nothing about Titus. I am but a soldier who obeys commands. I should not have mentioned him."

"Very well, Marcus; I respect your prudence. On we go."

It was not a great store of information, MacDougall thought as he strode briskly ahead, but better than nothing—except for Titus, whoever he was.

They approached the castle—fortress, rather, with its two massive stone towers, round, with crenelated walls on their flat roofs, and occasional high, narrow windows, a few with murky light coming from within. These formed the visible ends of the structure, with a smaller connecting building, also topped with battlements, between them. Torches burned in regularly spaced niches about thirty feet above eye level, doing little to dispel the general gloom, but serving to multiply the menace of great bronze figures of Roman soldiers with raised swords, standing at eternal watch within their glow. The entrance, with its huge black pillars, midway between the towers, was separated from the road by a broad moat and a raised drawbridge. A guard chamber set in the fortress wall completed the picture.

As Alan took in all of this, he felt it vaguely familiar and knew abruptly what it brought to mind. It suggested a Hollywood setting for a class B horror film.

They halted at the edge of the moat, and a challenge came from the guard chamber. Marcus Emilius identified the group; very slowly, creaking and groaning, the drawbridge descended.

As they waited, Alan, for the first time since entering Ochren, became aware of odors. From the moat rose a raw, earthy smell of decay, strong and unpleasant. As the bridge closed, and they started across, he looked down at the surface of the water ten feet below, reflecting the torchlight. The fluid seemed to emit a faintly phosphorescent glow; it was utterly still until a sudden movement broke its smoothness, as a thick, scaly tentacle thrust through green scum, then vanished, sending slow, oily ripples rolling into the darkness. He heard the faint swish of the wavelets lapping the rough stones of the outer wall and the moss-grown castle, despite the clatter of boots on the metal plates of the bridge.

At their approach, the great bronze door opened; they entered the castle of King Arawn, and the door thudded shut behind them. With the closing, Alan thought: No Hollywood set, this! Here was something no staging, no special effects, could create—an indefinable yet almost tangible impression of evil. It was in the very air of the place. He tried to scoff at the thought, but the feeling persisted.

With conscious effort, he turned his attention to the corridor along which they were walking. Walls and ceiling, though of rough stone, gave forth an eerie glow—enough light to dispel darkness, but not enough for comfortable seeing. Widely spaced lamps set above eye level aided vision—brass lamps in the shape of gargoyles, seven horned, with gas flames spurting from the horns. There was something familiar about the arrangement of the seven lights, three uniformly curved horns to the right and left of a taller central flame, like a mockery of the seven-branched candlestick, the menorah of Jewish worship. There were empty, glowing sockets where eyes should have been; evidently the tops of the heads were hollowed, allowing the pulsing light of the flames to dance in the openings. Repulsive, those lamps!

He became aware of the irregularity of the flagstone floor, as if a central strip of the slate had been worn into a foot-wide depression by endlessly scuffing boots and sandals through millennia of time. The centurion had taken the lead with Alan at his heels, and both walked in this narrow area. Alan glanced back, noting that the other soldiers followed in single file. Strange, he thought; as if they were keeping as far from the walls as possible. A second backward glance revealed an uneasy expression on the faces behind him, even the suggestion of an unnatural pallor.

A startling thought struck him. Never in the Four Cities of Tartarus had he seen similar time-worn floors. Certainly Ochren was no older than Falias and the others, yet it seemed incredibly ancient.

They passed two closed doors directly facing each other; regularly spaced along the corridor before them were others, momentarily suggesting a prehistoric motel. He noticed that his escorting guard tried to walk more quietly, seeming to listen. To Alan's ears came a distressing sound—as if a woman were trying to scream through tightly closed lips. The cry was choked off, muffled behind a closed door. MacDougall hesitated, thinking he heard a faint moan coming from the facing room. The Roman at his heels pushed against him.

"Don't stop!" the man said hoarsely. "Nothing you can do."

Reluctantly Alan went on, now listening as they passed each door. Strange were the sounds he heard—or thought he heard—none clearly, all muffled—the rhythmic clink of metal on metal and a cracking whip followed by a faint whimper. There were odors, some nauseating, others cloyingly sweet, and sounds he could not identify. All of them verified his initial impression of prevailing evil.

They reached a crossing corridor, and the centurion turned to the right, past more of the closed doors with their disquieting indications of hidden unpleasantness. Somewhere ahead must be the place of meeting with King Arawn of Ochren. As he thought of what he might face, MacDougall told himself he was being led like a lamb to the slaughter; and in view of what he had seen or, more accurately, heard, that might be an apt comparison.

What could he do? The armlet, of course, was his sole source of power. He had to depend on Lord Enki and Lady Inanna. It was strange to think of the jewel as twin personalities, but he'd better get accustomed to the idea.

Why not try now? Idwen the Seer, obviously prompted by Ahriman, had seen the coming of a man in black with yellow hair and beard. Why not show them someone different? He didn't know just how shape-changing worked, but the serpents should. He visualized Nuada as he had seen him several times, dressed all in white except for his bright blue cape, beardless, his thick shoulder-length hair almost as white as his garments, and his sword suspended from a broad belt of golden links. With this image firmly in mind, Alan grasped the armlet.

"Lord Enki, Lady Inanna—can you give me Nuada's appearance?"

"With ease," came the mental reply, "though you have the ability within yourself to bring about the change."

"I have?" MacDougall demanded incredulously.

"You have, indeed. But now is not the time to awaken and enhance these powers." With the thought Alan felt a flowing of his facial features and glimpsed out of the corner of his eye the white garments, blue cape, and sword of the King of the *Tautha de Danann*; he knew the transformation was complete. Inexplicably, he felt a momentary touch of fatigue, as if effort somehow had gone into the change. It passed in a breath. He heard gasps and a sharp cry, instantly cut off, from the Roman behind him. Marcus Emilius half turned, then spun around, his jaw slack, consternation on his face.

"No sound." MacDougall put all the authority he could muster into the quiet words. "I have assumed my true form to meet your king. I am Nuada, King of the *Tuatha de Danann*." He looked sternly into the centurion's eyes. "It will be well for you and your men to remember my powers when you present me. This is the only form you have seen. Remember! Now proceed."

Mutely Marcus turned, and the column moved on along another corridor and past other closed doors with their hints of enigmatic sounds. They made one more turn, this to the left, the hallway gradually growing wider, to end at a great bronze double door. Two Roman guards in the full regalia of their office, javelins in hand, barred the way.

Again Marcus explained their presence. One of the guards passed through the doorway. After what seemed an endless wait he returned, and the doors swung wide to admit them to what must be the throne room of the King of Ochren.

They stood alone in a great round chamber with a high, domed, phosphorescent ceiling, evidently in one of the great towers, probably one not visible from the front. The walls of the room were formed entirely of polished bloodstone, dark green mottled with sullen crimson, broken at regular intervals by tall, narrow window openings. High up on the wall, rimming the entire chamber, flamed gargoyle lamps like those in the corridor, fiery eyes watching from every side. The floor, of dull black stone, sloped upward from all sides toward the far wall where towered the throne—so all in the room, Alan thought, must look up to the King.

A striking thing, the throne dominated everything. Massively wrought of dull, red-yellow gold, it rested on a dais of jet black which rose a full ten feet above three backless silver seats at its base. About fifteen feet away from the seats stood a curving gray-metal rail, suggesting, Alan thought, a bar of judgment.

He followed the centurion as the man strode to the rail, then stood beside him, with the other soldiers forming a double row behind them.

"We wait," Marcus whispered.

Moments later, doors opened on both sides of the dais to admit two columns of Roman legionnaires, evidently the King's Guard. A hundred, fifty in each column by Alan's estimate, every man a picture of military splendor, they fanned out on both sides of the dais to form a broad V.

A door under the dais opened, and a single, gray-cloaked man with a troubled face emerged and took his place on the other side of Marcus—probably Idwen the Seer.

Moments later three dignitaries in black-hooded robes came through the same doorway, took positions beside the three silver chairs, and stood facing the throne.

In complete silence everyone waited.

MacDougall felt a slight nudge from the centurion and heard a faint whisper: "When the King enters, kneel!"

As the moments dragged by, Alan thought, Hanged if I'll kneel! I can't picture Nuada kneeling before anyone. Nor will I.

At last a narrow door in the wall behind the throne opened and King Arawn of Ochren appeared. Splendid was the only word for his dress: a full-cut robe of crimson velvet, thickly studded with pearls, with a long string of black pearls suspended from his neck, supporting a huge *crux ansata*—a looped cross, the Egyptian ankh—shaped from a single great black opal, flashing with incredible fires with every slightest movement. His crown outshone even this—dome-shaped, of glistening gold, suggesting a papal tiara rather than any kingly diadem; three bands of black opal cabochons encircled it, with another *crux ansata* rising from the pointed tip of the dome.

At his appearance there was concerted movement, a rustling, the clanking of armor as all the waiting men knelt—

All except Alan MacDougall.

With his face expressionless, his body erect, though not stiffly so, Alan looked steadily into the face of the King. The deep-set eyes meeting his were narrowed at first, then widened into a wrathful glare—pale gray eyes that intensified the blackness of the pupils. Alan became aware of the face as a whole. At first glance it had somehow reminded him of Ahriman, but actually there was little resemblance. King Arawn was tall and broad of shoulders; but where the Persian had seemed ageless, the face before him was deeply lined, gaunt, and heavy with eternities—the thought came unbidden—of evil. His nose was large and hawk-beaked, and his lips so thin as to be almost undetectable, twisted in a sardonic, somberly menacing half smile. But the eyes, malignantly glaring, seemed to be trying to force Alan to lower his gaze—unsuccessfully. Interest awakened, with perhaps a hint of uncertainty.

Finally the King spoke in a deep voice, anger and menace just below the surface.

"And who are you who dares to stand without permission in the presence of the King of Ochren?"

"King Nuada of the *Tuatha de Danann*," MacDougall answered with quiet dignity. "I kneel before no one, be he king or god."

Mac, he thought, that's big talk. But it wasn't bluff; he meant it!

Eyes still fixed on Alan's, King Arawn sank to a seat

on his throne. With a clap of his hands he exclaimed, "Arise!"

As quietly as possible, everyone stood up, the three black-cowled men, probably judges or counselors, taking their seats. Alan could sense the tension in the chamber; all were shocked at his bold and open defiance of the King.

Arawn turned his attention to Marcus Emilius, uttering a single harsh word: "Report!"

"Thank you, your Gracious Majesty," There was a tremor in the centurion's voice. He indicated the men behind him. "We were patrolling the assigned area when with no warning of any kind this man appeared in our midst." Seeming to gain a measure of confidence he continued, carefully recounting all that had happened—except the shape-changing—concluding, "And, your Majesty, we have brought him here without his once leaving our sight."

There were two weak links, Alan thought; the guards at wall number two and at the drawbridge had seen him in black. But there was no reason why they would be questioned.

The King addressed the man at the centurion's right. "Idwen, is this the man you saw in your dream? You spoke of a man in black."

Fear was evident in the Seer's hesitant reply. "I—I cannot be certain, your Majesty. I—the man in my vision was as tall, but his hair, I thought, *was* yellow—or so it seemed. Perhaps it was lighter. But he *did* seem bearded. And," he continued doggedly, "he *was* dressed in black." Weakly, he tried to defend himself. "But he *did* appear where I foretold—"

"So—you were half-right!" There was sardonic humor in the deep voice. "At the same time, you were half-wrong." After a pause, he turned. "Judges, your decision concerning Idwen the Seer? I am inclined to be merciful."

The three black cowls came together in inaudible conference; then the central judge rose, faced the throne, and bowed.

The King waved his hand. "You may speak."

"We recommend, Most Merciful Majesty, that he be permitted to live until such time as he makes another half error." As he resumed his seat, all of the soldiers murmured in chorus; "Our King is merciful."

Again the King's hand waved. "This is my decree. You may go. Hereafter consult your oracles more carefully." The Seer bowed and, with his gaze fixed on the floor, he backed away and out of the throne room, leaving by one of the doors that had admitted the King's Guard.

"And, judges, what of those who have executed my orders?"

Again the consultation and the obsequious decision, "Since they have done well, Most Merciful Majesty, we invoke your blessing upon them."

With another indolent wave of the hand, the King said, "So be it. Return to your quarters and await your next assignment."

Again there followed the murmured chorus, "Our King is merciful." Alan saw Marcus bow deeply and heard his escorts backing away and out of the chamber.

"And now—" Arawn's voice was icily cold. "What of this—visitor—who claims to be the King of the *Tuatha de Danann*?"

Again the three hooded heads came together—and instantly drew apart as MacDougall's voice echoed through the throne room with annoyance and anger in its tones— feelings that were not simulated.

"Enough of this silly game! Who gives any of you the right to judge me? I, King Nuada of the *Tuatha de Danann*, have come from the Great Above to visit Ochren— and, instead of the reception due a royal visitor, I am threatened by armed soldiers and brought as a criminal before common judges. This is not to be borne! I am tempted to return whence I came, and as I came, and so report to the Lord of Light. I suffered your soldiers to conduct me to you because it accorded with my purpose. And that purpose was to judge *you*!"

"Judge me!" The King half rose as fury blazed in his pale eyes, then sank back, iron control reasserting itself. "Assuming you are Nuada, as you say, why have you come from the Great Above to Ochren, to what you must consider to be Annwn, the Not-World? Why, as you say, do you seek to judge me?"

MacDougall had been wondering the same thing; and a sudden wild possibility flashed into his mind—perhaps not so wild in a place like this.

"It has come to our ears that there is revolution, near-anarchy, in your part of the Not-World, this island of Ochren. Your fitness to rule is in question."

King Arawn's expression remained unchanged; but Alan clearly heard sharply indrawn breaths from the three judges. Shock—or could there be truth in his guess? Could this explain the mysterious Titus?

He continued, "There is nothing to prevent my becoming invisible and conducting my investigation unseen. I prefer working with you—but if you wish to have me vanish—" Alan paused as though inviting comment.

"If you are Nuada that will not be necessary. But surely you do not expect me to accept your unsupported word. After all," Arawn said, permitting himself a half smile, "even gods have been known to speak other than truth. I must have proof. And fortunately that proof is readily available. Father of Nuada is Beli; and Beli, as you must know, dwells in his castle, *Dinas Affaraon*, which is little more than a sleep removed from *Caer Ochren*. I shall send for him and he will say whether or not you are Nuada. You should enjoy a visit with your father after what must be a very long separation." With thinly veiled menace in his voice, he added, "Of course, if you are *not* Nuada—but why waste thought on idle speculation? We seek knowledge."

He addressed the spokesman of the judges. "Febar, you will conduct our visitor to proper quarters so he may rest from his journey, which must have been a long one. You will also dispatch messengers to Beli and invite him to call—to meet his son. Tell him it is the wish of King Arawn that he come at once." He smiled thinly at Alan. "In Ochren even the gods honor the desires of their King ... Of course you will surrender your sword—"

"Of course I will do no such thing! As you must know, my blade is enchanted and cannot be defeated—if I am Nuada. If I am not King of the *Tuatha de Danann*, what matters one ordinary weapon against so many?" He waved his hand toward the Guard in obvious imitation of the King.

Again the narrowed eyes glared their wrath as, with evident effort, King Arawn said, "So let it be for now— except that I would hear more about this Great Above you speak of. Why have I not heard of this place during all the time since Ochren and its dwellers were removed from the world of men? And why has none seen fit to visit my realm before?"

Again Alan waved his hand in a noncommittal gesture. "Who am I to question the decrees of the Lord of Light? Or the time of his revealing or withholding knowledge? Surely it must be evident to you that I am not of this land." He paused as if in reflection, telling himself, Easy, Mac—say no more till you know what you're talking about. "I could tell you of the Land of the Four Cities, fair beyond imagining—but it might be wiser for us to defer further discussion until you are certain of my identity."

Unsuccessfully, King Arawn tried to conceal his frustration and anger. "I grow weary of all this. See to my commands, Febar."

Abruptly he rose and passed through the doorway behind the throne. In ordered fashion, the Guards withdrew, followed by the two judges, with Febar and MacDougall the last to leave.

Beyond the door under the dais lay a narrow hallway that led into a broader corridor which branched almost immediately. The two judges turned to the right while Febar led the way leftward. He and Alan climbed a wind-

ing stairway to a second level; and there the judge opened
a door into what must be a tower room, since there was
a narrow slit of an opening in the curved far wall. Like
the corridors, the walls were phosphorescent; and a single
gargoyle lamp burned above the door.

For the first time Judge Febar spoke, the rancor he
felt becoming evident in his tones. "If you need anything,
there will be a guard on duty at your door. You will be
summoned when the Lord Beli arrives. Do not attempt
to leave until you are summoned." He stalked out, closing
the door behind him.

MacDougall looked for a lock. As he expected, there
was none. No privacy could be expected here. No matter.
He did not intend to sleep; but this gave him an opportunity to do what was most important—get in touch with
Taliesin.

He stretched out on the bed and closed his eyes, the
better to concentrate. He recalled the time in Tartarus,
just before the battle between the forces of Nuada and
Balor, when he had communicated with the Bard. Then
he had, as he conceived it, "thought into the armlet."
Now it would be communication through the serpent-
gods.

"Lord Enki and Lady Inanna, I want to speak with the
Bard Taliesin." He visualized the round face with its per-
petually twinkling eyes; mentally, he called, "*Taliesin!*"

There was a hint of amusement in the Lady Inanna's
response. "Again you ask for help in an area well within
your own powers. Indeed, with a minimum amount of
guidance, you can become a skilled telepath. In this realm,
of course."

Startled, Alan grasped at the idea, to be interrupted by
the amazed, yet delighted, thought of the Bard of Bards.

"Alan! Is it really you? And where are you?"

*"It is really Alan, son of Dougall. And I am in a part
of your world, but in a place they call Ochren. You mean
you did not call me?"*

"Call you? Why should I? And Ochren—you said

Ochren? But that is a dreadful place, worse even than this accursed land. I should have suspected that it, too, would be under the aurora. How did you get there?"

In flashing thoughts MacDougall recounted—with one major exception—the essential details of what had happened, beginning with his awakening to find he had put on the armlet and his receiving what he thought was a call from the Bard—most certainly, it now appeared, a trick of Ahriman. He told of his passing through the second Gate and all that followed, describing the gray castle with its drawbridge and stagnant moat and what he knew about the land. He was careful to omit any reference to the serpent-gods.

The Bard's thoughts, responding, fairly seethed with excitement. *"Then there are other lands in this world! Probably four since you refer to four Gates—as did Caermarthen! But the Druid seems to have had all details wiped from his memory—he's only able to recall the Portals, but nothing beyond them."*

"Shall I attempt to come to you—?" Alan began.

"No," the Bard interrupted, *"I'll come to you and bring Nuada with me. I'll need his strength to make the transfer. He'll welcome the chance—a priceless opportunity to experience something new. And since you've adopted his appearance, better to have him there in person, dressed as you are. Before we come, I'll communicate with you to help me visualize your surroundings, though just to picture you might well be enough."* Alan could sense his excited planning. *"I'll come as a Norseman—no, better a Druid. I'll call Nuada immediately. Unless there is more?"* At MacDougall's negative response he concluded, *"Until I join you, friend, farewell!"*

Nuada—it was probably a good idea to have him with them. He was a fantastic swordsman with god-powers and an invincible weapon. Once Nuada, the King of the *Tuatha de Danann*, had come to Alan's rescue when three Norsemen had attacked him. Nuada had magically guided his arm in a fantastic display of swordsmanship. It had been a strange feeling—complete detachment during an uneven duel.

Alan heard a slight sound and raised his eyelids. The door had opened a mere crack as someone peered in. Suddenly it swung wide and the Roman guard stood framed in the opening, eyes wide, mouth open. Swiftly he drew his sword, then turned and shouted at the top of his voice; "Febar! Judge Febar! The man in black! We have him!"

CHAPTER 4

The Prison of Ochren

MacDougall stared at the soldier's back for an uncom-
prehending instant, then looked down at his own recumbent form. Black! He reached up to his chin and felt the
familiar beard. While he had lain with eyes closed, his
true shape had returned. He leaped erect.

"Enki!" If a mental shout were possible, Alan shouted
the name. "Quick—back to Nuada's shape! Now you've
gotten me into real trouble. What happened?"

He felt his facial features flow, and the return of Nuada's
form was accomplished. Again there was a brief moment
of energy loss, less noticeable than in the corridor. He
sensed the amused thought of the Lady Inanna: "My Lord
Enki, you should know better than to try to do several
things at one time. Maintaining the change while being
the channel for communication, plus other—diversions—
led to a lapse of attention."

Disgust and annoyance colored the serpent-god's retort.
"You know very well that despite the handicap of this
imprisonment, at this moment I am deeply involved in

the concerns of Nuith and Hadith in the House of Khabs—
as are you!" He addressed Alan. "No real harm has been
done. When you are taken before King Arawn, as you
will be, merely tell him you were practicing shape-changing
when the guard entered; and then we shall demonstrate
your abilities."

Sound of commotion came from the corridor; in
moments, Febar the Judge appeared in the doorway with
armed guards crowding behind him. At sight of a beardless
MacDougall in white and blue, he faced the man who had
given the alarm.

"You said you had the man in black—?"

"As I did, Master." The man pointed dramatically.
"There on that bed he lay—yellow beard and hair, and
all in black! I swear it by my head!" His face set stubbornly. "I know what I saw—and this I saw."

Febar's close-set eyes glared at Alan. "And what have
you to say?"

MacDougall smiled. He had but to deny, and it would
be his word against the guard's. He thought of Enki's
assertion. Better follow the serpent's lead.

"In truth he saw me as he said. I lay there amusing
myself by changing into different forms, including that of
the man whom your Seer described. As you should know,
any shape is possible for the gods."

The Judge scowled, his gaze shifting indecisively from
Alan to the soldier and back. Finally he nodded, his mind
made up.

"The King shall decide. Guards—to his Majesty's
chambers."

With Febar in the van, MacDougall behind him between
two guards, and a half-dozen others following, they
marched through a maze of hallways, deeper and deeper
into the castle. As they proceeded, Alan became aware
of a change in the character of the corridors; thick car-
peting covered the floor, tapestries hid the masonry, and
the number of lamps increased. Finally they halted before
a great bronze double door inlaid with ornate gold designs.

Before it stood two huge black men clad only in loincloths of golden fabric and gold-thonged sandals, each armed with a gleaming scimitar.

At sight of them MacDougall had to repress a laugh. Perfection! Nubian slaves—nothing else would have sufficed.

Febar spoke, his manner and voice subdued. "We wish to see the King."

One of the guards pressed a knob in the gold design; and Alan heard a faint chime beyond the door.

"Who seeks entrance?" the King's voice demanded impatiently.

"Judge Febar, with the visitor."

There was a sound of scurrying feet, a faint high-pitched giggle, then the harsh command, "Enter!"

As the double doors were drawn apart, Febar, Alan, and the soldier who had given the alarm passed through. Now Alan felt no inclination to laugh. A strangely revolting odor of incense filled his nostrils, and there was that feeling of prevalent evil. King Arawn, in red silken tunic and pantaloons, half reclined on a great mound of cushions; behind him, massive draperies covered the wall, the heavy folds still swaying; at one side was a low table, mere inches above the floor, heaped with food and wine in golden vessels. He looked older without his kingly trappings, wrinkled and almost bald.

They halted well away from the monarch, judge and soldier starting to kneel, when Arawn growled, "Stand!"

He scowled at MacDougall. "You again! Why?"

Hastily Febar told him what had happened, including Alan's explanation.

"Show me," the King demanded.

From the Lord Enki came the thought, "The King himself."

Alan commented lightly, "With your permission, your Majesty." And in moments he stood before the startled ruler as his perfect double. In the other's deep voice he said, "There is no form I cannot assume—including this."

With the flowing of his features, he became another Judge Febar. "But I prefer this." Again he assumed the guise of Nuada. "Do you still question my godhood?"

Visibly shaken, the King glared angrily, uncertainty evident in his manner. After a moment's thought he said, "I have summoned Beli. My decision is unchanged. He will pass judgment." To Febar he added, "Until Beli arrives, I believe our visitor will be more comfortable in Manannan's Masterpiece. See to it." He waved his hand in dismissal.

As MacDougall turned away, he felt oddly drained. Walking toward the door, he heard the shuffling of the other two as they backed after him. An oddity caught his attention. On both sides of the doorway were framed areas about eight feet square, smooth and white as new plaster—an anomaly in a place like this.

In the corridor, they assumed the positions they had previously held, following a different course, including descent of a long spiral stairway which must have gone far below ground level. Curiously, Alan thought of the odd title, Manannan's Masterpiece. Manannan? The name awakened memories out of his reading in Celtic mythology. The god of the sea, as he recalled it, was famous, among other things, for having built the fortress of Oeth and Anoeth, whatever that was. Supposedly it was made entirely of human bones. Could that be Manannan's Masterpiece?

As they left ground level and began their descent into subterranean depths, it became noticeably darker. There were no lamps and no gas flames to dispel the murk. The phosphorescence of the walls, extending now to the ceiling and stone stairs, seemed to grow stronger, though perhaps this was illusion created by the gradual adjustment of eyesight to the gloom. The downward spiral seemed endless; but at last they reached bottom, entering upon the level stone floor of a vast underground chamber. No walls were visible in any direction, only the luminescence of the floor providing light. Directly ahead, barely discernible in the distance, MacDougall thought he saw a faint glow, suggesting some sort of structure. A momentarily disturbing question came to Alan. This cold light coming from all surfaces—was it phosphorescence or radioactivity? If the latter, what could prolonged exposure do to him? Mentally he shrugged. There was nothing he could do about it.

Febar the Judge, quickening his pace to a brisk walk, led them toward the patch of light. Probably, Alan thought, with his destination in sight, he was anxious to deliver his prisoner and get back to the surface.

As they advanced, the light resolved itself into a white building of strange appearance. About ten feet tall, its walls followed a sort of zigzag pattern, somehow familiar. Still closer, Alan knew what it suggested—the end of a honeycomb with three faces of a hexagon, the recessed end of another, three more faces, and so on. Now he recalled that one writer had told of the prison of Ochren being shaped like a beehive. Perhaps a honeycomb instead? But what about the walls of human bones? Close enough now to make out details, Alan could see they were indeed there.

Forming the top edge of the wall was a row of carefully placed human skulls, face out, lower jaw included. About five feet above the base of the wall was a second row of rounded backs of skulls, like bone-white cobblestones. The rest of the wall was a mélange of bones of every description, carefully fitted together, mortared into a solid mass—ribs and thigh bones, arm and finger bones, vertebrae and pelvic bones, all emitting a phosphorescent glow.

Alan noticed a door at the end of each hexagon, tall, very narrow, its upper portion formed entirely of thigh bones standing on end, the natural spaces permitting sight into and out of the interior. Altogether Manannan's Masterpiece was a ghastly sight.

From around a corner of the structure came two men, drawn, probably, by the sound of the group's approach.

They halted, standing side by side, arms crossed over broad chests. Of medium height but massively built, they were dressed entirely in black, and both wore great, black beards. One was completely bald; the other had a mass of black hair, squarely cut at his shoulders. From the right wrist of each dangled the nine metal-tipped thongs of cat-o'-nine-tails. neither man spoke, but merely stood waiting.

Hastily Febar explained, "Lords Pryderi and Pwyll, we come on instructions from King Arawn, bringing a temporary—guest. He is to be held safely and unharmed until the arrival of the god Beli, who he claims is his father. At that time, an escort will come for him."

MacDougall felt the eyes of the two boring into his. Then suddenly the bald one raised his whip and roared; "His sword! Remove his sword!"

Uneasily the judge responded, "He wears it by permission of King Arawn, and he will not be long with you."

There came a deep rumble from the jailer's throat, and he stalked to a door five hexagons away and flung it open. "In here!" Moments later the door closed behind MacDougall, and he looked through the gruesome bars in time to see the bald one forming signs with both hands. Locking the door with magic, he thought; but what magic could do, countermagic could undo. He watched briefly as Febar and his retinue turned hastily and hurried back into the darkness. The jailers had already disappeared.

Scowling, MacDougall examined his cell, though there was little to see and almost no light to reveal that little. The room was indeed a hexagon, about fifteen by fifteen feet at its widest points, bare of furnishings except for a narrow benchlike bed in the middle of the cell; and this too, he realized, was formed of mortared bones. The most striking feature of the room was the repetition of borders of luminous skulls, grinning down from the top of the walls, with alternating central bands staring emptily at him. Reluctantly he sat on the bone bench.

A most unsettling spectacle, Alan thought, his imagination starting to work. Unconsciously he began counting skulls, thinking of the dead who had contributed to this structure—and with near-physical effort he checked his morbid thoughts. A little imagining of that caliber went a long way. After all, they were only bones.

Mac, he told himself decisively, you know you don't have to stay here. You can leave whenever you want to. He grimaced at the skulls. Then why stay? He addressed the serpent-gods. "Lord Enki and Lady Inanna, am I correct in assuming that you can whisk me out of here whenever I wish?"

Lord Enki answered. "If you mean can we counter the spell that locks the door to permit your escape, yes. But if you mean what I think you mean—one of those transfers to a distant point—the answer is no."

MacDougall felt his jaw drop. The answer was totally unexpected. He could hardly believe he had sensed the thought correctly.

"You mean you can't do what the gods of Tartarus can do with apparent ease?"

There was obvious annoyance in the serpent-god's response. "You seem to have forgotten that the Lady Inanna and I are imprisoned in this armlet under specific restraints—or perhaps we failed to make this clear. The abilities we once had—powers beyond your conception which we once controlled—have been greatly curtailed. Were this not so, think you we would remain here?

"As for what you have come to think of as transference, you must realize that to move you would require the expenditure of great energy. You would have to be the source of that energy, hence the obvious limits."

"But the gods—Nuada, Balor—why can *they* do it?"

"You are not thinking," Enki chided. "Recall your conversation with Ahriman in his golden tower. He spoke of the power everywhere in limitless supply—but he spoke also of the *powers* that control it. Those powers and the limitless power are accessible to the gods of Tartarus, but because of limitations placed upon us by the Lord of Light, not to us."

MacDougall tried to keep his disappointment from appearing in his thought. "But Ahriman referred to his revealing to me, under certain conditions, all the powers, the properties of the armlet—powers exceeding those of the gods of Tartarus—"

"We *have* abilities and powers, important to you, mental and psychic, which you can command: shape-changing, as you know; invisibility; the countering of magic or illusion; creating illusions of your own fashioning; thought exchanging; sight beyond normal physical barriers and over great distances; and, perhaps the most important, the ability to develop those powers within you."

The Lady Inanna interjected a mocking thought, "As for whatever Ahriman said, one should remember that the truth is not always in him."

Alan ended the mental interchange, aware of a sudden letdown. Ever since the serpent-gods had revealed themselves, his imagination, despite himself, had been working. Like a child with the promise of a new supertoy, he had anticipated using god-powers in the Other World. And they were there—within limits. One of those limits was the availability of energy—*his* energy.

He listened. He had been aware of faint sounds, as of conversation; and now he began to understand words, coming through the walls. Of course—there had to be others in this prison. Somewhat reluctantly, he sat on the bench-bed and closed his eyes, the better to concentrate on the sounds and to shut from his sight those empty eye sockets.

He heard: "A new prisoner, I tell you. I *know*. And he came armed. I heard Pryderi bellowing about a sword. Would that I had a sword and a chance at the fat pig!" There followed a dim, meaningless mumble, evidently a reply from a neighboring cell.

Curious, Alan crossed to one of the back walls and held his ear close to the surface. The sound of heavy snoring came faintly to his ears. About to return to the bench, he noticed a perpendicular line about two feet from a corner, a sort of door with a slightly protruding bone, an apparent handle. He drew it toward him, revealing a narrow cubicle with a round hole in the floor. He heard the sound of flowing water far below. Primitive, he thought with a grimace, closing the door and returning to the bench.

He considered exploring the prison of Ochren through the powers of the armlet, viewing the other prisoners, assuming this could be done, but decided he was not sufficiently interested. He was curious, however, about what lay behind those mysterious doors in the corridors of Arawn's castle.

"Lord Enki and Lady Inanna," he addressed the serpent-gods. "If this lies within your powers, I should like to see what is concealed within the rooms of the castle, those lining the hallways. Any room; you make the selection."

"You concern yourself with matters that mean nothing to you." Enki seemed annoyed. "But if you insist—"

In Alan's mind appeared a picture of a small, shadowed, square chamber, dimly lighted by glowing stone walls, its corners veiled and misty, as if obscured by dusty cobwebs. It was empty, except for a naked man in the center, curled into a ball, arms covering his head. He writhed and twisted and cringed, seeming to attempt to escape from something causing exquisite agony, for from his lips came groans and screams and faint, hoarse cries for mercy. It was strangely eerie and completely inexplicable.

Revolted, Alan shut the picture from his mind and exclaimed in wonderment, "But why—"

The Lady Inanna interrupted. "That is what is actually there. This is what the man thinks is happening, all very real to him."

The same room appeared, but now the area seemed vastly expanded, a veritable amphitheater, with the circling seats filled with screaming multitudes of Romans in

holiday dress. And in the center of the arena cringed the
lone man, surrounded by mightily muscled men, naked
to the waist, wielding whips which lashed out with blows
without number, striking without order or rhythm—or
mercy. Again MacDougall thrust the picture from his mind,
more puzzled than before.

"But why—?"

"He was an overseer of slaves who thoroughly enjoyed
his work. Many died under his whip for his own strange
pleasure. He found enjoyment in inflicting pain. Now time
for him has stopped in his own small world; and blow for
blow returns to his back. The fiery pain of the first lash
is no more nor any less unbearable than the last—and
the last—and the last. Forever."

MacDougall shuddered. All those doors—and certainly many others he had not passed—!

Enki's thought was faintly amused. "Shall I show you
others of Arawn's toys? Perhaps the butcher who dis-
membered children—slowly. Or the witch whose hungry
covens—"

Hastily Alan interrupted, "No more. No doubt they
deserve what they are getting, but I have no stomach for
such spectacles." A phrase Enki had used came to the
fore. "Arawn's toys—what do you mean by that?"

Another picture formed in Alan's mind, a view of the
room in which he had seen the ruler sprawled on his
mound of cushions. Now King Arawn was not alone; with
him were a score of houris, scantily clad, fawningly eager
for his caresses. But he was ignoring them, his eyes gloating over something before him. One hand held a golden
object suggesting an ankh which he waved now and again.

The view changed; and Alan seemed to be looking over
the King's shoulder, seeing what held Arawn's hungrily
fascinated attention—the two white squares on the wall
on opposite sides of the door. But they were no longer
blank; rather, like two giant television screens, they held
action scenes of the private hells spawned in the minds

of occupants of those countless rooms. A flick of his looped cross changed the view on one or the other screen.

Apparently Enki had selected one of the less gruesome spectacles to show Alan; for a few revolted, horrified moments he watched, then blotted out the sickening images.

The Lady Inanna commented dryly, "One sows one's seeds; they sprout and ripen; and at the harvest, each must eat the fruit of his own planting."

With amusement Lord Enki added, "The arrogant Arawn has an insatiable lust for the sufferings of those who have condemned themselves. Yet his sleeps are never free of a haunting dread, of a certainty that eventually, even for him, time will end, and he will reap and consume what he has sown."

MacDougall stared without seeing at the ghastly wall of his cell, questions rising in his mind. Why was Arawn— he groped for the word—custodian of these tortured souls? It seemed as if the castle with its countless rooms had been designed for its present use. Why was Arawn chosen, and not one of the other gods of this dark realm? He directed his questions to the serpent-gods.

The Lady Inanna responded. "We have not the answers, but a bit of delving in the mind of Arawn should reveal what you wish to know."

MacDougall sat waiting with eyes closed, shaken by all he had seen and been told. Why *me*? he demanded. What had he done to be chosen from all the billions on earth to undergo this experience? If this were a part of hell—and it certainly had all the earmarks—why couldn't he have delayed his entry until he had died? On second thought, he told himself with grim humor, it was better this way. Barring mischance, he could leave!

After what seemed an unusually long time, the Lady Inanna's thought came to MacDougall, bearing, it seemed to him, a note of surprise.

"If Arawn is typical of the gods of this land, they are more complex than I expected. We of the ancient times

were gods from the beginning. Arawn was first a mortal
who achieved power through the worship and belief of
many. This, I perceive, is true of all the gods of this part
of Lucifer's creation. And not always was Arawn as now.
Though he was a god of the dark realm, Annwn, he dwelt
at times among men, and then he had within him some
of the virtues esteemed by men, even compassion and a
degree of honor. But power was his, power over the living
and the dead; and as that power increased and his subjects
multiplied, he became arrogant and merciless. Even before
this island came to be and he became King of Ochren, he
began to enjoy and gloat over the suffering he inflicted.
His becoming as he now is was of his own choosing.

"His was the design of this castle and his the consigning
to the torture chambers those whom he judged. For, since
he is King, these too are his subjects."

There was a pause in the flow of thought, then Inanna
continued, revulsion in her words. "His selection of those
who must suffer was made, not necessarily on the basis
of those most deserving of judgment, though all here have
earned what they receive, but those who would provide
him the greatest entertainment!"

Incredulously Alan asked, "You mean the mental reliving of their past by the judged was Arawn's doing?"

"It seems incredible," the goddess answered, "but he
certainly thinks so."

Lord Enki interjected: "I have followed your probing,
Inanna, and Arawn is only a willing tool. Behind all of it
is the Great One, working, I believe, through Ahriman,
who in turn manipulates the King of Ochren."

The sudden entry of an external thought into Alan's
mind terminated the dialog. *"Alan—Alan MacDougall—
we are ready to join you. Exactly where are you?"*
Unquestionably it was the Bard, Alan thought, wondering
how Ahriman's impersonation could have deceived him
on that distant night in *The Red Bull of Ballydhu.*

After acknowledging Taliesin's call, he mentally pictured where he was, starting with the interior of his cell,

and traversing in thought its location underground, its position in relation to the castle of Arawn, on back to the spot of his entry into Ochren.

"*I doubt that I needed all that,*" Taliesin commented, "*but better an excess of information than not enough. We should be with you in moments.*"

MacDougall moved away from the bench, providing as much open space as possible for the arrival of the Tartarians. What would happen, he wondered briefly, if, during that magical transfer, they landed in an area already occupied—by the bench, for example? Of course, efficient magic could not permit such disastrous bungling. This fleeting thought was dispelled by the sudden materialization of the two Tartarians, Taliesin and Nuada.

For a moment the three stood motionless. Then as one, Alan and the Bard, smiling broadly, flung their arms around each other. Taliesin spoke enthusiastically as they drew apart.

"It is good to see you again, son of Dougall, though I hoped you would never have to return to this depressing place."

Alan shrugged. "I really had no choice."

Nuada, who had been examining the interior of the cell with fascinated attention, exchanged greetings with MacDougall, eyeing him quizzically, then exclaimed, "A striking imitation, friend MacDougall, but now that I am here, one of me should be enough."

"True enough," MacDougall agreed somewhat absently, at the same moment flashing a thought to Lord Enki: "Back to myself." Aloud he admonished, "Hold your voices down; sound travels through these walls." Even as he spoke he was aware of physical change, of a return to Alan MacDougall.

After further brief conversation, MacDougall said, "I left you in the middle of a war, with the leader of the opposition trying to follow me into the Other World. How did it end—assuming it did end?"

The King of the *Tuatha de Danann* waved his hands

expressively. "It ended as it inevitably had to. We won, of course. With the failure of their ambush at the crossroads and with both Balor and Morrigu slain, it was impossible for the Fomorians to win. They are fierce fighters, and of course the casualties were heavy, but we finally drove them over the hills back to Murias. The clean-up of bodies seemed endless," he added cheerfully, "but the war gave the Norsemen and the Ch'in something to talk about for a long, long time."

Finally MacDougall asked, "Now that you are here, what do we do? I certainly don't intend spending much time in this cell—nor in Ochren itself, for that matter. I still haven't got a clue as to why Ahriman tricked me into coming here, but I'm getting tired of letting him lead me around like a dog on a leash."

Again Nuada answered. "Taliesin has told me everything that happened, except perhaps for the fine details." A note of enthusiasm entered his voice. "Most important at the moment is our need to learn as much as we possibly can about this place. Imagine—a completely unknown world! What we've learned from you—even this very prison, which we had heard of in the Olden Time, but had never seen—makes our own Island more inviting. So I suggest to begin that I take your place and meet my long-lost father, Beli. I wonder what he looks like now."

Surprised, Alan exclaimed, "He wouldn't have changed that much—" He paused, then continued with understanding, "I see—here all of you have received new bodies, the old ones having died. But I had thought maybe your new ones were fashioned after the old."

"As they were," Taliesin interjected. "But a lot of time has passed, and we change with the centuries. Not aging in the same way we aged in the Olden Days, but subtle changes occur, none the less."

"So that means, Nuada," Alan concluded, "that Beli may not recognize you as his son—"

"Hardly that—except of course, with the power of shape-changing, what one sees is always suspect. But if there is any doubt, there are things out of our mutual past which only he and I know. He'll be convinced. If I receive a fatherly welcome, perhaps we'll visit his castle. Tell me what we should know about Beli's arrival and what will follow."

"There is little to tell," Alan replied. "With his coming, I understand an escort will be sent for me—which group you will meet. His castle, *Dinas Affaraon*, according to King Arawn, is a sleep away from here, which means at least two sleeps, with the messenger going and Beli's travel time for the return. Crazy way to measure time." He added, "One other thing you should know." Briefly he told of his claims—his having come from the Great Above to judge the King's fitness to reign in Ochren, of a revolution, of confirming signs that his guess might be true. "You may have to back up my story."

"The two of us," Taliesin commented, "will watch that meeting—invisible, of course. We'll be guided by whatever develops. Meantime, while we await the coming of the Lord of Death, I suggest Nuada and I do some exploring. Invisible and traveling the easy way, we should be able to learn a great deal in a very short time. You will wait here for the escorts. There should be ample time for us to explore, but I'll keep in constant touch so that, if there is any need, we can make an instant return. A good plan, I think. Are you ready, Nuada?"

"Ready." The two joined hands.

"But—" Alan began to protest, annoyed at the Bard's high-handed planning, then said no more, because Taliesin and the god had disappeared.

Well, Mac, he told himself ruefully, you're the victim of a thirst for knowledge. He sank to a seat on the bench-bed, trying to see his visitors' side of the matter. A new country to explore after fourteen centuries would be a break in the monotony of existence. If he were in their shoes, he'd probably be just as curious. And he had to admit there was merit in Nuada's plan to meet his own father, a test that he, MacDougall, would probably have failed.

His thoughts returned to his interchange with the serpent-gods, dwelling particularly on the need for his supplying the energy for whatever physical magic they performed. He had to admit it was logical. Access to unlimited power on their part would have enabled them to have escaped the confines of the armlet ages ago. He had been expecting too much. This simply meant that he had to depend on himself and his own wits and abilities, something he had been doing all his life.

Inevitably he thought again of those closed rooms in the castle of Ochren and of King Arawn and his prying eyes. He felt utter loathing for the sadistic monster. In spite of himself he began imagining what must be in those chambers; with almost physical effort he shut out the thought.

Idly his gaze rested on a fold in his black cape draped over the bone bench. Better change back to Nuada's form, he thought, in case one of the jailers might look in on him.

Perfectly timed, a hoarse roar came from the direction of the door as it was flung open and one of the bearded jailers burst in, his whip hand raised high.

"Up! Enough of rest. Time for dancing." He halted, staring at MacDougall in unbelief. "Who are you? Where is the white-headed one?"

At the first sound, Alan had leaped erect; and during the slight pause, he dove for the other's legs, striking him just above the ankles in a vicious tackle. The massive form fell forward, barely missing MacDougall, the elbow of the upraised arm receiving the brunt of the fall. There was a howl of pain as the jailer writhed over on his back. Alan leaped erect, saw the exposed jaw, and with all his strength swung the side of his heavy hiking boot against the bearded chin. The man slumped and lay still.

Only then did Alan think of his sword or the armlet with the possible use of magic. He stood rubbing his shoulder. A football tackle worked better when one wore shoulder pads.

There came another sound from the doorway and the second jailer, the bald one, stood in the entrance. He saw his companion's recumbent figure and sprang forward, crouching. "Pwyll, what happened?" He dropped to his knees and touched the younger man's forehead.

About to leap from behind, MacDougall, on impulse, flashed the thought, "Invisibility, Lord Enki!"

At that instant Pryderi stood up, whirling, his whip lashing out. Instinctively Alan dropped to the floor and heard the metal-tipped thongs whistling above his head. He saw the jailer spin wildly around, seeking his invisible prisoner.

"You must be here!" he howled, looking everywhere. He halted, his gaze fixed on the cubicle in the corner; he moved swiftly toward it as MacDougall watched. Suddenly he spun awkwardly around, his neck wrenched to one side, his black beard pointing upward, a shocked curse escaping him.

And as suddenly he was gone!

Where Pryderi had been, Nuada and Taliesin appeared out of thin air. The King of the *Tuatha de Danann* laughed heartily with obvious self-satisfaction.

"That was too easy," he exclaimed, "and rather unfair. But for me to fight him would have been equally unfair. And I couldn't let him swing that lash of his. Someone might have been hurt." He added, "You can appear now, MacDougall."

Alan stood up, canceling his invisibility. "What happened to the jailer?" he asked curiously.

"I dropped him into the moat," Nuada said casually. "That should keep him occupied for a while." He looked at the unconscious Pwyll. "Should I send him to join his father?"

"That's hardly necessary," Taliesin commented. "And if the shock of the water didn't awaken him, he'd probably drown."

Fleetingly, Alan thought of the scaly tentacle he had seen in the oily water of the moat. "We can tie this one up with his own whip," he suggested. "And even I have enough magic to put him into a deep sleep." Drawing a sturdy pocketknife, he cut off four leather thongs and knelt beside the jailer. Hesitating, he looked up wonderingly at Nuada.

"You say you dropped the other one in the moat? You mean you were able to transfer him through this wall, the ceiling, and the masonry of the castle?"

"Of course," the god answered smugly. "How this is possible, I don't know. But if you'll recall when we transferred you and four others from the road north of Findias, we materialized *inside* Darthula's home. This meant passing through a wall. We might well have encountered clumps of trees on that flight. And moments ago when we returned here—as when we left—we passed through the wall. All matter is alike to the power."

"Amazing," MacDougall exclaimed as he fell to work with the cords. He addressed Lord Enki, "You *can* put him into deep sleep—I hope."

The answer came. "With ease."

"You've been busy," the Bard exclaimed. "I watched your little adventure. You had the situation well in hand, so we wouldn't have returned this quickly, except that Beli has almost reached the castle of Arawn, and we had to be here to play our part."

"Beside that," Nuada added with a chuckle, "I couldn't let you have all the fun. Pryderi has not had his beard pulled in a long time."

"Beli almost here?" MacDougall demanded, ignoring Nuada. "But how is that possible? Unless it's the crazy time in this world."

"No—he started even before Arawn's messenger was dispatched. We heard him discussing it with one of the Druids, a man who had been told in a dream that the god was sorely needed at Arawn's castle! He made the journey underground, by the way, traveling with his own retinue of fully two hundred Druids and a small army of soldiers— all on horseback, of course."

MacDougall scowled blackly in growing anger. "Again we see the meddling figure of Ahriman, using dreams to manipulate his puppets. I wonder if these two jailers are also in his scenario."

"Be that as it may," Nuada interjected, "we'd better prepare our own plans. You, MacDougall, had better be invisible while Taliesin takes on the appearance of one of the two warders. He'll greet the escorts and I'll leave with them. Understood?"

They were ready and waiting when two quaternions of soldiers came marching to the prison, and everything went according to schedule, with Nuada leaving with the Romans after being delivered by the spurious jailer. Moments later the invisible pair fell in behind them.

They followed without incident across the plain, up the spiral stairway, and through the corridor into the throne room. They approached it from the rear, entering by the doorway which previously had admitted the King's Guard, the invisible ones slipping in while Nuada momentarily delayed his entry. The King of the *Tuatha de Danann* was led by his escort to the same position MacDougall had occupied before the judgment bar. Minutes later the cer-emonial army marched into position. Standing to one side, the silent and unseen pair watched.

Alan noticed a change in the setting. Where three chairs had awaited the coming of the judges, there were now five, the central one larger, more ornately decorated and raised above the others. With the soldiers in position, the door beneath the dais opened, and four gray-cowled Druids entered and stood before their seats.

After a noticeable interval, the door behind the throne opened and King Arawn, in his customary bright red, entered. As on signal, everyone—except Nuada—knelt; and only then did the god Beli enter, taking his position before the central chair and immediately seating himself, his eyes fixed on Nuada.

Alan watched the King, whose face grew livid as he glared viciously at Beli's back, then transferred his furious attention to Nuada. The King of the *Tuatha de Danann* met his glare with a faint smile. Clearly Beli's actions were not according to protocol; his delayed entry had been a deliberate affront.

While the tableau held, MacDougall examined the god with avid interest. He was a most impressive figure, taller than Alan or Nuada, massively built, with a broad, prominent nose, deep-set, pale blue eyes under bushy red brows, thin-lipped mouth, bristling red beard, and luxuriant red hair falling well below his shoulders. His short-sleeved vesture of vivid green, gold trimmed, gaped to expose a muscular, hairy chest. Knee-length black breeches, and black boots ending at mid-calf completed his dress. A broad belt of gold circled his waist, supporting on his left side a long-handled mace and on his right a great broadsword, sheathed in gold.

Taliesin's thought came to Alan: *"He makes the King look shoddy. No love lost between them. Now I see why he brought his Druids and army. It would seem he doesn't trust King Arawn."*

Finally Arawn spoke, anger evident in his manner and voice.

"Tell me, Beli—is this your son? He claims to be Nuada, King of the *Tuatha de Danann.*"

The god of the Underworld ignored the King, addressing Nuada.

"You say you are my son. I confess there is some resemblance to the Nuada I knew."

Nuada smiled faintly. "And you appear in large part as Beli did in the long ago. But as you well know, when we were given new bodies, the Lord of Light may not have recalled exactly what had been buried in the earth. Perhaps this will be closer to what you remember."

As he spoke, his features changed subtly, became more regal, stronger. Otherwise they remained unchanged.

"The passing centuries have had a mellowing effect," he added.

"And then there was this," he continued, holding out his right hand. Slowly it became metallic silver—the hand, Alan recalled, fashioned by Diancecht the Healer to replace the member lost in the Battle of Moytura. This had earned him the name, Nuada of the Silver Hand. His clothing remained unchanged.

The new—or old—Nuada met Beli's gaze for seemingly endless moments; then he returned to his former shape.

Beli's face remained expressionless. "Where have you been since the long ago? Certainly not on this island."

Smoothly Nuada answered, "I have been in the Great Above, where lie the Four Cities, Falias, Murias, Findias and Gorias, a world of no night, of unending day. Some might call it the Blessed Place; and there dwells the Mother Danu, as well as the Dagda, and others of the gods whom you have not seen since the Olden Times."

Beli's eyes narrowed and momentarily his jaws tightened. "Danu—" he began, then seemed to change his mind. "Why have you come here?"

Nuada answered promptly. "To judge Arawn's fitness to rule. There are reports of revolution, and the Master is not pleased."

Beli snorted. "The rebellion of these Roman soldiers is not a danger, merely a nuisance." In silence he stared at the other, seeming to think things over. Finally he said, "If you are my son, you will remember, during the great battle with the Fomors, when, with a single well-cast stone, I put out the death-dealing eye of Balor and turned the tide of battle."

Nuada chuckled. "I remember it well—but your memory has betrayed you. It was not you but Lugh of the Long Arm who cast that magic stone. Perhaps you, my father, will recall the time when, as a very young lad, I tricked you into hiding in the House of Math, whence you escaped with only—"

"Enough!" Beli interrupted. "A tale better left untold." His rugged face broke into a smile. He rose and faced the throne.

"Arawn, without question this is my son. And of course he will return with me to *Dinas Affaraon* as my guest."

King Arawn gestured with both hands, palms upward. "Take him and welcome. I certainly do not object—"

A deep bass roar raised in fury interrupted him. The voice came from beyond the bronze door at the rear of the chamber. Every eye turned toward the sound.

"Open that door! I must see the King—now! Open, I say!"

The door swung wide to admit the water-soaked, bedraggled figure of the bald-headed keeper of the prison of Ochren. His black cape hung heavily from his broad, squat frame; his whiskers and garments were fouled with the oily green scum of the moat. With him came the heavy odor of decay.

Catching sight of Nuada, the man raised his right hand and brandished his whip.

"I'll kill him!" he cried in a frenzy of wrath.

CHAPTER 5

In the Abyss

Shocked silence followed the wild outcry; even the warder himself was speechless, as if realizing the enormity of his offense. King Arawn and the god Beli were on their feet, motionless. The King finally spoke, his expression grim, his tones somber.

"Pryderi, advance and explain your actions."

Slowly the jailer approached the bar of judgment and halted beside Nuada, bowing deeply.

"I crave mercy, your Majesty. Even in my anger, I should have shown respect for your presence. I beg—"

"Enough! Tell me what happened."

Obsequious now, Pryderi told of his entry into the "white head's" cell after hearing a shout from his son Pwyll. Instead of the prisoner—pointing accusingly toward Nuada—he had found a man in black with yellow hair and beard; and on the floor, unconscious, lay Pwyll. He had stooped over to examine him, and when he stood up, the prisoner had disappeared.

"Then someone grabbed me by my beard—and an

instant later I was struggling in the water of the castle moat. That monster had almost caught me, when the sentry pulled me out. Had it not been for him, I would have died. And this one," he said, glaring at Nuada, "must be behind it all!"

King Arawn, still standing, fixed narrow eyes on Nuada. "Again the man in black! What have you to say?"

Nuada shrugged. "I say your warder has spent too many years underground. His mind is gone. He is seeing things that are not there." He drew away from Pryderi, wrinkling his nose. "Only a madman would go swimming in that stinking moat."

The King gesticulated wildly. "Take him away! Pryderi, chain guards to his wrists and ankles and lash him until he tells the truth—"

"Hold!" The god Beli's voice was only slightly louder than Arawn's. His words came clearly, quietly, but with cold finality and absolute authority. "This is my son. He goes with me. My Druids are down below, all two hundred of them, and at my word, with their combined power, they will open every door and free every prisoner in this castle from his spell and from his cell. In the mind of each will be planted the knowledge that you are responsible for their tortures. And you know I can do as I say." He spoke to his four Druids. "Freeze the soldiers where they stand."

With a wave of his hand, he said, "Come, Nuada."

Side by side, the two gods passed through the doorway under the dais, the Druids following closely. At their back hastened the invisible pair, hands clasped. As the outer door closed behind them, Alan heard Arawn shout to his Guard, but there was no apparent response.

Beli seemed to know precisely where to go; without wasted motion, they found the spiral stairway and descended into the depths. There they strode purposefully through the gloom toward the faint sounds of horses and occasional voices raised in conversation. They reached a low, stone-walled enclosure. Within it, Alan judged, were about three hundred men and their mounts, about two-thirds of the men in the white robes of Druids and the rest Roman soldiers.

"We ride at once," Beli called out, his voice echoing hollowly through the vast chamber. "Bring one of the extra horses for my son Nuada."

"Extra horses. Good!" Taliesin's thoughts came to MacDougall. *"Somehow we must get two of them so we may follow."*

"We'll find a way." MacDougall moved to the edge of the milling herd, watching as Nuada, Beli, and the men mounted and started out. The gods led, with the Druids behind them and the soldiers in the rear. At the very back rode two men leading a tandem string of eight riderless but saddled animals.

Mentally Alan addressed the serpent-gods. "My Lord Enki and my Lady Inanna, can you help us get two of those horses?"

Impatiently Enki answered, "It hardly takes two of us for so trivial a task. The men have already forgotten their count. I shall hold their attention while you mount the last two animals."

In moments they were astride the horses, detaching the tether lines and coiling them around the saddle horns.

"It might be well," the Bard silently suggested, *"if the horses like us were invisible."* Alan agreed, and this too was accomplished.

Gradually they fell back, permitting the body of horse-men to get farther and farther ahead, satisfied to keep them in sight as a moving gray-white mass, clear against the darkness. They had quickened their pace, and the sound of iron-shod hoofs on the stone floor came back clearly.

For a time they rode in silence, eyes fixed on the horse-men ahead, matching their pace, each busy with his own thoughts. Alan became aware of something heretofore unnoticed; at widely spaced intervals rose great, round, stone pillars, phosphorescent like every surface in this place, merging with the ceiling far above. It was comforting to know that adequate supports held up the incalculable weight of the surface world.

Taliesin was the first to speak, his tones solemn. "I have thought and thought since I first learned you were here—and, Alan, I feel strongly that at the very first opportunity you should return to your own world and stay there. No matter what the cost. I have gained new knowledge—"

A sudden sound behind them interrupted his words. With one accord they drew rein and listened. Rapidly it grew louder, the distant roar of many galloping horses.

The army of King Arawn was in pursuit.

"Quick!" Alan spurred his horse into action. "We don't want to be caught in the middle."

They raced at top speed, closing the gap. They saw the forces of Beli pause, evidently listening, as the sounds of pursuit as well as their own approach were detected. Alan checked his mount, pulling up. The horses of Beli, they saw, had come to a dead halt. Were they going to fight?

Taliesin was the first to see their defense.

"Fog!" he exclaimed. "The Druids of Beli at work."

From the massed Druids came rolling banks of heavy fog, sweeping over the floor, in seconds blotting out all sight of the horsemen, rising to fill the vaults above, and spreading out on every side. As the gray cloud cloaked every surface, it spread darkness.

It engulfed MacDougall and Taliesin—blinding fog and darkness that concealed everything, destroying all sense of direction, rolling on to swallow up the army of King Arawn.

Now ahead, muffled and muted, they heard the hoofbeats of Beli's horses, again in motion.

"Quick! Better visibility now," Alan cried. "The cord that fastened your horse in line—pass it to me. We must follow the sound. If we lose it, we're really lost—and I hate to think what that would mean in a place like this."

Somehow they succeeded in passing the cord and, held together by the line, they started after Beli. For a time they were able to hear and follow, though attempting to keep up in the blind dark lacerated their nerves; then suddenly the faint hoofbeats seemed to come from several different directions at the same time. Confused, they halted, realizing that, with a possible change in surroundings or entry perhaps into a corridor, their guiding sound echoed from every side. As they hesitated, the sound was fading. It became fainter; then all was silent.

They were lost indeed!

Alan drew his flashlight from one of his pockets, pointing the beam toward Taliesin. Despite the powerful ray, he could barely see the Bard and his horse, nebulous in the fog. "I don't suppose it's possible for you to transfer us out of here?"

"Not possible," Taliesin answered regretfully. "Perhaps our combined strength—?"

MacDougall shook his head, then, realizing he could not be seen, spoke aloud. "This is not one of the powers of the armlet. Perhaps guidance out of this mess would be possible." He directed his thoughts toward the serpent-gods.

"Lord Enki and Lády Inanna, can you lead us out of this fog?"

For the first time the mental reply came hesitantly. "We sense tides of power from many minds, and they confuse and mislead. We might be able to direct you back to the skeleton prison or the castle of Arawn, since these are strong in influence. It would be better if we were farther away from the army of Druids."

So there were other limits to the armlet's powers, Alan thought. "We have no wish to go back to Arawn's domain." He said aloud, "Let us continue as we are, in tandem, giving my horse his head. Perhaps the animal has a sense of direction, and since he came from *Dinas Affaraon*, he may go back there. At our slow pace, the Druids and their spell should be getting farther and farther away from us.

We certainly can't wait here for the fog to clear. Don't ask me to explain, but, because of the mental influence, the confusion created by all those Druids, the power of the armlet is not sufficient to guide us safely out of this. Not now."

Lightly Alan spurred his mount, flicking off the light; there was no point in wasting current. Reluctantly, it seemed, the horse moved into the darkness, Taliesin following. Though nothing could be seen, not even his hands on the loosely held reins, MacDougall kept peering intently ahead, straining to see *something*.

There was almost no conversation. At one time Taliesin grumbled, "This is worse than anything in Tartarus. I don't plan other visits to Ochren. I prefer monotony to this."

Alan grinned into the darkness. "I recall a time when you created a bit of fog yourself. I was glad when it lifted."

They rode on in silence for a time, letting the lead horse set the pace. Something, half-remembered, kept prodding Alan, and finally he recalled it.

"Taliesin, just before we heard Arawn's horsemen, you had begun to tell me something. You started to say, 'I have gained new knowledge—' and then we were interrupted."

"Did I? Perhaps I'll recall it—later." An awkward silence followed.

It was an eerie feeling, this riding into unbroken blackness. Alan thought of his escape from Murias under cover of magic fog, but there he had been following a road by its sound, and there was light behind the fog. Here was utter darkness and nothing whatever to indicate direction. There had been no apparent order in the spacing of the pillars he had seen. He hoped instinct would guide his horse around them.

Then ahead he detected a faint glow.

"Light!" he exclaimed in sudden relief.

It was so. Moments later, they rode through a wide doorway into a great, boxlike chamber filled from end to end and side to side with tier upon tier of symmetrically arranged shelves, reaching to the very top of the high ceiling. On the face of each tier on wide walks extending from end to end, about six feet apart, one above another, were scores of women busily engaged with something on the shelves before them. All had shoulder-length hair and wore identical sleeveless gray shifts ending at the knees.

The two halted just inside the doorway, and though there were women less than ten feet away, they were ignored. Finally Alan called out. "Hello!"

There was no response. "Weird," he said aloud, then rode up to the nearest woman and looked over her shoulder. She was busily harvesting mushrooms, placing them in a tray suspended from a cord across her shoulders.

"Mushrooms!" MacDougall exclaimed, then leaning forward he gently turned the woman and looked into her face. Hastily he released her and drew back. Her face was an expressionless mask, her eyes staring emptily! As if nothing unusual had happened, she continued her work.

Momentarily Alan was speechless.

"Very logical, mushrooms," Taliesin commented casually. "We raise grain and fruit and harvest fish. Here in a dark world they grow mushrooms."

"But these women—like puppets—"

"Like living dead," Taliesin added. "But since this obviously is a source of food, we must be near a castle, perhaps a city. Let's continue."

"Wait." MacDougall had caught sight of a worker entering a distant doorway, hauling a cart heaped high with something dark. "Let's see this whole operation. Since they don't seem aware that we're here, let's explore."

He led the way through the long central aisle to the far doorway, the woman and her cart having turned into an intersecting lane. Even as they approached the opening, they heard strange flapping sounds and a high-pitched chirping, barely within the range of hearing. They halted and looked into a second chamber, this one in total darkness, no glow coming from floor, walls or ceiling. Alan drew out his flashlight and circled the room with its beam.

As one, he and the Bard cried out incredulously. "Bats!"

Every square inch of walls and ceiling hung thickly with furry brown-black bats, a nightmare horde. And soaring erratically in and out of the beam were hundreds on the wing, all apparently entering or returning through a great doorway leading into a third chamber. The air was heavy with the odor of decay. The floor, Alan noticed, was thickly covered with bat guano; and in the midst of all this, like a blind mole laboring in the dark, one of the women wielded a shovel, busily filling her cart!

Unsuccessfully MacDougall tried to see into that third chamber, then mentally addressed the serpent-gods. "Lord Enki and Lady Inanna, can you show me what lies in that third room?"

"If you wish—though I must say you have the strangest desires." A picture formed—a great writhing mass of offal and refuse—in the midst of the mass suggestions of fleshless bones, some obviously human; and pouring into the foulness from openings in the walls came more of the same. The mound seemed to be heaving with internal life; with sudden nausea, MacDougall realized the reason for the ferment. Insects by the millions infested the place, some rising and hovering in clouds, eddying and drifting— and feeding the bats!

Abruptly Alan cut off the vision, spurred his mount, and led the way out of the mushroom plant.

"I've seen enough," he said, "and if this is the food of Ochren, I want none of it." Briefly he described to Taliesin what he had seen in the third chamber.

"Very logical," the Bard commented in amusement, "but not something to stimulate one's appetite. Probably there's one of these systems for each castle or center of life."

Outside, they faced the wall of black fog, no less dense than before their entry into the mushroom chamber. Again they started, MacDougall leading. Lightly he spurred his mount, little more than a nudge, and the darkness closed about them.

After a time, their course seemed to slope downward, though Alan could not be certain. Perhaps the impression came from a slight but constant flow of cooler air touching his face, the draft possibly indicating an opening to the surface somewhere ahead. At the moment, he was more interested in what seemed to be a strangely mottled glow in the distance, a probable sign of thinning fog. As they rode on, more and more of the glowing surface appeared.

Without warning their way dipped sharply, the horses suddenly scrambling and sliding, struggling to regain their footing. The steep descent ended, and, though the gradual downward slope continued, their way seemed smoother and the breeze stronger. Now the normal yellow-green glow began to appear. Yet Alan's horse seemed to hesitate, his steps tentative, uncertain. Then MacDougall caught sight of something puzzling—a glowing wall close to his right side.

"Pull up your horse," he called sharply. "We're stopping. With the thinning fog my flashlight should help—and I'm puzzled."

He brought out the torch and flashed it ahead. The powerful beam cut through the dark, but if a wall lay ahead—as it must—it was too far away to be seen. He swung the light downward to the road—and stiffened from head to foot, catching his breath, his free hand clutching the pommel of his saddle.

They were perched on a road no more than four feet wide, running along the face of a cliff. To their left lay a sheer drop into black emptiness and certain death.

After one quick glance into the abyss, Alan kept his beam—and eyes—trained straight ahead. He heard Taliesin's weak attempt at levity. "For this we should have magic wings—or change into a hoodie-crow as Morrigu used to do."

MacDougall drew a deep breath and tried to speak calmly. "No reason to panic. We can't go back—no space to turn around. But as long as this road continues, we can go on. I'll walk ahead, leading my horse and lighting the way." He hesitated. "If the road should end—but let's not consider that."

He spoke soothingly to his mount, patting the smooth neck, while he considered his next step. If he dismounted on the left, any move of the animal could push him over the edge; holding the reins, he slid off on the right and without mishap made his way to the head of the horse. Facing forward, beam on the road, he said quietly, "Let's go."

This began what seemed the longest walk of Alan MacDougall's life. Time stood still as he led along the tortuous way, downward, deeper and deeper, around corners that almost defied passage, along straightaways, into dips and rises, following that circle of light that marked their course. Not for a moment could he relax his concentration, nor could he forget that black gulf at his left.

They halted only once, at Taliesin's sharp exclamation; "Listen! What was that?"

Out of the blackness of the abyss came what Alan thought of as a loud whispering. As he listened he knew it was not one voice, but many—a multitude, a vast, whispering chorus—like the hubbub of sound in a packed football stadium, but reduced to a mighty whisper. The volume rose and fell but never ceased—and never rose above that loud whisper.

Alan caught himself listening for individual voices, as if trying to follow a single instrument in an enormous, macabre symphony orchestra. Almost he heard a high-pitched cry, the words barely eluding him, a dry sobbing, and a wailing lament. Pictures began to form in his mind, awakened by almost-identified voices: the hopeless keening of a mother bereft of her child; the anguished, quavering moan of a centenarian in unending remorse; and a grossly wrathful mouth that cursed and cursed and cursed endlessly, an eternity of imprecations.

He felt a strong urge to turn his torch toward the sounds,

but a strange dread restrained him. Finally he forced himself to train his beam into the Stygian source of the ghastly chorus. For a fleeting instant, he saw, or thought he saw, like swirling eddies of tenuous fog, unimaginable multitudes of transparent, spectral figures, human and naked, yet distorted and intertwining, ghost merging with ghost in an indescribable fusion. An instant—then as if dreading the light, the cloud of—souls?—fled deeper into the dark, the whispering fading into near silence.

"God!" MacDougall exclaimed, more prayer than curse. "What was that?"

Taliesin answered in a subdued voice. "This can be none other than Annwn itself, the Abyss, the lowest level of Lucifer's domain. The Unrimmed Place where wicked souls betake themselves after death, awaiting another body—if perchance they are to receive one." Dryly he added, "What a delightful place Tartarus is becoming!"

Mechanically Alan groped for his canteen, took a substantial swallow to moisten his mouth and throat, and swallowed again, realizing he had not had water since entering Ochren. "Water, Taliesin?" He held his canteen aloft.

"I have my own," the Bard replied; and he too drank.

Alan resumed the long walk, his torch fixed on the road. "Annwn," he repeated, trying to lead his thought away from that ghastly, ghostly cloud and to shed its spell. "That sounds familiar. I believe I read about it in a book on the mythology of ancient Britain—which reminds me, Taliesin. I brought two books for you from the Other World. They are our version of a scroll. They've been weighing down my robe during all of this, and maybe you can decipher the language. Remind me to give them to you when I have opportunity."

Genuinely interested in the prospect, the Bard began asking questions; but, in a very short time, memory of the eerie living cloud checked conversation.

Alan picked up their pace, but his mind was not on the journey. Those sights and sounds in the darkness—could they have been illusion? The serpent-gods—maybe they could tell him more.

"Lord Enki and Lady Inanna—what did I really see and hear?"

The answer formed in his mind. "You saw and heard precisely what you seemed to see and hear. Do you wish to have a clearer view? We can provide it if—"

"Indeed, no!" Alan answered hastily. "I have seen enough."

On they rode, the path maintaining its four-foot width, the breath of breeze slowly intensifying; and constantly at the edge of consciousness hovered that dreadful, rustling whisper. Only once during the remainder of their descent did it approach more closely; a sweep of Alan's beam sent it scurrying into deeper shadows. Evidently light was anathema.

The road leveled at last; after a long, wide sweep to the right, they entered upon a luminous plain. They had reached bottom. And directly ahead, a mile distant at the most, rose a domelike glow, suggesting the lights of a village on a moonless night, the welcome and welcoming sign of life.

Alan flicked off his torch and dropped it into a pocket. "Better we approach cautiously," he said. "Maybe on foot till we learn what we face."

Taliesin gazed toward the distant glow. "Certainly we can go most of the way on horseback without being detected, thus having the animals available and nearby when we need them. Especially if we and the horses are invisible. After we arrive and learn what we face—"

"We can do better than that," MacDougall interrupted, suddenly recalling the serpent-god's probing into the castle of King Arawn. "I think the powers of the armlet can do our advance investigating for us."

Mentally he called, "Lord Enki and Lady Inanna, we plan to visit whatever produces that light ahead. It will help greatly if we know in advance what we will encounter."

After a slight pause the Lady Inanna answered, amusement in her thought. "The Lord Enki is deeply involved at the moment, so I have investigated—and I find it quite amusing. What fools these mortals be.

"Ahead is the encampment—I suppose that is the correct term—of a once-famous Roman ruler, Caesar Titus Flavius Sabinus Vespasianus, to give him his full name. He thinks he has been very badly mistreated by the powers—the Lord of Light, really—and his talents unrecognized. He, Titus the Conqueror, should be King, he feels, not that weakling Arawn, as he thinks of him. He has gathered from among the Roman soldiers an army of dissidents which for ages has been making attacks on the castles of Arawn, Beli, and Manannan, with no one ever gaining a decisive victory. Indeed, they are just on the verge of attacking *Dinas Affaraon*, having learned of Beli's absence. Final preparations are almost completed."

"This encampment," MacDougall asked, "is it a village, rough shelters, or just how do they live?"

"That is what I find so amusing. They live in illusion. You shall see."

MacDougall seemed suddenly to be hovering above the most anomalous vision he had seen thus far in Ochren— a delightful little town of tile-roofed cottages, hundreds of them, lining a street as broad as a modern highway which passed through the middle of the town. At its center, in a wide circle marking an intersecting street, stood a castle of white marble, rising high into the upper reaches of the Underworld, a fairyland structure of towers and pointed spires. Gas lights atop slender marble pillars lined the streets, sending their radiance through the area.

Along those broad streets, men and women walked or stood and talked, uniformed soldiers and their robed companions, for all the world like those in an ancient Roman village.

Beyond the village, merging with the darkness, were soldiers and horses whose numbers Alan could not estimate.

"Incredible!" he exclaimed. "But you said—illusion?"

"That village," said the Lady Inanna, "is what they think they see—where they think they live. And of course for them, the image is the fact. This is what is really there."

Alan's mental view changed. All that remained of the former scene were the gas lights—and they were simple pipes with flared tops, projecting from the stone floor. Of cottages and castle there was no trace—only regularly spaced pallets on the hard floor; and in the center was a roughly built seat of heaped-up stones on which sat a man in the garb of a Roman ruler. There were other soldiers in the picture, most noticeably a group gathered before the central figure; but nowhere was there trace of a woman.

As the vision returned to that of the village and its castle, MacDougall demanded,

"How can that be? How is such illusion possible?"

"They have with them a god skilled in creating illusion, his name Amaethon, whose sole task is to maintain what you now see. Only the Emperor Titus, beside Amaethon himself, knows the truth. This god, by the way, is a son of Nuada, and forever the enemy of Arawn."

"If the two of us enter the village, what will we see?"

"You will see the illusion, as does everyone else. The spell is strong and not easily countered."

Alan opened his eyes and stared toward the distant lights. The Bard had dismounted; Alan joined him, glad to stretch his legs.

"I have the necessary information," he reported. "The leader of the revolution—and there appears to be a perpetual revolution of a sort—is a one-time Emperor of the Roman Empire. He is Titus Vespasianus, and if I remember my history, a most unpleasant individual. He sacked Jerusalem in the first century, led successful campaigns of conquest into Germany and Britain, and was honored with a great Arch of Triumph erected in Rome. He was made Caesar following in his father's steps, and ruled the Empire until his own death. He has with him at least one god, Amaethon, who supplies him with strong magic. There may be others, Druids as well, though that remains to be seen."

Briefly he described the illusory Roman village as created by Amaethon, and told what was really there. He concluded with a question. "What should be our next step?"

Taliesin looked quizzically at MacDougall. "What do you suggest?"

Alan frowned. "Since I've learned what we face, I have a question. Can you think of any logical reason for our risking a confrontation with Titus Vespasianus?"

The Bard pursed his lips. "N-no, there is no real reason. I would like to see his encampment—and we must find a way out of here. There certainly is one, since no army could enter or leave by the way we came; but a meeting is neither necessary nor desirable."

"In short, we and the horses become invisible again. We ride as far as we may safely go, see what is to be seen, find the exit and leave. We either use these horses or others, if need be—borrowed, of course." He chuckled. "If this were the Old West, we'd be in danger of being hanged as horse thieves. I've been stealing horses ever since I arrived on Tartarus. Seriously, to stay together we'll hold the lines as we did on our way here."

According to plan, they set out toward the distant glow. At first, they spurred the horses to a brisk pace; but soon, becoming aware of the clatter of hoofs, they slowed to a walk. At Alan's leading, they veered to their left, approaching above the encampment, aiming toward the area where he recalled seeing the soldiers and their horses.

"If we can get close enough for our horses to join the other animals," he said to Taliesin, "we can restore them to visibility and have them—or others—close by when we need them."

As they drew near the pseudo-village, the wisdom of his plan proved itself. There was sufficient commotion among the assembled horses to hide their approach, the last fifty yards on foot. The animals, saddled and bridled in numbers impossible to estimate, were milling about in a rough enclosure formed of long, stone feeding troughs. Beyond them, well out of earshot, were the Roman soldiers. From somewhere came the sound of splashing water.

With their horses safely corralled, they approached the illusory village. They reached its edge and stood marveling at its perfection. Close by, they saw a fully caparisoned Roman soldier in animated conversation with a handsome woman who, Alan knew, was not there. Mind-boggling! How far did the illusion go? It was pointless to speculate.

The castle caught and held their attention, and they made their way toward it. They passed several soldiers who, of course, ignored them, and they reached the marble steps leading to the castle entrance, guarded usually by soldiers bearing lances. They began mounting, stepping carefully to avoid making a sound. Suddenly, as if electrified, the soldiers sprang to attention.

"Halt!" one cried, leveling his lance; and shouts came from every side. Before Alan could begin to grasp what had happened, except that they could now be seen, they were seized and held by strong hands.

"Spies!" someone exclaimed. "Take them to Caesar!" In swift response, they were hustled through the doorway, along a marble-walled corridor, and into a smaller version of King Arawn's throne room, this one seeming of marble and gold.

On a gold-inlaid throne, resplendent in royal purple, sat the Emperor Titus. Before him, in uniforms of high rank, stood what appeared to be his corps of officer.

"Lord Enki!" MacDougall cried mentally, even as they were hurried along. "Our invisibility—what happened?"

"A counterspell, obviously—which I admit I should have been prepared to check. I could restore—"

"To what purpose? They have us now."

At the first sound of commotion, Titus stood up, his officers quickly turning, all looking in wonder at the strangely dressed visitors firmly held by castle guards.

The monarch, tall and black-bearded, scowled imperiously, then demanded, "Speak! What means this?"

One of the officers, apparently in command, began, "We saw these spies suddenly appear—"

Loudly Alan interrupted, pushing to the fore.

"Indeed I shall speak! This treatment is intolerable. We have come from the Great Above to consider your claim to the throne of Ochren. When we appeared on the steps of your castle, we were violently seized by your soldiers without an opportunity to speak a word. We demand an explanation!"

To Taliesin he added, "*I don't know how far bluff will go, but we can't hope to fight. Have any ideas?*"

"*I'm trying to reach Nuada. Maybe he can lift us out of here. He has the power—*"

The Emperor's exclamation interrupted. "My claim to the throne?" He stared at MacDougall with piercing eyes. "My claim to the throne? Who are you?"

"One-Sent-To-Judge," Alan answered in impressive tones. "The emissary of Ahriman himself." He waved as best he could toward Taliesin. "And this is the Ruler of Tartarus. We have honored you with our presence—only to be seized and accused without a hearing."

The Emperor glowered at his prisoners, his eyes moving from MacDougall to Taliesin. "We shall learn the truth of this matter."

Impatiently he called, "Simon! Simon—at once!"

The draperies behind the throne were parted by a small man, white robed, crowned with bushy white hair, and stooped with years. His only ornament was a silver ankh suspended from a golden chain around his neck.

"Yes, your Majesty."

"What can you tell us about our visitors? They come with a strange tale."

The ancient Seer faced Alan and Taliesin, his deep-set eyes staring fixedly. Slowly he raised his thin arms in a wide half curve, reaching toward the two, the white, full-cut sleeves dangling like strange wings; his bony fingers spread far apart as if to draw from them the information he sought. Quite a showman, MacDougall thought, as the Seer held the position interminably.

At last he spoke, his voice surprisingly deep and resonant. "They are not of Ochren. One—the one in black— is not of this world, nor did he enter as we did. I see them riding and coming by the Forbidden Way! I see the living cloud—" His words broke off, hastily changed. "I see Arawn and Beli—they have been with them. I also see Pryderi and Pwyll, though not clearly." He paused, his position unchanged, tension mounting; and no one moved.

"Now I see them walking—invisible until they reach the castle steps—then my protecting shield destroyed their spell." The thin lips curved in a smile, almost senile in its self-satisfaction. "None can withstand the powers of Simon Magus."

"What of his claim to have come to judge my fitness to rule?"

The Seer seemed to concentrate even more intently; finally he spoke with smug satisfaction. "I see no truth in this. No truth at all."

During all of this, the restraining hands of the soldiers had not relaxed; now Alan felt the fingers tighten as Titus exclaimed, "Spies! And they shall be treated as such! Simon, check their power—" He halted with a gasp; and MacDougall saw his eyes widen with consternation, their gaze fixed over his shoulder. He half turned to stare at the empty hands of the soldiers.

Taliesin had disappeared!

"A third man," Titus gasped. "For a moment there was another. Now both—are gone!"

For a timeless instant MacDougall's mind was blank, then his thoughts raced. Nuada! The Bard had reached Nuada, and the King of the *Tuatha de Danann* had appeared to transfer him elsewhere. Maybe he lacked power to take both—but more likely he lacked the inclination. He owed Alan nothing; could gain nothing from him or his rescue. Grimly Alan realized he was on his own.

These flashing thoughts took mere seconds; he felt the grasp on his arm unconsciously weaken. With sudden violence he wrenched himself free, leaped at Simon Magus and sent him sprawling, then dashed for the exit, drawing his sword as he ran. If he could only pass beyond the old Seer's sphere of influence and become invisible again—

The clamor of shouts and pounding feet rose behind him as he reached the doorway—only to face several surprised soldiers mounting the stairs. Viciously he swung his weapon in a wide arc, sending the newcomers reeling backward. The slight delay brought his pursuers upon him; he spun to face them, each threatening with a drawn shortsword.

Behind them rose the shout of Titus: "Take him alive! I want him alive!"

At the same instant, with his sword flicking and darting, MacDougall mentally cried, "Enki—a diversion! Now! Counter Amaethon's illusion of the village! If you can."

"If we can!" The serpent-god's answer was derisive.

At the same instant, the white castle, its marble steps, the tile-roofed cottages, the broad streets, and even the marble pillars with their gas-flame crests all vanished. Left in their stead were a mound of rocks on which Titus stood, the pipes with their gas lights, and long rows of pallets.

The floundering Roman soldiers were shocked beyond expression and in utter pandemonium. With the vanishing of the steps, the soldiers fell sprawling. MacDougall, half-prepared for the change, managed to remain erect and, with a single wild shout, he darted out of the central area, thinking, "Invisible!"

With the thought, he glanced at his feet and realized he could not be seen. He took a few more steps, then stopped short. Silence now was all important. No sound must alert recovering pursuers, though their recovery would not be that quick. Stepping carefully, he headed for the horses. Once he glanced over his shoulder. The Romans in what had been the village seemed in a state of complete confusion, with no apparent thought of him.

He looked for the gray he had been riding and saw at once that finding it would be well-nigh impossible. Take a good one while you're at it, he thought. In moments, he saw the horse he wanted, a magnificent roan, standing well above his fellows; if the ornate silver harness meant anything, the steed was that of an officer, perchance that of Titus himself!

Carefully, he moved through the herd, grasped the stallion's reins, and led him out of the corral. Minutes later, unseen horse and rider moved away from the encampment.

"Lord Enki and Lady Inanna," he addressed the serpent-gods. "My appreciation for a timely task well done. And now I need more help. There must be a way out of this pit, and I haven't the vaguest idea where it is. Can you direct me?"

With evident annoyance the Lady Inanna answered. "Merely because we told you of certain limitations placed upon our powers is no reason for you to question our abilities with each need. Of course we can guide you to the surface. Your horse will find the way for you. At our direction, of course."

The Lord Enki added, "Has it never occurred to you that you, too, have the ability to influence these horses mentally? They, as other animals, are receptive to mental commands, responsive to stronger minds."

An interesting idea, MacDougall thought, but hardly the place and time to discuss such possibilities. Especially—from behind him he heard the sound of hoof-beats—with Roman soldiers in pursuit! He could not be seen, but he could be heard, hence followed.

How urge the horse on to greater speed when he had neither spurs nor whip? As if in response to the wish, the big stallion leaped ahead, quickly leaving the lights of the rebel camp behind them, then veering to the left and starting up a long, wide incline.

The sound of pursuit persisted but grew no louder. The roan ran tirelessly on. It would take an animal with unusual speed and endurance to catch him. Ahead loomed a perpendicular wall, faintly glowing and vanishing into the murk far overhead. They were dashing straight toward it; then at its base, MacDougall saw either the mouth of a cave or the entrance to a tunnel.

Tunnel it proved to be, roughly fifteen feet wide, with symmetrically arched walls and ceiling, and a floor of sandy white gravel. Alan's horse continued into the opening with unchanged pace, his hoofbeats now somewhat muffled. The sound of pursuit died with entry into the tunnel, though after a time it could again be heard. The noticeable grade continued unchanged, but Alan became aware that their way followed a serpentine course, curving alternately to left and right, a way cut through solid rock. What an engineering feat, he thought. And to what purpose?

"Lord Enki and Lady Inanna, I am puzzled. I am grateful for this way to the surface—but why was it constructed? Of course it was Lucifer's doing, but to what end?"

The serpent-god answered, amusement in his thought. "How else would the famous Emperor Titus Vespasianus reach the surface to attack Arawn or Beli or Manannan?"

"But surely," Alan objected, "you can't mean the rebel army is part of Lucifer's plan?"

"Why not? Discontent—futile attacks by an army that never wins, with no reward for their efforts. And on the other side, the annoyance of a persistent enemy who is always there through slowly passing ages. As you will learn, Titus controls the largest group in Ochren. And now you enter the scene; as in Tartarus, you have introduced new elements—the disappearance of the Roman village, for example. We have permitted Amaethon to reassert his spell, and Caesar's palace rises again in all its splendor. But seeds of doubt have been sown in every rebel mind. Even Titus is uncertain now. Can he trust Simon Magus and his prognostications—or are you whom you claimed to be?" Enki's amusement increased. "Indeed, no matter where you go, you make your presence felt. Permanently."

MacDougall scowled, then shrugged. Too bad—but he hadn't asked for any of this.

Sight of a half circle of bright light ahead caught Alan's eye, that mysterious beam of radiance from the black sky, revealing the end of the tunnel. Moments later as he emerged on a grassy plain, the light winked out, and he brought his horse to a halt to give his eyes time to adjust to the dim light.

Which way to go? He was in the middle of a plain, the twilight gray merging on every side with the black, dimly lit auroral sky. All directions were alike. Let the horse decide. Invisible, he could not be seen by his pursuers; but even invisible horses left tracks. An idea—

"Lord Enki, can you—rather, will you—create an illusion in the minds of the oncoming soldiers? Tracks leading into several different directions?"

"Indeed. They will be utterly confused."

With a slap on the stallion's rump and a mental "Go!" they dashed across the meadow into the semidarkness.

CHAPTER 6

Taliesin's Trouble

A bright beam of light lanced out of the black sky ahead and far to Alan MacDougall's right, revealing at its edge a long white structure, too distant to be identified. At last, Alan thought, a sign of life.

Bringing the stallion to a halt, he faced the way he had come and peered into the murky distance, then circled the horizon with his eyes. There was no motion anywhere, no sign of pursuit. He was alone on a flat and featureless plain, an expanse of gray-green turf.

A slap on the horse's rump and a mental command sent his mount moving toward what finally resolved itself into a great white stone block, long, low, and windowless. Suddenly Alan gave a short, rueful laugh. This was another Hall of the Dead, like those on Tartarus, rising starkly in solitary isolation, with thousands of cold cadavers awaiting animation by the spirits of the newly slain. He checked the stallion. No reason for going there. It was not a place to visit.

The circling beam reflected brightly from an expanse

of rippling water between him and the Hall of the Dead. He rode closer, halting at the shore of a lake, an oval about a hundred yards in length. The surface was in constant motion, waves moving out from the center where the water spouted upward as from a fountain. Annoyingly, at that moment the light winked out. After his eyes had adjusted, he saw that four narrow streams flowed from the lake, one from the left end, one from the right, and two from the side he faced, their regular positioning indicating planning. This was the water supply, he decided, for the four areas of life on this island; that at the right end flowed to the castle of Arawn, and the next to the outlaw encampment. He had approached between these two streams. The other two in front must flow to Beli's castle and to that of Manannan in the North.

Dismounting, MacDougall removed the harness from the stallion, talking quietly to the great animal as he did so. "You're quite a horse," he said softly, "and you need a name. If this harness says anything, it tells me you belonged to the outlaw Emperor. So I'll call you Caesar. After all, he has more names than anyone needs—Caesar Titus Flavius Sabinus Vespasianus. Agreed? I'll appreciate it if you stay close by. Beside which, there's no way I can anchor you, the grass is the same everywhere, and we have a good water supply." Newly named Caesar headed for the lakeside and in moments was drinking thirstily.

Alan dropped to a seat on the thick turf, leaned back on one elbow, and stretched out his legs. It felt good. He was tired and—suddenly he realized it—sleepy. Little wonder; a lot had happened since he had bade farewell to the Camerons so long ago. He drank freely from his canteen; before he left the lake he'd refill it. With thirst satisfied, he became aware of hunger; gratefully he recalled the food that Norah had insisted he take and retrieved it from the pockets in which he had stowed it.

Sitting cross-legged, Alan hungrily attacked the viands, the slices of roast lamb and oat cakes proving especially satisfying. As he ate, he mentally reviewed all that had happened since his entry into Ochren: his fantastic adventures; those appalling torture rooms of King Arawn; and that skeleton-jail and its grim jailers. Grinning, he pictured furious Pryderi, green with the slime of the moat, then the blind wandering in the fog, the triple mushroom caves, the Forbidden Way and its ghastly living clouds, Titus and his rebels, and his arrival at the lake. A lot had happened.

One question repeated itself over and over. Why? Why? He had been tricked into entering Ochren, so this was part of the plan. Plan? What plan? And whose? Ahriman in his golden tower must be responsible—and behind him Lucifer. But none of this told him why! And there was that interrupted remark of Taliesin: "I have gained new knowledge—" Knowledge of what? And the Bard had repeatedly urged him to return to his own world. Again, why? Frustratingly, there were no answers.

He thought of Taliesin's disappearance. That at least could be explained; Alan could reach him mentally and find out what had happened. He closed his eyes and centered his thoughts on the Bard.

"Alan—are you safe?"

"Quite safe in the middle of nowhere. Quite surprising, your sudden departure. Couldn't Nuada handle both of us—or were you his only concern? And should I start out to join you? I've acquired a horse."

The answer came hastily. *"No—stay where you are. I can't explain now; but we'd better continue this later. I am being questioned by Beli at this moment and need to give him full attention."*

"Later, then—after I have slept."

MacDougall opened his eyes, staring unseeingly into the gray distance. Taliesin had seemed uneasy. But then, Beli was an intimidating character. Well, it was not his problem. He yawned and stretched. Time to prepare for sleep. Removing his cape, he folded it into a makeshift pillow, then thought of his saddle, a far better head rest; he draped the cape over it. Removing his riding boots and placing his sword conveniently close, the belt under his pillow, he stretched out on the thick turf. At a sudden recollection he sat bolt upright. The scorpion he had seen in the grass during the approach to Arawn's castle!

"Lord Enki, since apparently you never sleep, I will appreciate your keeping watch for anything like scorpions disturbing my slumbers."

There came an impatient, "Sleep in peace." Alan sank back on the turf. He hadn't realized how tired he was—and his eyelids were heavy, closing in approaching slumber.

A confused blurring of thought came, as of scores of dreams seeking the stage of his mind, or of many silent voices crying for attention. One gained ascendancy and registered clearly, obliterating the others.

"*Dagda, have you noticed the absence of Nuada and Taliesin?*" Alan recognized the words as those of Danu, mother of the gods, coming just as others had during his stay in Tartarus, reaching him in the moments of drowsiness just before slumber. He seemed to have an unsought ability to eavesdrop on mental conferences among the *Tuatha de Danann.*

"*No, I haven't. I have been visiting the Trolls under Findias. They at least still have some creativity—*" It was the familiar, quiet, measured reply of Dagda.

"*I received a call from Nuada,*" Danu continued, "*and he has a fascinating tale to tell. Alan, son of Dougall, has returned to our world, though not to this island—to another which can only be Ochren, yes, even Annwn, the accursed place. Nuada and Taliesin joined Alan there.*" There followed a sequence of flashing images, thoughts too rapid for verbal form, Nuada's report of what he had seen and experienced.

A third god, one unfamiliar to Alan, raised a question. "*Is there anything we should do?*"

"*I think not, Diancecht. Action on our part without Nuada's request would be unwise. I suggest we maintain vigilance and remain in close communication in the event we are needed."*

There was more dialogue, but it was of little interest to Alan; and in the midst of it he slept.

When MacDougall awakened, he was lying on his back. He opened his eyes and stared into the shifting sheet of aurora that was like a dim veil of light stretched over the velvety black sky. As always with him, waking was instant, and he needed no time to identify his surroundings. He stretched the kinks from his muscles and sat up.

Out of the corner of his eye he saw movement. Swiftly drawing his sword, he leaped erect, facing south. He stared wide-eyed at a column of twelve helmeted and armored Roman soldiers, fully equipped, marching single file around the far end of the lake. When they reached the stream, they turned and followed the edge, ignoring MacDougall completely. Astonished, he watched as they moved steadily across the plain, becoming smaller and smaller, vanishing as did the stream into the darkness.

For the first time Alan noticed the footpath on which they marched; with his eyes he followed it back around the lake and saw it join a wider, central path that led back toward the distant Hall of the Dead. In his mind's eye he saw the great, frigid hall north of Findias in which he had been trapped, with the newly animated Vikings leaving, walking zombielike past him on their way into the city.

The riddle of the marching twelve was a mystery no longer. They were replacements, heading for the castle of King Arawn. Perhaps there had been an encounter between the forces of Arawn and Beli despite the fog. And if there had been casualties in the god's forces, they might have marched by while he slept. It was an uncomfortable thought, despite their being oblivious to everything around him. If true, how had they crossed the southern stream and that leading to the rebels, to follow the proper one? Then he saw that a stone slab parallel to the edge of the lake bridged the brook. Enough! He'd better prepare for whatever lay ahead.

The horse! To go anywhere he'd have to be able to ride. Of course, there was always walking... With relief he saw the stallion grazing about thirty yards away.

"Caesar," he called, "come here."

The animal raised his head, tossed it in seeming greeting, and ambled slowly toward MacDougall, stopping to nibble clumps of grass on the way. Handy thing, this mental rapport!

After filling his canteen, he took a dip in the lake, followed by brisk calisthenics to dry his body before dressing, then ate a hearty breakfast. With regret, he noted at meal's end that only three oatcakes remained. These he stowed in one of his pockets. Then, again sitting cross-legged on the grass, with eyes closed he reached out mentally to Taliesin.

After greetings the Bard began somberly. *"I am in trouble. Short of calling Danu and the rest of the gods into this, I don't see a solution. I am being held in a prison in Beli's castle while he decides my fate. At the moment, escape is impossible. When you called me earlier, I told you I was being questioned by the god.*

"In response to my call to Nuada as we faced the Roman Titus, he had transferred me to his room. Unfortunately, at that moment the god Beli appeared at the door. He had come to escort his son to a banquet already prepared. He did not appear happy about my being there; and when Nuada began introducing me as the Bard Taliesin from his own land, Beli cut him short and simply said, 'The Bard will join us.' Immediately we were led to a large banquet hall."

"A banquet?" Alan had to interrupt. *"On mushrooms?"*

"Mushrooms that had passed through Beli's cauldrons, which transformed them into all sorts of delicious dishes. A banquet which included the two hundred Druids and the officers of Beli's elite Guard. I confess my first

mouthfuls were hard to swallow; but I was hungry, and the taste was good.

"After we had eaten, Beli questioned me. I had decided on a story which left you out of the picture. I had merely followed Nuada from Tartarus after he had been gone for what I felt was too long a time. Unfortunately, there had been no opportunity to consult with Nuada—and when I tried mentally at the dinner, the power of the massed Druids blocked my thought. Hence I didn't know that he had been forced by those same Druids to tell the truth.

"My lies angered Beli. He considers you a menace, and of course thinks I am your accomplice in whatever mischief you are planning. I told him about the attack planned by Titus and his rebels, but he only laughed and said, 'He will never learn!' So here I am! And through the constant attention of those Druids, all my powers are held in check. Your armlet, not any ability of mine, makes this interchange possible."

After a long pause, Alan commented, *"I'll have to think of something. There's always a way. Tell me, just where have they put you in Beli's castle? Can you describe just where your prison is?"*

"Don't try it, Alan." Taliesin's thought was insistent. *"Take my advice: don't concern yourself about me; just get out of Ochren as quickly as you can—and stay out!"*

Making no effort to conceal his annoyance, Mac-Dougall answered, *"Why are you so anxious for me to leave? Does it have anything to do with that sentence you left unfinished, 'I have gained new knowledge—'? If so, tell me what you know. When we parted before my return to my own world, you seemed to expect me to return. If it's just your interest in my welfare, thanks—but forget it. I'm a stubborn Scot! Ahriman and his trickery annoy me, and I'm determined to find out what's behind it."*

"I am sorry I can't convince you." Alan could almost see the Bard shrugging his shoulders. *"I am confined in a room on the first underground level. There are lower ones. A spiral stairway leads down from the banquet hall."*

Carefully he described the position of his prison. *"There are Druids in the three rooms surrounding this one, several in each room, and two in the hallway guarding the door. All are alert to anything I may try."* He added a faintly facetious thought. *"If you can get me out of this, you're a magician."*

Reluctantly Alan broke contact. He remained seated, staring unseeingly into gray distance. There had to be a way to free the Bard, and he had to find it. He needed something to distract the Druids, to get their attention away from Taliesin. The ordinary magic spells, such as fog, fire, darkness, an indoor storm, even a rain of blood—he had read of all of these—would simply be ascribed to Taliesin and countered. Mass illusion would fail for the same reason. Counterspells... That raised a question.

"Lord Enki and Lady Inanna, I need information in several areas. The great power of Beli's Druids—what is its source? And why is it so great?"

The answer was delayed, as if the serpent-gods were considering the matter. "None of them alone has unusual strength—psychic strength, I think you would call it—but they have been trained to combine their force on any need that arises. They react instantly, each mind attuned to the others."

"If several crises should arise at the same time, let us say, an earthquake, a rain of fire from the sky, soldiers going berserk and attacking Beli, and so on—all magically caused—what would be the result?"

"Initially there would be confusion, but in a very short time smaller mental groups would form, each concentrating on one problem, and under most conditions they would counter all of them."

Alan saw a glimmer of light touching his dilemma. "You used the words 'react' and 'counter'. Does this mean—?"

"It means they do not initiate action unless instructed to do so by Beli. They do not act, they react. And if there were a sufficient number of different distractions, the powers of each unit, obviously, would be greatly reduced, and their effectiveness diminished. Their strength lies in numbers."

"Thank you. You have been most helpful."

With fingers intertwined behind his head, MacDougall lay back on the grass and considered the situation. There was a germ of an idea in what the serpent-god had told him; he need only develop it. Several plans suggested themselves, to be discarded immediately as too uncertain—not that certainty, he knew, would be assured with any idea. He tried to plan systematically. First, he needed a place of concealment in or about the castle where he could observe without being detected. Then he needed something unusual to distract the majority of the Druids, plus another diversion to seize the complete attention of those guarding Taliesin, all before he could think of rescuing the Bard. Alan grimaced. It was a tall order.

A hiding place. There might be a spot made to order for his purpose! With suppressed excitement Alan grasped his armlet.

"Lord Enki, I have not seen *Dinas Affaraon*; but on the outside wall of King Arawn's castle there are regularly spaced niches containing guards or images of guards. Is this true of Beli's castle? And—most important—are there any empty niches?"

"Both castles have their guards of bronze figures, and both have vacant niches, probably statues displaced through the passage of time."

"Am I correct in assuming that you can change my appearance to match that of one of the bronze figures, without the rigidity, of course?"

"You are correct. Indeed, you should be able to do it without my help, providing the influence of Beli's Druids does not interfere."

Another idea came out of nowhere. "What progress has the rebel Caesar, Titus Vespasianus, made in his planned attack on Beli's fortress?"

"You do jump about! They have left the Underworld

and are even now riding toward *Dinas Affaraon*. Your sudden departure from before Titus helped precipitate his move, since he thinks of you and Taliesin as spies. They are well on their way."

Excellent, MacDougall thought jubilantly. This could well be the main diversion. Certainly the Druids would be involved in resisting any attack on the castle. He could hardly have planned anything as effective as such an actual physical presence which could not be ascribed to magic. He supposed Beli had an army to call on, but surely the Druids' abilities would also be called into play.

Now if he could introduce something into the rooms surrounding Taliesin's which had the same qualifications—something unusual. The bats from the mushroom cave? No, too ordinary. Or the bugs from the next cavern—millions of them? Perhaps they would do, if they were of a stinging variety, but that was too much to hope for. If only they were bees... Bees! There were bees on Tartarus, uncounted numbers to pollinate the orchards—but little good they'd do here. What about local stinging insects—other than scorpions, which were more than he wanted?

"Lord Enki, as you know, the bees in the orchards of Tartarus are stinging insects. There would hardly be bees here in Ochren where no flowers or fruit grow, but are there any other insects equipped with stings? As I think of it, I believe I caught a glimpse of a scorpion near Arawn's castle."

Surprise was evident in the serpent-god's reply. "I must say you have a most devious mind, but I begin to see the direction of your thinking... and I appreciate your confidence in my having universal knowledge. To answer your question, yes, Ochren has great numbers of wasps, insect-eaters who keep the beetles under control. They in turn are attacked by certain of the beetles which prey on their larvae, since the wasps nest underground."

So far so good! "A final question. Can you control

large numbers of the wasps, causing them to swarm into the castle?"

Response was slow in coming; Inanna finally answered, "My Lord Enki is testing your request. It has been long since we were involved with influencing insects. Animals, yes—but not insects. I must say you have unusual and interesting ideas."

The thought of the serpent-god reached Alan. "You will be pleased to learn that, though the wasps do not have minds as we think of them, there is an area of control that can be reached and influenced. We will be able to do what you wish, causing them to swarm and arousing their irritation. They are naturally savage creatures, easily annoyed."

"Thank you, my Lord and my Lady!" Alan was jubilant as he severed mental connections. His plan should work. He scowled at a sudden thought. How could he prevent the wasps from stinging Taliesin—and himself for that matter? He shrugged. He'd have to find a way.

Caesar, as if knowing they were about to leave, had taken a last drink of water. With the big animal saddled and bridled, MacDougall mounted, glanced about to be certain he had forgotten nothing, and started out for Beli's castle, or on a course he thought would lead there, the path following the third of the four streams. He thought of checking with the serpent-gods, but stubbornly rejected the idea. He had to be right.

He rode with eagerness that seemed to be shared by Caesar, who broke into a brisk canter. As the miles passed, Alan thought over his plans, a feeling of excitement gradually awakening. For the first time since entering Ochren, he was pitting himself against one of the dwellers in this section of Lucifer's domain. Not unassisted, he had to admit; the armlet would play an important part—but the serpent-gods were merely equalizers. After all, his opponent was an old-time god with two hundred Druids to aid him.

He tried to visualize coming details. First he'd have

to be invisible during the approach. That included Caesar. Then he'd have to find a place for the horse to wait, preferably among other horses.

"Lord Enki, is there a corral somewhere on the surface near the castle?"

The serpent-god's answer came promptly. "Though the Romans' horses are quartered underground as you might expect, those of the Druids are in an enclosure within the wall. There's a gate, but there is also a guard."

Alan grimaced. He had to expect difficulties. So he'd have to get around the gate and the guard—and the moat, of course—then hide in a vacant niche. Why the niche? why had that idea suggested itself? Invisibility should be concealment enough; but on second thought, he realized the Druids would be more likely to counter invisibility than shape-changing. Ruefully, he added, perhaps both.

MacDougall scowled into the distance. It was stupid of him to attempt to plan details in advance, especially since he had seen none of what he faced and could not possibly anticipate every exigency, every circumstance. He'd have to play it by ear, but he'd win in spite of Beli and all his Druids. It would take more than an ancient god who had died at least fourteen centuries ago to stop him!

He seemed to have spent hours on the monotonous way when he saw the bulk of a castle looming ahead, its top lighted by a flickering red-yellow halo, and paler lights in tall, narrow windows standing out against the gray silhouette. He checked Caesar's pace to a walk. Invisibility was in order. "Enki," the thought came, followed immediately by a defiant, "Do it yourself!" He recalled his first experience with the magic spell when he was trapped in Balor's apartment. At Taliesin's instruction, he had thought of light passing through or around him, of complete transparency, centering all his faculties on the armlet. He recalled his practicing before the mirror in Darthula's room. Now he concentrated his thought on the concept that here, in this ensorcelled world, invisibility would work—

for *him*. He and his horse *would* be invisible. And instantly they were.

An approving thought came from the serpent-god. "Excellent. You learn. The Lady Inanna and I have merely been catalysts. Your powers grow."

MacDougall fixed his attention on the castle. Unlike that of King Arawn, this consisted of a single, round, gray stone tower, massive and tall, topped by six pointed spires uniformly spaced around the edge of its roof. A succession of gas torches, set just below the roof, shed light all about the tower; and just above the circling high stone wall, Alan could see the heads of the bronze soldiers in their shadowed alcoves. The stream running parallel to the path he had followed flowed into a wide-mouthed conduit that vanished under the wall.

As he drew closer to the castle, MacDougall became aware of a strange sensation, a growing mental turmoil; and he noticed Caesar beneath him seemed to be fluctuating between solidity and invisibility. The Druids and their counter spell! Grimly he set his will to resist, then addressed the serpent-gods. "Lord Enki and Lady Inanna, can you help? I have trouble maintaining invisibility."

"Our rigidly held wills in combination should be able. Accept no negation."

The fluctuation ended.

MacDougall was approaching from one of the sides, midway between two great barred iron gates, their spiked tips rising well above the wall. A substantial distance away, he rode completely around the castle, carefully inspecting it. There were two entrances on opposite sides, north and south. The southern gate was the larger, the doorway into the castle more ornate. The horses were quartered close to the north gate, and that was where Alan's interest lay. He rode to the gate and peered through the bars.

A white gravel road about thirty feet long led up to a well-filled moat with its upright drawbridge at the castle end. A cubicle built into the wall housed a uniformed guard. Three-foot-high walls, each with its barred gate, bordered the road, forming enclosures for the horses.

As Alan studied the situation, he wondered how on earth—or in Ochren—he could climb into one of those niches. There were vacant ones, as Enki had said, but they were at least five feet higher than he could reach. Yet there was no other vantage point from which he could watch developments, unless he entered the castle and watched through a slit of a window.

Then he noticed a narrow ledge, at most eight inches wide, running along the inner edge of the moat, the top of what appeared to be a foundation wall. It would provide a precarious way to circle the castle and perhaps to climb into a vacant alcove. Neither the circling nor the climbing was at all enticing.

As an alternative, he could climb to the top of the outer wall to watch—except that, if invisibility failed, he would be a sitting duck.

First he'd have to get past the gate. He rode to one side, close to the wall and out of sight of anyone within the castle, and dismounted, still conscious of the effort required to remain invisible. Well hidden, he relaxed the spell on the stallion; and suddenly an idea formed.

A stray horse trying to enter to join the others, especially one as handsome as Caesar with his splendid trappings, might tempt the guard. With reins hanging to one side, he led the horse to the gate, planting the idea that he should try to enter. He had no difficulty in doing this; it was fully in line with the stallion's own instincts. Then he waited. If this worked, he'd not only get inside, but he'd have his mount in a safe place while action developed.

Caesar helped, whinnying and striking the gate with a forehoof. Almost immediately there was reaction. The door of the guard house opened and a Roman soldier appeared, gazing curiously at the riderless horse. Finally he lowered the drawbridge and slowly approached, muttering, "Where did you come from?"

Reaching the gate he peered cautiously through the bars, looking to right and left, his gaze finally settling on Caesar's handsome equipment. After another precautionary look, he slid back two massive bolts and swung the gate open wide enough to admit the stallion—wide enough, too, to admit the unseen MacDougall, sliding in on the opposite side. With the gate secured, the guard led Caesar through one of the smaller gates and into the corral; Alan walked on the gravel only as the Roman walked.

With a furtive air, the soldier removed the saddle and bridle and carried them across the drawbridge into his cubicle, Alan following as a shadow, step by step, until he stood safely at the castle entrance.

Safely? With distaste he eyed that narrow stone ledge. It was either that or entry into the castle—and the latter might mean waiting interminably for someone to open the door. Certainly for him to open it—if he could—would arouse unwelcome suspicion. That left only the ledge and a climb up the wall to a vacant alcove.

"Lord Enki and Lady Inanna," he thought earnestly, "I don't know what, if anything, you can do to help me follow that ledge—but whatever it may be, it will be appreciated. Above all, keep me invisible."

The Lady Inanna replied, faintly amused, "Since you include me, I'll concentrate on keeping you on the ledge while my Lord Enki resists Beli's Druids."

MacDougall swung his sword around to the middle of his back, drawing his cape to his side and fastening the sword belt as tightly as he could. Then, with set jaw and arms outstretched, he faced the rough wall and stepped out on the ledge. Slowly and silently, toes pointed outward, he began the nerve-wracking trip.

At first he made good progress, but he had a long way to go; after a time, his leg muscles became cramped, and he had to resist an overwhelming desire to change position. He knew he was in no physical danger, but a slip would mean a thorough soaking and the certain ruin of his plans, not to mention probable capture. But at last the cramp in the calves of his legs made a change imperative; and hugging the wall, he swung his feet inward and stood motionless on his toes. This provided momentary relief. Gritting his teeth, he continued his awkward slide.

An encouraging thought came from Inanna. "You have gone more than halfway. And there's an empty niche just to the right of the main drawbridge."

At last the trip ended, and he hugged the wall directly below the alcove that was his destination. A dozen feet ahead lay the main entrance to the castle, with its guard cubicle and open drawbridge. Alan considered covering the remainder of the ledge and resting at the entrance, but a word from the serpent-god canceled the thought.

"The army of Titus is fast approaching. It would be wise to make the climb without delay."

Without comment, Alan looked upward, groping overhead for a hand hold. He was not a climber, and his hiking boots were not designed for climbing. Only the roughness of the stones made success remotely possible. Taking a deep breath he started. Inch by inch he climbed.

With barely a foot to go, his fingers groped in vain for purchase. The builders had found flat rocks, fine for building but worthless for climbing. In desperation he sent a mental cry to Lord Enki.

"I'm stuck! Now it's up to you."

Incredibly MacDougall felt his muscles tense for one supreme effort—and somehow he found himself, arms outstretched, flat on his stomach, halfway into the niche in the wall. Gasping, drained of strength, his heart pounding, he lay there interminably, finally dragging himself over the edge and struggling erect. Exhausted, he leaned against the wall. Looking down he caught a glimpse of himself.

Bronze, the greenish brown of ancient metal!

"You became visible, so we made the change," Enki commented. "Better try to take your position, erect and holding your sword at your waist, blade pointing upward."

Mechanically MacDougall assumed the position, his

thoughts on that last superhuman lunge. "Lord Enki and Lady Inanna, I did not—*could* not—make that final leap upward."

"We helped—but you supplied the energy, as you must be aware. Now you know why we cannot move you as Nuada and the others do." Resentment entered the thought. "Though there was a day when it would have been as nothing... But our visitors arrive. Look to the south."

Strength returning, MacDougall peered across the gray plain, seeking sight of the army of Titus.

He had not long to wait. He first glimpsed the approaching soldiers as faint flickers of light rising out of the distant dark, the aurora reflected from helmets and armor. This grew clearer with the passing moments, becoming the wavelike glimmer of a thousand polished helmets, undulating with the movement of the horses. Because they rode over smooth turf, their approach was almost soundless, only an occasional metallic clink heard in the stillness.

Then out of the blackness above the aurora flashed that unpredictable searchlight beam. It flared toward Alan's right, then circled out of sight behind the castle; but in its passing it left a clear image of charging armored cavalry and of a forest of lances drawing swiftly nearer.

Others than Alan had seen the approaching horsemen. There came a shout from the guard in the tower at the drawbridge; the bridge clanked down, and across the metal plates thundered the hoofs of the mounted defenders in an incredibly rapid response, as if they had been awaiting attack. They rode five abreast, a seemingly endless horde. They fanned out in orderly ranks, forming a front wider than that of the attackers, curving inward at the ends, row upon row upon row, with fixed lances and poised shields, charging with absolute abandon.

The armies met with a thunderous crash, with shouts of men and shrill neighing of horses, and with the clash of steel on steel. In moments, lances in the front ranks, having done their deadly work, were replaced by flashing swords and hand-to-hand combat. But behind them, from seemingly limitless reinforcements, poured more and more of the defenders, charging into the bloody mêlée. Men were falling everywhere, to vanish screaming under metal-shod hoofs as the battle intensified.

Watching, carried away by the fury of conflict and carnage, MacDougall could hardly remain motionless, and momentarily forgot his plan. Where—where in the castle behind him could this horde of men and horses have been quartered?

"Lord Enki—this seems impossible. Whence come these men and horses?"

In surprise, the serpent-god answered, "Have you not guessed? See it as it really is."

Where there had been at least three thousand horsemen, MacDougall now saw only the original forces of Titus, fiercely battling—nothing! Yet their blood spurted; they were falling, dying.

"For them, their foes were real—real enough to kill."

The Druids! The Romans were battling illusion, created by Beli's two hundred Druids! All were occupied now with the battle, with meeting slashing sword and darting spear. It was a far better diversion than any he could possibly have imagined.

"Lord Enki, Lady Inanna—the wasps! Will it take long to assemble them? Now is a perfect time to send them on their mission."

"Assemble them?" Enki's thought was impatient. "That was done long before we came under the Druids' influence. Watch."

From somewhere above MacDougall, clearly visible against the glow of the torches, came a swirling black cloud, hovering, weaving, reeling, much like a swarm of bees Alan had once seen. From it came a high-pitched, angry buzzing, audible above the bedlam of battle.

Alan was aware of Inanna's amused thought. "You

recall, my Lord, during our days in Egypt we controlled the plague of flies?"

"Yes—and locusts and frogs... But to business. My messengers have been waiting impatiently on the face of the tower for my command. Where shall I send them?"

"As you must know, Taliesin is imprisoned on the first underground level, with Druids in each of the surrounding rooms and in the hallway guarding the door. Send them into these surrounding rooms and the hallway."

The Lady Inanna responded, "We see the Bard—and fortunately there is ample room under the doors for the entry of the wasps. Our little messengers are on their way."

With a crescendo of buzzing, the deadly cloud swept down, through one of the narrow windows, and into the castle.

Jubilantly, MacDougall sent an excited thought to Taliesin. *"My friend, things have begun to happen, as you will soon learn. Are you alone in your cell?"*

"Indeed—but I can sense my guards, Druids behind, beside and before me, and their pressures have never weakened."

"They will weaken and soon vanish altogether. You will hear a commotion. The Druids will have a problem like none they have ever faced. Even now, thousands of angry wasps, assembled by the powers of the armlet, are in the castle, directed toward the rooms around yours. When they attack, your guards will forget all about you.

"And there's more! Titus and his rebels have attacked and have been met by a phantom army created by Beli's Druids. So they are well occupied and won't have spare thoughts to expend on a hypothetical attempt to release one prisoner. We'll have you out of there—and soon!"

Taliesin's response was jubilant. *"The wasps have begun their work! I hear shouts and curses—and better, the mental pressure is diminishing. Your diversion is working."*

Alan had another thought. With a hasty, "*Sit tight*," to the Bard, he addressed the serpent-gods. "Where is Beli?"

"He and Nuada are watching the battle from an upper window, with him the officers of his personal guard."

"Where are the other soldiers?"

"In the rear of the banquet hall, watching the Druids—all of them seeming to be doing nothing."

Alan grinned with satisfaction. "Can you send your little messengers among them? I believe you have an ample supply. This should create a bit more confusion so that none will possibly give thought to Taliesin—or to general counterspells, including invisibility and shape-changing. And just think of what it will do to the phantoms on the battlefield!"

"A devious mind."

MacDougall inhaled deeply. He had no feeling of animosity for the Druids; maybe this action was not necessary—but on the other hand, it was time someone took them down a peg. An arrogant bunch. Time they learned to respect Alan MacDougall! The thought surprised him, but he stuck to it stubbornly.

Briefly he turned his attention to the battle on the plain. At first nothing seemed to change; then he saw the first indication of confusion among the defenders. Horses and soldiers were standing idly; others simply vanished.

Then a sharp thought came from Taliesin. "*There's bedlam all around me. I've heard doors open and men running down the corridors. And such cursing you never heard. They've forgotten all about me. I have checked and my powers are unimpaired. There is no restraint. Isn't it time to move?*"

"*Yes. Can you get out of your cell?*"

"*Without difficulty. The door is locked by Druids' spell which now I can negate.*"

"*Your great concern should be the wasps. Invisibility may be enough to escape their attention. In any event, you will want to be unseen as you make your way through the castle. We'll meet at the rear entrance, the corral where the Druids' horses are housed."* In swift thought he described the situation including his own position. *"Go out through the main doorway, since that drawbridge is down, and circle around to the rear. Remain invisible. As quickly as possible, I'll appear there as a Roman officer. Good luck."*

He turned his attention to the battlefield. Utter confusion prevailed with the soldiers of Titus in combat with their own men. Below him, two castle guards stood on the drawbridge watching the strange conflict, fascinated.

Enough of watching—his sole concern now was getting down from his perch. First, he must return to his own shape and invisibility. No difficulty there; all restraint had been lifted. But—how to get down?

"Lord Enki, you helped me to get up here, but I don't see how the procedure can be reversed."

"It cannot." There was smugness in the serpent-god's answer. "Look to your left. There are rough stones in the wall providing excellent foot and hand holds. Beyond them is one of the chains supporting the bridge. I suggest you move over to the chain—and the rest should be obvious."

MacDougall looked where Enki indicated and grinned in relief. A simple solution. "Thank you, my Lord." Carefully, but without difficulty, he crossed to the massive iron chain, and descended hand over hand to the bridge.

He passed unnoticed within a few feet of the Roman soldiers; any sounds he might have made were concealed by the noise of conflict. On the thick turf he headed toward the rear of the castle. Out of the range of their vision, he assumed the form and uniform of a Roman centurion and dashed toward the corrals. As the drawbridge came into view, he waved toward the soldier on watch and shouted; "Quick! I need two horses at once, fully equipped."

Startled, the guard came out of his cubicle. "But, sir—"

"No buts. A special order from the god Beli, a mission to King Arawn. There are problems with the battle."

Uncertainly, the soldier entered his quarters, and the drawbridge began descending. MacDougall breathed more easily and moved among the horses. He saw Caesar immediately and quickly selected another likely looking animal, calling them to him, and led them onto the road.

"And that special harness that you have hidden—get it! And another saddle for the spare."

The guard's jaw sagged and, obviously frightened, he tried to explain. "I had put it aside for the Lord Beli—"

"Enough. You were seen and will be dealt with. The saddles."

Hastily, the man entered the castle and brought out gear for the second horse and, from his guard chamber, that for Caesar. With trembling hands, he saddled the second mount, while Alan attended to the stallion. As he worked, MacDougall felt an unseen grip on his arm and knew that Taliesin was there. Moments later, in the saddle and leading the Bard's mount, Alan rode through the gate. Halting long enough for Taliesin to mount, he spoke to the flustered and still-frightened guard.

"I shall report your fine cooperation; and perhaps the matter of the gear may be overlooked. Return to your post."

As he turned his back, MacDougall set out swiftly across the plain on what he hoped was a northerly direction toward Manannan's castle, since there was no other place to go. Minutes later, he addressed the apparently empty saddle.

"You *are* there, I trust, my friend."

Instantly, the welcome form of the Bard appeared. The two men clasped hands warmly, and Taliesin exclaimed in wonder, "I didn't think you could do it. I still don't see how you succeeded. I can only say you certainly have mastered the powers of the armlet."

MacDougall grinned. "I wish I could claim credit for everything, but I had nothing to do with the cooperation of Titus Vespasianus and his rebels. The attack made it a certain success." He urged his horse into a gallop. "I want to put as much distance as possible between us and Beli. He won't appreciate what I've done."

CHAPTER 7

Beli's Dragon

They rode in silence for several miles; then Alan recalled his books.

"I have brought you something from my world. I'll be happy to transfer the weight from my cape to yours." Slowing his horse to a walk, he brought out the Bible and *Mythology of the British Islands.* "You will recall that I mentioned them before. I think they will really test your skill in deciphering hieroglyphics. We call them books, and they are manufactured by the billions."

Briefly, he explained what each dealt with; and the Bard stowed them away, marveling at his new and fantastic possessions. Taliesin expressed his appreciation and voiced his eagerness to get to work on the books; but far more quickly than Alan expected, he fell silent.

Not till then did MacDougall realize that the Bard was deeply troubled. "What's the problem, my friend?" he asked at last.

Taliesin delayed his reply, staring straight ahead. "Frankly," he finally answered, "I am worried about

Nuada. Oh, I know—he's a god, with god-powers, and he carries an invincible sword—but I can't help feeling his powers can't stand up against those of Beli's Druids. And I'm afraid that Beli will vent his fury on him, even if Nuada is Beli's son. I'd feel much better if he were with us."

Logical reasoning, Alan thought. He should have realized this himself. Maybe the serpent-gods...

"Lord Enki and Lady Inanna, what can you tell us about Nuada?"

After a brief pause the serpent-god answered. "Nuada is in trouble. He and Beli are surrounded by all the Druids, and they are concentrating their powers on keeping him there, preventing his transfering himself elsewhere. The attackers have fled, leaving many dead. Some of the castle guard are gathering the bodies and dropping them into the moat. Other soldiers are herding the surviving horses down a ramp into an underground enclosure. We have guided most of the wasps into the open and released them. A few have escaped us."

Alan reported to the Bard. "Nuada is being—restrained. The forces of Titus have fled in defeat and all the Druids are centering their attention on Nuada. I don't see—"

Taliesin thrust up a hand for silence, bringing his horse to a halt, his face set in a deep frown as he seemed to be listening. At length he said gloomily, "I managed to reach Nuada, and it is as I expected—but worse." He paused, his brow furrowed. "I still say this is not your problem, so I urge you to return to your world. The armlet should guide you."

Impatiently, MacDougall exclaimed, "When will you decide that I am seeing this through to the end? What did Nuada say?"

"Beli is beside himself with rage. He ordered Nuada to tell us that unless we return—and at once—he will skewer his son with his own invincible sword. He already has the weapon and he will use it—this is not an idle threat. I know Beli. He has mocked the King of the *Tuatha* by saying he can always hope for a new body."

MacDougall stared blankly ahead. He really had no choice in the matter. And he had been so pleased with himself! He had worked everything out to perfection— except that Beli held the winning card. Blast it! He hadn't asked Nuada to come to Ochren. That had been his own idea—or had it? Not really. Taliesin had invited him, and he, Alan, had called the Bard; if he hadn't, they wouldn't even have known this place existed. But why kid himself? He'd have to go back. He clutched the armlet.

"Lord Enki and Lady Inanna, Beli threatens the life of Nuada unless Taliesin and I return to *Dinas Affaraon*. I feel we have to go back. A question. What protection can you give us? Or do his massed Druids make you completely powerless?"

The serpent-god's reply fairly bristled with indignation. "Powerless? Thrice their number could not do that! All the gods of Ochren and Tartarus together could not make us powerless. *I*, who have been Kaliya, and Muchalinda, even Shesha, the world-serpent himself?"

Equally annoyed, the Lady Inanna added, "Powerless! *I*, who have been Tiamet, the Dragon of Chaos? Merely guard yourself against folly."

It was a wise answer, Alan thought. Just don't make a fool of yourself. But he felt vastly more confident now.

"Let's go," he said to Taliesin as he swung Caesar about. "We have no choice." The Bard, shaking his head in silent protest, joined him, his face a picture of gloom. On sudden impulse Alan faced skyward and spoke aloud, defiantly, "Are you watching, Ahriman? Is this part of your plan? Or are things getting out of hand?"

Grimly and in silence, they set out, each occupied with his own black thoughts. Unaware of the passage of time, they were surprised to see the castle looming ahead. As it came into view, scores of Roman horsemen sped toward them. In moments, they were surrounded, and rough hands seized their reins. Cords were flung around them, drawn tight, and menacing swords rose on every side. Without ceremony, they were hurried into Beli's council chamber and brought to a halt before the two gods, Beli and Nuada, seated side by side no more than ten feet away. Nuada's sword lay across Beli's lap. Standing, crowding closely in a rough circle, were Beli's Druids, and behind them, also in a circle, the Roman guards.

As the escort drew back, there was an instant of silence; then from the Druids rose an angry growl that grew louder and louder every instant until it became a roar of hatred. MacDougall, smiling grimly, stared at the gray-robed figures behind the gods, noticing the depredations caused by his diversion. His smile was forced; there was nothing amusing about the situation. He saw great welts, ugly swellings, and puffed lips everywhere; on every livid face were hatred and wrath, scarcely contained—fury that needed only a spark to set off an explosion of violence.

"Hold!" The great voice of Beli burst through the bedlam. The roar died slowly, an indication of the depths of the Druids' anger. When all was silent, the Lord of the Underworld fixed his intense blue eyes on MacDougall, ignoring Taliesin. His face was a rigid, frozen mask; but Alan noticed the veins standing out on his neck, the nostrils of his wide nose distended, and his red beard seeming to bristle more than usual.

"So you thought to outwit Beli! You thought with your puny magic to defy me!" The voice was bleak; though there was almost no inflection in the tones, there was something dreadful, evil, and diabolically menacing in the man and his message.

Alan felt a dryness in his throat, and it required all his strength of will to keep his face impassive, his gaze unwavering, meeting the hard blue stare. With steady voice, he answered, "You held my friend; I had to try to free him. If there was any failure, it lay in the weakness of your—tools."

Anger flaring, Beli rasped, "Those—tools—felt your gentle touch, and those tools will name your punishment."

His gaze swept over the ranks of the Druids as he called out, "What is your wish?"

"The dragon!" Hungrily, as one, they roared the words. "Let him feed the dragon!"

"What shall be done with his companion?" The god Beli waved toward Taliesin.

"The dragon!" they cried again.

Beli's expression had not changed, though Alan thought he saw a gleam of satisfaction flash in his eyes. "So shall it be!" He faced Nuada and smiled mirthlessly. "And you shall watch with me, my son. It is only fitting, since they purchased your life with their returning. And it will be a fair contest. You—" He indicated MacDougall. "You shall retain your sword." He turned to Taliesin. "And you shall also receive a weapon."

He called one of his officers by name. "Your sword for the prisoner." He added grimly, "You will regain it after the contest." With the weapon in the Bard's hand, Beli cried out, "Take them away!" He stood up in dismissal, towering over them all.

"One moment!" Nuada shouted, leaping erect. An unnatural pallor whitened the god's face as he stepped to Taliesin's side and faced his father. "I join my friends. Whatever fate they meet, I meet also." He forced a hint of a smile. "As you pointed out, if I lose the life of this body, another probably awaits me."

Beli stared at Nuada in momentary unbelief; then his mask, so rigidly maintained, fell away, and Satanic fury flamed in his eyes. Jarringly, he laughed—dreadful laughter in which were mingled frustration and gloating.

"So that is your choice! I permitted you to live so that you could lead me to this Island of yours. And you choose death. May you find it enjoyable. I'll find this land without you."

With a mocking bow, he held out Nuada's sword, hilt first. "At least, you shall have a fighting chance—a test for your invincible blade." He glowered menacingly at each of the three in turn.

"Lest you think to attack me—me, the god of the Underworld—I warn you that if, for any reason, I change my mind, I will give you one at a time to the Druids and my Guards to do with as they wish." To the Druids he added, "Take them to the dragon's lair."

Turning on his heel, Beli strode toward a great arched doorway, gray-robed men parting hastily before him.

The circle closed, and clutching hands reached out for the three—only to meet an impervious barrier. Frustration and awe appeared on the nearer faces; and Alan sensed their attempts to break through, to counter whatever barred them from their quarry. In vain.

Faintly a derisive thought touched Alan's mind: "Powerless?"

Pressed in as they were by at least two score Druids, MacDougall had no means of seeing where they went, except that the way led downward, around a long spiral stairway and along a low corridor to a wide bronze door. Heavy bars sliding into metal sockets reinforced the barrier; after they had been thrust through the doorway, they heard the clang of the bars sliding into place and heard the scurrying feet of the Druids rushing away.

Instantly, the three with swords in hand faced whatever the chamber might hold. For a moment nothing moved. They were in an oval room about the size of a football field, its floor of gray flagstones, its walls, about thirty feet tall, of closely fitting masonry, with regularly spaced gas torches set well below the arched ceiling. Completely encircling the room, just under the ceiling, were a succession of foot-high openings, and at each appeared a face, dimly seen—the spectators.

"So that's why our guards rushed away," Alan growled. "To get a good seat to watch the fun. A dragon fight."

"A dragon!" Nuada scoffed. "Seems Beli should have something more original to perform his executions."

Taliesin commented soberly, "Joining us was a fine thing to do, Nuada, but I fear it was most unwise. Certainly your sword gives us greater strength; but swords against a dragon—"

"Speaking of the dragon," Alan interrupted, "unless I'm mistaken, we'll soon know what we are facing. I see movement."

At the far end of the chamber something stirred, a huge, shapeless mound slowly rising out of the shadows, reaching higher and higher, taking form. As it grew, tall as three men, it began moving toward them, lumbering at first, as if just wakened from sleep, then with ever increasing speed. Like a great grotesque bird preparing for flight, it thrust out huge, membranous bat wings, flapping them noisily, beating the air. Its fearsome, thickly toothed jaws, like those of an enormous crocodile, opened wide, beginning to glow redly; and a whiplike tongue lashed out and back, to be followed by a deafening roar. Two long arms, level with the wings, reached menacingly, great, clawed talons extended like three-fingered hands. Scales of a cuprous green color covered body, arms, trunklike legs, and long, twitching tail, merging to white over the belly.

Alan saw all this in a flash as the juggernaut bore down upon them, flames suddenly erupting from the cavernous mouth. Barely aware of the intruding sound, he heard screams and shouts from the watchers.

He heard Nuada cry, "You two attack right and left; I'll go for the middle—and I'll control your sword arms!"

With heart pounding, muscles tensing, and breathing checked, Alan's left hand grasped the armlet in desperation.

"Enki, Inanna—do something—and do it now!"

The attacking monster, almost upon the three crouching men, suddenly halted, actually sliding several feet across the smooth floor. The mouth closed, the talons relaxed, and the wings folded back. Incredulous silence fell as the dragon slowly backed away, halting, eyes staring—as all eyes stared—at a form taking shape between the men and the monster.

Materializing out of nothingness, there appeared a great,

coiled serpent, its scales burnished gold, its head rising majestically up and up, until jewelled eyes were level with those of the dragon. In his mind's eye, MacDougall saw again the serpent in his room in the *Red Bull of Ballydhu*—except that one had had two heads. As though to explain, slowly solidifying, there appeared a lovely woman, perched on the serpent's head, a woman with raven hair, deep brown eyes, and skin of rose-tinted ivory, dressed in a cobweb robe of palest blue. A sparkling silver crown was on her head, deep blue jewels about her neck, and gold breastplates, gem encrusted, visible though her robe—the vision of the Lady Inanna as he had seen her walking toward the Great Below.

A movement, a change, in Beli's dragon caught Alan's attention. In an inexplicable metamorphosis, the near-caricature form was losing its savagery, its fire snuffed out, claws and jaws shrinking, and its massive body, legs, and tail suddenly half their bulk and becoming graceful in line. The head was now a face, reptilian but intelligent. The changes, Alan suddenly realized, the growth of one and the shrinking of the other, were synchronous. The serpent was drawing energy and substance from the dragon!

And with all this, MacDougall sensed a fantastic conversation—a succession of flashing thoughts.

First the Lady Inanna cried in joyful question, *"Ninshubur—in dragon form! Is it indeed you? My faithful messenger, Ninshubur, after all these centuries!"*

The dragon exclaimed in unbelief, *"My Lady Inanna—and my Lord Enki! Here—in my prison!"*

There followed an interchange of thought too rapid for verbalizing, only moments in duration; out of it the one important thought reached Alan. Ninshubur, condemned for playing a part in the confusion of Lucifer's dividing the Great Above from the Great Below, had been a dragon through millennia—but was no menace to them.

A sound penetrated MacDougall's concentration on the communication of the gods—a swelling roar of anger.

Above it rose the bellow of Beli. "Guards! Call the guards. Smite them with your lances. Slay them and the dragon!"

The serpent-gods also heard. Instant transformation followed. The dragon was again her fire-breathing self— larger, reaching the ceiling; the lovely Inanna was gone; the serpent, now two-headed, rose menacingly, flames blasting from two red maws.

For an instant, they seemed to Alan less solid, almost ghostly; the thought vanished. With thundering roar and screaming serpent hiss, they swept side by side around the windows, flames lancing through every opening, searing all they touched, clearing every watcher from his post.

The flames died. Slowly the giant serpent faded, then disappeared; and again the great dragon alone stood towering before the three rigid men, who had been frozen during the entire dramatic magic display.

"Time you go," Enki's thought came to MacDougall, "before they recover from their panic." In amusement, he added slyly, "Powerless, did you say?"

Uncertainly, Taliesin and Nuada, swords still poised, backed slowly toward the bronze door, looking intently up at the giant reptilian figure. Only Alan knew they had nothing to fear from the monster.

He spoke reassuringly. "Don't worry about our little playmate. She's on our side. Our problem is getting out of here." Even as he spoke, as if to verify what he said, Ninshubur sank back on her massive tail, folded her wings, crossed her green-scaled arms over her white belly, and grinned down at them.

Taliesin responded with awe in his voice. "I suppose you know what you are talking about. I won't ask how you did whatever you did—but I have never seen magic to compare with your serpent."

Defiantly, Nuada waved his invincible sword. "I still think we could have handled that beast ourselves." He added grudgingly, "Though I suppose we might have been singed a bit in the process." Suddenly he brightened. "Getting out is no problem. Watch this."

Facing the bronze door, he swung his sword mightily at the edge of the barrier. With the clang of metal came a blinding green flash, and a long jagged gash appeared. A second and third blow followed; and with a single powerful kick, Nuada opened the way to freedom. He spoke triumphantly to MacDougall.

"You see? You have been underestimating my sword."

Duly impressed, Alan raised his brows as he stared at the glittering blade, no trace of nick or scratch marring its perfection. "I certainly have."

The Bard moved quickly toward the opening. "No reason for us to dally here," he said—then spun around as did the other two at sound of a high-pitched, almost childish voice.

"May I go too?"

The dragon! Head bent far forward, she held out her arms as if begging. "I have been here *so* long."

Alan was first to recover from his surprise. After all, this had been Inanna's messenger. And a talking dragon was no more surprising than his armlet. "But you'd never get through the doorway, nor the corridors."

"I *did* help you." How incongruous, that plaintive pleading from the cavernous mouth. "They brought me here through the hallways."

At this irrefutable logic, MacDougall shrugged. "Why not?" For that matter, how could they stop her?

Taliesin chuckled. "Can you picture us going through the castle with the dragon leading the way? I don't think anyone would challenge us." He glanced questioningly at Nuada, who nodded.

"But we go first," he added hastily, "until we have passed through all the narrow ways."

Quickly the three moved out. When well into the corridor, Alan looked back to observe an incredible sight. Ninshubur was exhibiting fantastic flexibility, her great body seeming to shrink to half its normal size and extending itself in serpentine fashion, yet almost filling the corridor. But she was getting through.

Inanna's thought came to Alan. "At the next branch, turn right. This will lead you to the ramp they use for horses, more comfortable for Ninshubur. From there on, let her lead, and I will guide her."

When finally they moved into the wider hallways on ground level, the dragon in all her might took the lead. Her crocodile jaws gaped redly, with torrid tongues of flame lashing out of plumes of black smoke to lick up anyone who might seek to bar their way. Incessant roars echoed through the corridors and rooms. The three men followed, swords poised; but any soldier or Druid who came within sight fled with frantic haste.

They met their first resistance when they entered Beli's council chamber. They were greeted with a shower of lances hurled by massed and waiting Romans. The missiles glanced harmlessly from Ninshubur's metallic scales and passed by the crouching three. A second shower was no more effective. Then the soldiers charged from every side; and Alan found himself wielding his sword against Roman weapons.

To his surprise, his blade swept aside darting steel with amazing skill; he realized that Nuada had at last found use for his prowess, guiding Alan's sword arm, even as he himself fought. And he also controlled Taliesin's blade, no doubt.

The dragon was not idle. The great head swung swiftly from side to side in great arcs, and screams of pain rose from attackers' throats to mingle with their shouts as searing flames swept through their ranks. Then, perhaps stung by sword points, the mighty tail became a gigantic flail, striking out and flinging aside all it met. Alan found himself clinging to massive scales on the huge trunk, hanging on with all his strength, his sword pressed between him and the dragon. He caught a glimpse of the Bard in a like position. And Nuada! Sword raised high, the god of the *Tuatha de Danann* straddled the juggernaut, shouting his defiance.

In seconds the fight ended, and Ninshubur, roaring

triumphantly, swept across the chamber. As they left it, Alan caught a glimpse of the god Beli standing on his dais, arms crossed, with scores of cowering Druids behind him, his face a mask of frustrated fury.

Without further incident, they found the rear exit. At a shouted command from MacDougall, the drawbridge was lowered, the ancient structure groaning under the dragon's weight as they crossed. Quickly, they secured horses, Alan looking in vain for Caesar. The terrified guard supplied saddles, and they were ready to go.

Outside the walls, astride their mounts, the three faced Ninshubur, and Alan spoke. "Here we have to separate. Thank you for your help."

The great creature looked down at them, her head drooping, and a sigh of regret, hot and sulphurous, came from the gaping mouth. "I suppose we must," the little voice said. "It was fun while it lasted."

"*Farewell until another time*," the serpent-gods' thought went out to Ninshubur as the dragon turned away and, in a slow, shuffling trot, headed into the deepening darkness.

Alan, Taliesin and Nuada sat silently watching the monster grow smaller with distance. Then they faced about with a final glance at Beli's fortress and without sight or sound of pursuit, they rode northward.

"I think," Alan said quietly after a prolonged silence, "that Beli has had enough of us for a while."

Taliesin said nothing, slowly shaking his head, eyes and face expressing growing wonder.

Nuada stared at MacDougall as if he were seeing him for the first time. "I won't ask how you did it. If I hadn't seen it, I wouldn't believe it. I'm still not sure it happened."

"Don't be surprised, Nuada," Alan said slyly, "at anything I do."

CHAPTER 8

Manannan, God of the Sea

The castle of Beli lay far behind the three riders when Alan MacDougall called a halt. Since their escape, they had held the horses to a steady trot, intent on putting all possible distance between themselves and the angry god, even though they thought pursuit unlikely. There had been little conversation, each occupied with his own thoughts.

"I believe," Alan said as they drew rein, "we need to make some decisions before we continue. Why are we heading for the third castle—assuming we are so headed— the castle of the god Manannan? We had a bad experience with Arawn, a worse one with Beli—and for all we know, the next may be the worst. I'm about ready to call it quits here and move to Tartarus, if you, Nuada, can carry us there."

The King of the *Tuatha de Danann* gave a short, unpleasant laugh. "I don't see why you should be concerned. No matter what we face, you are equal to the occasion. Your magic seems invincible." He shook his head in mock wonder. "To think I have had to fight your duels for you!"

"This would hardly have been a duel," Alan said grimly. "Three swords—even including your invincible blade— against that dragon, whether part illusion or all reality, would not have been a contest. I appreciate your guiding my sword arm when I needed it; but I believe in using whatever is available when facing a fire-breathing dragon." He eyed Nuada speculatively and was suddenly aware of the god's problem. Pride! He resented losing the chance to show his prowess in handling three swords at one time. That little episode in the council room hardly counted. But there was this to be said in his favor—he had cast his lot with the apparent losers.

The Bard looked at Nuada in surprise. "I for one am glad Alan's magic worked. Not his, really, but the powers of the armlet. I knew they were great—but not *how* great."

Nuada forced a smile, trying to hide his annoyance. "Don't misunderstand me. I'm glad we're out of that monster's den. As for our visiting Manannan, I think we will be welcome there. I remember him from the old days— god of the sea with wondrous tales to tell. We were friends. As I recall it, there was no love lost between Manannan and Beli. And since I doubt that I'll ever visit this dark land again, I'd like to see the whole of it while I am here. By the way, we *are* riding in the right direction. Were we not, I would know and would have told you."

Alan turned to the Bard. "Your opinion, Taliesin?"

"Everything considered, I should say we go on."

"So be it." Alan shrugged. "Before we continue—" He dug deeply into a pocket. "—perhaps a bit of food might be welcome." Casually he drew out the three oatcakes left from his breakfast and divided them. "Food from the Other World," he said.

Curiously, the others bit into the unfamiliar cakes, then

ate with enjoyment. "I had forgotten how these tasted," the Bard commented.

Nuada's thoughts were elsewhere. "I am puzzled by Manannan's being here in Ochren. He hardly seems to fit into the company of such as Arawn and Pryderi—and even Beli, though he be my father. Rather, I can picture him as one on our own Island."

Taliesin smiled quizzically. "There was much that could be said in Manannan's favor; but have you forgotten his darker side? His fiery wrath knew no bounds; and in the Olden Time, he was said to be joint ruler with Pryderi over the dark realm, Hades. It was he who built the prison of bones to hold those who aroused his displeasure."

Stubbornly Nuada shook his head. "Manannan here and Balor with us? Not my idea of justice."

"Lucifer's sense of humor," MacDougall commented.

Again conversation died as they rode on across the gray plain. Alan thought about the newly revealed facet of Nuada's makeup. Jealousy? Most likely. His powers usually prevailed; and suddenly he had not been needed. And Taliesin—why his constant insistence on Alan's returning to his own world? What prompted it?

He thought of that fantastic dragon, incredibly Inanna's messenger in the strange tale from six millennia in the past. He felt a sudden chill as he thought of the meshing, the interweaving of so many seemingly unrelated threads. Behind everything—Lucifer?

His soliloquy ended as Taliesin exclaimed, "What was that?" They checked their mounts and listened. Now Alan heard it, as did Nuada—a faint and distant sound, suggesting the clamor of a gaggle of geese in migratory flight, the baying of a pack of hounds, or a strange combination of the two.

The sound grew stronger as they listened, drawing steadily nearer; and there was something about it that raised the short hairs on the nape of Alan's neck. Then from the south where sky and plain met, they saw something emerging from the dark. In moments it resolved itself into a single gray horse with a red-clad rider, followed—no, preceded and surrounded—by a pack of great, snow-white hounds. White? They were a glistening white except for their great ears, which were a brilliant red, like flapping, bloody appendages, the color of the rider's garments.

"Gwyn and his Hounds of Death!" Taliesin cried, spurring his horse, the others dashing after him.

The baying of the hounds intensified, now a bedlam of eager, hungry sounds. The horses needed no added spurring; terror was driving their racing hoofs. Alan looked back. The pursuers seemed no closer; they were holding their own. He thought of the pack of pseudowolves following him in the fog during his flight from Murias; he wondered if these hounds were also the result of shape-changing. Taliesin's words suggested otherwise.

"Gwyn!" Nuada's voice rose angrily. "Gwyn!" he repeated. "That's my son! First my father, then my son—and both hostile." He turned in his saddle and shouted, "I am Nuada, your father. Why do you pursue us?"

There was no indication that he had been heard. The horseman and his hounds continued their headlong pace, the baying undiminished.

"*Taliesin,*" Alan addressed the Bard mentally, "*you seem to know the red rider. Is he in truth Nuada's son?*"

"*Almost certainly he is Gwyn the Hunter—red-hooded, riding a gray horse, the white hounds with glistening red ears. In the long-gone days, he was god of war and the dead, and Nuada's son. He haunted fields of battle to escort the souls of those slain into Annwn, where he ruled over them. Here—who knows? Nothing is the same.*"

Nuada spurred his horse and drew closer to Alan. "Well, MacDougall—is it not time for more of your magic?" There was a suggestion of a sneer in his voice.

"What do you suggest?"

"Why not stop the hounds?"

"I'll think about it," Alan said lightly. He grasped the armlet.

"Lord Enki and Lady Inanna, would it be possible to slow down or stop the hounds?"

"Not only possible but easily done, even though Nuada is concentrating all his powers on preventing its accomplishment. However, since Gwyn has no desire to catch you, but is merely intent on delivering the three of you to Manannan, which is your own destination, you need but slow down your horses and travel at your own pace. The Huntsman will adjust to it."

Immediately MacDougall checked his headlong flight, drawing back on his bridle and leaning over to speak soothingly to the animal. "Slow down, my friends," he called. "Gwyn will do likewise." Casually he added, "The hounds will remain at their present distance."

His horse slowed to a canter; and in moments, though with apparent reluctance, and with anxious looks behind them, Taliesin and Nuada fell back to join him. Though the volume of the hounds' baying remained unchanged, they, too, slowed, drawing no nearer.

Taliesin's admiring thought reached Alan. *"I suspect Gwyn does not really want to catch us. But how did you know?"*

Alan answered with mock solemnity. *"Just a guess, of course."*

Nuada said nothing, keeping his eyes fixed steadily on the darkness ahead.

Interminably, they continued in this fashion, the ceaseless bedlam of sound becoming more and more nerve-wracking; but even though the tiring horses moved ever more slowly, the distance between the three and Gwyn's hounds remained unchanged. Twice during the ride, the erratic beam lanced out of the sky, revealing only the monotonous landscape. At last MacDougall saw their destination rising before them, a great square castle with a huge central tower jutting up to blot out a portion of the dim aurora.

A new eagerness entered the cry of the hounds, but, strangely, as though on a collective leash, they maintained

their distance. Ahead lay a high, straight, sea-green wall—
and the hounds now veered to the left, blocking the way,
as if herding their quarry. Their directed course led around
a sharp corner of the wall, toward a double bronze door
like the one before Arawn's castle.

Startlingly then, lights flared everywhere, more light
than MacDougall had seen since his entry into this dark
land. Tall, narrow windows were set in an oblique line in
the sea-green castle, suddenly aglow; torches flamed at
the top of the central tower and lighted a bridge across a
wide moat inside the wall.

There was something strange about that castle—not
its shape, but its substance. It appeared to be seamless
and glass-smooth, as if it had been molded in one great
casting! And moving now into Alan's field of vision came
the gleaming castle entrance, rimmed by torchlight.

Moving? The entire castle was revolving!

Taliesin exclaimed in wonder, "*Caer Pedryvan*, the four-
cornered glass castle on the Isle of the Strong Door, which
revolves ceaselessly—so it was in the Olden Time."

"And," Nuada added triumphantly, "it was the dwelling place of Manannan, as it is now."

As they approached the great gate, Alan saw, high
above in the spaces in the crenelated wall atop the castle,
helmeted archers with drawn bows—images probably,
though he could not be sure with their faces shaded from
the light of the torches on the higher tower. The three
slowed their mounts to a walk, ignoring the red rider and
his hounds.

The bronze gate opened at their approach. Standing
rigidly at attention on either side of the white pebble walk
appeared six Roman guards, resplendent in full uniform,
including chain mail armor and proudly tufted helmets,
shields over left arms and lances held upright beside them.

Nuada took the lead as they entered upon a broad
expanse of gray-green lawn, through which stretched the
wide, white road of the bridge. A drawbridge over a moat;
it was already lowered, as if they were expected—per-

haps announced by the baying of the hounds. Behind them came the hounds and their master, to speed off toward the far end of the courtyard, where MacDougall saw a stretch of still water, evidently a pond.

They swung from their mounts, and from behind the gate appeared two grooms who led the horses toward the distant pond. Nuada, again taking the initiative, strode toward the bridge.

"We'll have to wait for the entrance to come around again," he said, then added, "I told you we'd be welcome here."

Alan and Taliesin exchanged glances, the Bard shrugging faintly.

At length the entrance to the castle reappeared; and MacDougall now saw two guards standing stiffly at the great iron doorway. A smooth stone platform lay before them; as the three leaped upon it, the door moved slowly upward into a hidden recess. Out poured a flood of light. As the barrier rose above eye level, they came face to face with a most unexpected sight.

Six beautiful women smiling their welcome, standing side by side, formed a lovely barrier across the width of the brightly lighted corridor. They were dressed in a fanciful adaptation of Roman armor, completely feminine, with ornamental, delicately wrought, high-plumed helmets, cloth-of-gold vesture, silken green kirtles ending at mid-thigh, and silvery latticed sandals. Each bore a highly polished, round, bronze shield, delicately pierced and filagreed, more ornamental than utilitarian, and a short, slender lance. They parted, three moving to right and three to left.

In harmonious unison they exclaimed, "Welcome to *Caer Pedryvan*."

The three entered, and heard the door slide shut behind them. Nuada addressed the girls. "I am Nuada, King of the *Tuatha de Danann*, and these are my friends. We have come from other lands and would speak with the god Manannan."

"You shall," the six answered as one, "but now is his time of entertainment, and he may not be interrupted. But as his guests, you may also enjoy watching. Follow."

As the women led the way along the corridor, Nuada flashed a triumphant glance at Alan; but there was a doubtful expression on the Bard's face as he mentally exclaimed, *This seems too good to be true.*

"*I fully agree,*" Alan answered. "*I just can't believe it. I'm ready for anything. After all, this is Ochren.*"

Near the end of the hallway they heard faint sounds of exotic music, the rhythmic plucking of strings mingled with high-pitched piping and, beneath these, the rumble of muted drums. The passageway ended in the usual bronze double doors; the music came from beyond the barrier. Closer now, they heard it more clearly, but still muffled.

Two of their escorts stepped to the doors and slid them silently aside, providing an opening just wide enough for the visitors to see and hear, then stepped back, index fingers laid on carmined lips. The music poured out its strange and plaintive chords.

Alan gazed into a great circular chamber like a huge amphitheater, its domed ceiling far above them, glowing with internal radiance. Where ceiling ended, torches flamed, completely rimming the room. Recessed alcoves of identical size lined the walls at floor level, their ceilings domed like the hall itself; and within each sat a cluster of musicians, all of them women in flowing, delicately pastel robes. Twelve alcoves, Alan counted, six on each side. Above them, barely visible in deep shadow, were small niches, each holding a single white-clad man. Directly opposite the doorway through which Alan peered, against the far wall on a black dais, occupying a gem-encrusted golden throne, was an audience of one, evidently the god Manannan. And in a wider niche, high above him, sat three immobile, white-clad figures.

In the center of the chamber, weaving and gyrating in time with the music, were three score dancing girls, draped in cobweb-thin veils that floated and fluttered around them as they dipped and whirled. There was a wild beauty about the spectacle, quickening the heartbeat; the tempo of the music seized the feet, awakening in MacDougall an almost irresistible urge to dance.

Now the tempo quickened, the dance growing wilder; some of the dancers produced hand cymbals, others sistrums, these adding their rhythm to the torrents of sound. Suddenly as one, the dancers released hidden clasps; with unbroken steps, they danced out of their veils, and spun, twisted, and writhed in complete nudity before their god.

"Most interesting—" A quiet thought from Taliesin reached MacDougall. *"—those instruments. At least three kinds of harps—one the Highland clairsach—an Egyptian nefer, flutes, trumpets, horns, tambourines, and of course the drums—and with twelve groups, all in tempo and harmony. Fascinating."*

Just in time, Alan checked an impulse to burst into laughter. Incredible—the Bard commenting on the musical instruments with scores of naked dancers cavorting before him! Through his mind flashed a television commercial and its punch line: "Thanks! I needed that."

Mentally he replied, *"I find this quite unbelievable. It seems utterly foreign to everything we've seen in Ochren. And that applies to musicians and dancers alike. I wonder—"*

"Hold!" The stentorian voice of Manannan, sounding above the music, cut off his thought. The god had arisen, both hands held high. Nuada, Alan now noticed, had slid through the opening and stood clearly revealed, white hair, blue cape, and white garments standing out sharply against the bronze of the door.

The towering figure dropped his arms and called out, "Dismissed!" Instantly, the dancers caught up their veils and darted into the nearest alcove, where the musicians were already vanishing behind the dark draperies that covered the rear walls. In moments, the great hall was empty except for Nuada, Taliesin, and Alan, who stepped inside, and the god Manannan. Not quite empty! Alan noticed that the half-seen figures in their cubicles still remained.

"Approach," Manannan called out. As they did so, there emerged from each of the alcoves a tall, fully armed and armored Roman soldier, moving quietly toward the dais, converging on the three. As they halted before the god, the soldiers formed a half circle about ten feet behind them.

Intently and in silence, Manannan examined his visitors with frosty green eyes. Tall, with blue-white hair rising to form a crest, matched by carefully trimmed blue-white mustache and beard, he wore a dark green cape reaching to his ankles. Now he flung this aside and stood revealed in a white tunic, knee-length pleated kilts matching his cape, and gold-mesh boots that seemed to emit a pale blue glow. Truly, Alan thought, he was a fitting figure to be god of the sea—but oddly dressed even for a god intent on entertainment.

"Who are you?" Manannan demanded, his gaze fixed on Nuada. "And whence have you come?"

"I am Nuada, King of the *Tuatha de Danann*," the latter answered with dignity and firmness. "These are my friends, Taliesin, the Bard of Bards, whom you once knew; and Alan, son of Dougall, a visitor from the Other World. Taliesin and I are of this world, but from another island, where dwell most of the family of Danu. We apologize for our interruption of your entertainment—which I for one found most enjoyable. We have come in friendship and with the hope that we will be treated as friends. Elsewhere in Ochren we have met with violence and treachery."

Keen interest appeared on Manannan's face. "The interruption is of no importance. One wearies of music and dancers. But—another island? In this world? Where can it be?" As if just beginning to grasp the significance of Nuada's statement, he stared incredulously. "With my coracle I have explored all of the sea surrounding Ochren.

I have been to the very edge of the waters, even to the brink! But we shall speak more about this later. The Other World?" He looked keenly at MacDougall. "You mean he comes from the world where we once dwelt? In the Olden Times? Not—as we came?"

Nuada nodded. "He has not died. And he can return . . . As for our island, it is far more pleasant than this one— the Land of the Four Cities. We too have our problems, of course." Boldly he added, "You and I knew each other in the long ago, Manannan. Many are the tales I heard you tell. And there is much for both of us to add from the times that have passed since last we met."

Manannan seemed to be weighing what he had heard. "Nuada, once of the Silver Hand . . . Then Beli is your father and Gwyn your son."

"True—but you know my father's temper. Just now I am not in his favor. As for Gwyn, I have not had words with him, though he and his hounds—escorted—us to your castle."

"Gwyn is very strange, though he does his job well," Manannan commented absently, then suddenly seemed to come to a decision. "But come—there are places more comfortable, and we have much to discuss. There are steps around to the side. Follow." He drew aside the heavy drapes behind his throne and led the way into another corridor. Alan glanced back, looking for the six lovely guides. They were not to be seen, replaced by two burly Roman guards.

They had gone only a short distance when, suddenly breaking the quiet, they heard voices, laughter, and even the happy shouts of children! In moments, the sea-god and his retinue entered a room resembling a lounge; here and there were comfortable chairs and tables holding games with people playing. As Manannan entered, silence fell, and all motion stopped. It suggested to Alan the freezing of a scene in a motion picture—the absolute cessation of movement and sound. Completely ignoring the strange spectacle, Manannan crossed quickly and passed through

a doorway into the next room. One of the guards closed
the door behind them, and somewhat muffled voices burst
forth as if nothing had happened. Passing through this
second room, rather sparsely furnished, they entered a
third and halted. Here were appointments appropriate for
a god.

Manannan spoke to Taliesin and MacDougall.

"You will be conducted to rooms which will be yours
while you are guests in *Caer Pedryvan*. You will find
everything you may need to refresh yourselves. Later you
will join me for a welcoming dinner. I wish to speak briefly
with Nuada before he, too, goes to his quarters."

The guards motioned for Alan and the Bard to follow,
then briskly led them to adjoining rooms on a level above
and, with a bow, left them. A quick glance revealed to
Alan all there was to see in his quarters—a low-lying bed,
a small table, a low-backed metal chair, and in one corner,
a cubicle which proved to be the necessary but primitive
plumbing he had come to expect in Ochren. There was a
vessel of water and a coarse cloth, evidently intended to
serve as a towel. Everything seemed strictly utilitarian.
A single torch provided light; and in the far wall was one
of the high, narrow windows, about six feet tall and a foot
wide. Crossing to it, Alan looked out on the endlessly
passing landscape—at the moment a dark expanse of tideless sea.

A thought came from Taliesin: *"Well, Alan, what think
you of Caer Pedryvan and Manannan?"*

*"Surprising, to say the least. I haven't really begun to
think about the god or his castle. It certainly differs from
what I expected. All these people! What is your impression?"*

There was amusement in the Bard's answer. *"Have
you not realized that most of what we've seen is illusion?
Beautifully created. Simulating life itself—but illusion."*

Through Alan's mind flashed a picture of the non-
existent underworld village of Titus Vespasianus, the
Druid-created army of the god Beli, and even those ghastly

rooms in the castle of Arawn, with lone occupants sub-
jected to tortures of their own creation.

*"Of course! I should have realized it. But it has been
so impressive. Those musicians and their music—the
dancers—"*

*"Beautifully done! But all creations of the mind—and
magic. Did you not notice those men in the niches above
the alcoves, the three above Manannan? Each individual,
I am certain, created a different group of musicians and
their music, and the three, the dancers. They—or others
like them—formed our charming guides and the busily
talking family groups in that room we passed through."*

*"You say illusion. You mean they were not there? That
we merely saw what we were supposed to see?"*

Taliesin's thought was emphatically negative. *"No
indeed; all were solid enough—as were Beli's soldiers,
who could kill the attackers sent by Titus. I doubt that
there is an analogy that would make their form under-
standable. As to why—I believe we shall learn that there
are very few real people in this castle. Magic makes it
appear that Manannan is surrounded by a multitude of
subservient subjects.*

*"How has this been accomplished? In the long-ago
days he was one of the greatest of all magicians. His
fame had spread through every land. From wood chips
cast on the waters, he could form a fleet of vessels of
war. There was little his powers could not accomplish.
And he was noted as a great teacher, proud of his ability
to impart his knowledge to his pupils—always, of course,
maintaining his own superiority. If the truth becomes
known—and it may not be—we may well learn that Manannan has taught his magic arts to a gifted group, perhaps many through the centuries, and these now serve
him, producing the spectacles we have seen."*

"What of Nuada?" MacDougall asked.

*"Who knows? Obviously he has found favor with Man-
annan. Time alone will tell what, if anything, this means
to us."*

The mental dialogue ended. After freshening up, Alan stretched out on the bed to relax, but not to sleep; he was wide awake, his mind intensely active. Nuada—for some reason he felt uneasy about the god's actions. He seemed honest enough, but, Alan reminded himself, this was a world under Lucifer's control, a world of his creation, and its dwellers were his subjects. A grim and sobering thought came unbidden: was not that also true of many people in his own world? But Nuada—he closed his eyes and grasped the armlet.

"Lord Enki and Lady Inanna, I should like to see what Nuada and Manannan are doing. Can you help me?"

There was no verbal response from the serpent-gods, but instantly a picture formed in Alan's mind, Nuada and the sea god walking side by side through a brightly lighted hallway; and, as if he were there, he heard the excited voice of Manannan: "You really mean this son of Dougall has never died? That he can enter and leave this world at will?"

"Exactly." There was obvious envy in Nuada's manner. "It's the doing of that enchanted armlet he's wearing. But it won't help you and me. Some of us thought we could go with him through the Gate; but these bodies cannot exist in the Other World, and we would become disembodied spirits. And here through the armlet he has developed unbelievable magic powers. It is a long story. Sometime I'll tell it."

The sea god looked at Nuada curiously. "Has no one tried to relieve him of his jewel? I should think it would be tempting."

"One tried, a Druid named Arias, now dead. It could not be done without removing his arm; with the powers he now has, I for one would not consider trying."

Listening, MacDougall grinned broadly.

Manannan changed the subject. "There are two more of my many possessions I want you to see—mine from the long ago. Both are outside the castle. *Wave Sweeper* and *Splendid Mane.*"

"Wonderful!" Nuada exclaimed. "Who could forget your famous coracle and the horse like no other?"

They were passing the end of a branching corridor, descending at a sharp angle; and Manannan said, "That leads into Lochlann, an undersea city. The buildings are still there, but now all are deserted, those who dwelt within them when I came to Ochren long since removed. This castle was built for me," he added proudly, "for my dwelling as administrator of Lochlann and for those who served under me. It duplicates the one I had in the Other World. Lochlann itself is—strange; not suited for any save the Fomorians for whom it was designed. Later you shall see it."

They reached a door that opened at their approach, stepped out onto a wide stone platform, and waited. The castle in its turning brought them to a drawbridge, already lowered, and they quickly crossed over. Beyond, at the end of a fifty-foot path, lay a wharf of age-green bronze; moored to it was Manannan's coracle.

As they approached it, the sea god gestured dramatically and announced, "*Wave Sweeper*! Never in the old world or any other has there been a craft its equal—or its like."

MacDougall, the invisible watcher, had to agree that at least it had no counterpart. But why it was called a coracle was beyond him. As he recalled it, a coracle was a short, wide boat, usually of skins stretched over a frame. This was a sleek, graceful vessel about thirty feet in length, not unduly wide, formed of polished copper. Even in the half-light of this land, it gleamed like a jewel. Only magic could have maintained that sheen.

The prow rose high above the water, curved like a scimitar curled backward, its figurehead a beautifully sculptured likeness of a spirited horse, neck arched, nostrils flaring, mane swept back, and forehoofs raised in mid-leap, the rest merging with the prow. It was the personification of speed. Nestled below the prow lay a small cabin, its sides an extension of port and starboard bows.

In a smooth, graceful curve, the railed sides met at the stern, rising and curving like the prow to about half its height. Depth of keel could not be discerned; the bottom was concealed by the deck. All, including the deck, was wrought of gleaming copper. And strangely, nowhere was there sign of rudder or helm, mast or oar.

"No ship as swift sails any sea," Manannan boasted proudly. "It goes where I will, as swift as the wind. It obeys only me. It is well named *Wave-Sweeper*."

"Beautiful," Nuada breathed, obviously impressed.

"Later we shall circle the island—and still later, I hope, visit your island, taking with us whom we choose. Though how that may be done I cannot imagine. Before you go to your room—as you should, since the banquet will soon be served—I want you to see my horse."

They left the wharf and crossed the turf to a square, stone building—the stable that housed Splendid Mane. The sea god called out sharply, and two grooms appeared, leading a beautiful snow-white stallion, his mane instantly revealing the source of his name. Unusually long and of luxuriant growth, it was as white as all the rest of him. And this horse, Alan recalled from his reading, ran with equal swiftness on land or water. The horse was a fitting steed for a sea god in an ensorcelled world.

Manannan ran his hand along the smooth neck. "Never has he borne saddle or felt the touch of bit or bridle. Nor will he. And he, too, takes me where I will."

There was more conversation as Nuada expressed his admiration for the truly beautiful animal; but Alan decided there was little more for him to learn and cut off the vision.

With eyes still closed, MacDougall tried to think about the fantastic copper coracle and enchanted horse; but one thought drove everything else from his mind—Manannan's exclamation: "You mean he has not died? That he can enter and leave this world at will?"

If only the latter were true! At will? Surely—but not *his* will. The will of Ahriman in his golden tower? Or that mighty figure somewhere in the background behind Ahriman—Lucifer? Was Lucifer another name for—Satan? It was a most disturbing thought. Yet this hardly matched the popular idea of hell, though Ochren in some ways came close. He knew little enough about such matters, and there was a time when he couldn't have cared less. He'd better start caring; he was in the middle of something far beyond his depth.

Why me? It was a question he had asked before, and there was no answer. Was it that at some time in the past a remote ancestor had become involved with the dark powers—and "the sins of the fathers visited upon the children"? Somehow he couldn't buy that. Or was it simply that he happened to be in the wrong place at the right time? If only he hadn't put on that armlet! It had looked innocent enough. How was he to know about its powers, about its being the prison of serpent-gods?

Round and around and around—

There came a sharp knock on the door, repeated on that of Taliesin. As Alan sat up, his door opened and a Roman soldier stood in the entrance.

"You have been summoned by the Lord Manannan."

Alan moved into the hallway, where he met Taliesin, emerging from his room; side by side, they were led to a large chamber on the ground level. There was a brief mental interchange on the way.

Alan said, *"I observed Nuada and Manannan while I rested and saw the sea god's coracle and horse. Quite impressive."*

"I spent the time with your books," Taliesin told him. *"Fantastic and fascinating. But to master them will take a great amount of time and effort."*

Just outside the dining room, they met Nuada emerging from a branching corridor with his escort; after exchanging greetings, they entered together. Apparently they were the last to arrive except for Manannan, for there were only four vacant chairs at a table for ten to which they were ushered. The chair at the head of the table, more ornate than the others, evidently was reserved for the sea god. There were four seats on each side and another at the far end. Nuada was seated in the first chair on the right, and Alan and the Bard in the remaining seats, facing each other. There was a very lovely woman at the foot end. Alan glanced quickly around the table; as expected, none of the faces were familiar. No one spoke; accordingly the newcomers also remained silent.

There was another table in the room, long and narrow, occupied by thirty white-robed men, each with a silver chain and ankh around his neck, fifteen per side, seated on backless benches. They, too, were silent. Alan was reminded of the half-seen figures in the niches above the musicians' alcoves.

He sent a question to Lord Enki. *"Are any of these people illusions, or are they all real?"* Assurance came; all were dwellers in *Caer Pedryvan.*

Finally Manannan entered, unattended and regal in a flowing, dark green tunic, unusually long, with threads of silver skillfully woven through the fabric, forming designs appropriate to the sea—stylized waves, tridents, dolphins, a many-armed kraken. As he appeared, everyone rose, arms raised in salute. The three visitors quickly followed suit.

"Sit!" the deep voice directed, though all waited until he had seated himself at the head of the table before they took their places.

"We have three visitors," Manannan announced. "For their and your benefits I shall introduce each to you. First, at the other table are my Druids, the most skilled at their craft in all of Ochren—aye, more skilled than any I knew in the Olden Days. They have had a long time to perfect their abilities.

"At this table, seated at my right hand is Nuada, King of the *Tuatha de Danann,* visiting from another island in this world, an island of perpetual day, and one which, in due time, we in turn shall be able to visit. On his right sits Mathonwy, Master Magician in whose charge are the

Druids. On *his* right, visiting with Nuada, sits Taliesin, the Bard of Bards—"

As Manannan went on with his introductions, Mac-Dougall studied each one. First was Mathonwy, dark-haired, dark-eyed, handsome despite a sardonic half smile. On the other side of Taliesin sat Gwyn the Hunter, red-clad, thin of face, hawk-beaked like a dark bird of prey, deep-set eyes never still. At table's end was Fand, Manannan's wife, fair of face and hair, her smile somewhat vacuous. At the sea god's left sat Ler, Manannan's father, ancient, grizzled, gray-locked, and weather-beaten. Then came Saint Caradoc—

When he heard his right-hand neighbor introduced, MacDougall had difficulty in hiding his incredulity. *Saint* Caradoc! What was a saint doing here? Alan studied him with great interest out of the corner of his eye. The saint had the face of an ascetic: long, thin, gray hair carefully parted in the middle; high, narrow forehead; shaggy gray brows, shading piercing, deep-set, faded gray eyes; sharp features; cruel, thin lips, drooping at the corners; and small, receding chin. He frowned through the whole procedure in utter disapproval. Incredible, Alan thought. It was a face, if that were possible, without a single redeeming feature. And he was called a saint!

His own turn came; as Manannan referred to him as "from the world where once we all lived—but one who has not died," the green eyes of Caradoc widened with intense interest, and the man turned full-face to examine MacDougall. Eager words seemed ready to burst from his tightly compressed mouth. Alan met the probing gaze with bland indifference.

The tenth at the table was Idris the Astrologer—a small man who looked most miserable, with the kind of face that would vanish in a crowd of three. Alan repressed a grin. No wonder he was unhappy. Imagine an astrologer in a world where there were no stars!

With the introductions completed, Manannan motioned to some unseen servitor, and two groups of men entered, some carrying bowls and ladles to each table, and others pushing a great, polished copper caldron on a wheeled platform. A savory aroma, not readily identifiable, filled the air. With the skill born of long practice, the men served, starting with the sea god. Each guest, as a bowl and spoon were placed in position, was asked, "Your wish, Sire." The varying selections were brought out of the same pot.

When Alan's turn came, he said, "A savory beef stew would please me greatly." A generous portion of what looked and smelled very like beef stew was placed before him. The aroma was so irresistible that, though he knew the food originated in a mushroom cave, MacDougall was able to ignore the thought and begin to eat.

As if this were a signal, the man at his right, the one introduced as Saint Caradoc, began to speak in high, nasal tones, leaning close as if confiding in him, though he made no effort to speak softly.

"You may wonder, my friend, at my being in this dreadful place, among these warlocks and infidels. Indeed, it troubled me for a very long time until I realized that here, even as it was in Alba and Erin, I had been called to minister. I was being tested—and as you will surely realize, this is a most difficult field of endeavor. When I spoke of the Blessed Mother, they told of Danu, mother of the gods, older and more powerful.

"Then I found the Fomorians living in the undersea city of Lochlann. They wanted nothing of the Virgin— but they also hated Danu. That was a good beginning. Here was a fallow field for my labors. Long I ministered among them. One less dedicated would have despaired, yet my zeal never abated. But when it seemed I was about to reap the harvest of my sowing—though it is true that one with a less discerning eye might not have detected those subtle indications of response—it was then that, as one, the Fomorians vanished and Lochlann was left an empty shell. And so it has remained."

His voice sank to a low grumble. "Before they disappeared, we had honest fish to eat, better than this magic stuff."

"You mean they are fishermen?" Alan asked, trying to picture the Fomorians at labor.

"Not in the usual way. They lured fish into traps with their sorceries. And I almost converted them."

Caradoc paused, staring blankly ahead. Alan had continued eating during this strange monologue, trying to ignore it. He saw again the sullen, grotesque Fomorians, and he simply could not conceive of the monstrous race responding to anything. "I wonder that Manannan tolerates you," he said bluntly.

"*Tolerates me!*" There was venom in the thin voice. "He finds me *amusing!* As do all of them." Suddenly a beatific smile appeared. "But one day judgment will fall on these warlocks, and I should not be surprised if I were called to administer that judgment. Then *I* will be amused!"

He paused, then sounded pensive as he continued. "I have often wondered if the powers of this place, aware of my approaching success in converting the Fomorians, decided to remove them from my influence. It seems so logical—and a compliment to my abilities."

MacDougall gave him a sidelong glance. Could he be serious? Incredibly he appeared to be so. Now Caradoc's voice fell to a near-whisper and he leaned even closer.

"Never have I seen a man as angry as Manannan when the Fomorians disappeared. I heard him curse the powers that had treated him thus, making unspeakable threats, which, of course, he could not carry out. There were many people here then, under his control, but now there are few. He has Gwyn constantly searching for stray travelers to add to his subjects; but the dead are not replaced, and now he fills his halls with phantoms. It is the beginning of judgment."

He broke off suddenly and glanced furtively around. "Do not mention this. I was unwise to tell you. But it is so unusual for me to find one of the same faith." Intently he looked at Alan. "You are *not* a worshiper of the Dark

One, are you?" A fanatical light appeared in his eyes. "We burned such in my day."

Emphatically MacDougall shook his head. Worship Lucifer? "Hardly!" Curiously he added, "You say you burned such in your day?"

The man called a saint smiled gloatingly. "When first I became a priest of the new faith, there were few who believed. They tried to overcome us with their magic—but we fought fire with fire." Again there appeared that faraway look, the beatific smile reappearing.

"I remember well the day we built our first wicker giant. We learned how from the Druids. You have not seen such things?" At Alan's negative response he added, "Perhaps they are not needed in your time. We built giant, hollow men, twenty feet tall, woven of willow withes, and we filled them tightly with the witches and warlocks. The giants were cleverly made, with little platforms on which the chosen stood. We built mounds of dry faggots around them—and I had the privilege of striking flint to the first fire. It would have done your heart good to hear them scream for mercy." There was unholy glee in the thin voice.

In utter revulsion MacDougall stopped eating and pointedly turned his back to Caradoc, who, none the less, continued talking. In Alan's mind had appeared a picture of the small room in the farmhouse of Duncan Cameron with the big Bible opened on the lap of Elspeth, the reverence, and the simple prayer. Yet this monster supposedly professed the same faith!

He spoke to the little man at his left, Idris the Astrologer. "You read the stars, I believe. Isn't that a problem here?"

"Oh yes!" Idris answered, eager to talk. "A problem where there are no stars. I have tried to read the secrets of those faint lights in the sky and the blinding beams that come and go, but they have no order." He looked hopefully at Alan. "Tell me—this land of constant day from

which yonder King of the *Tuatha de Danann* has come—
are there stars in that sky?"

MacDougall shook his head regretfully. "None. But,"
he added hastily to blunt the disappointment, "the dancing
lights are strong and form many patterns, however fleeting, and it might well be that you could find omens and
portents in their formations."

Idris attempted a weak smile but the gloom persisted.
"Thank you, but with my luck, if I ever visit that land,
the lights will go out."

Alan stared into his bowl as he thought of the time
those auroral lights *had* gone out, leaving terrifying blackness, turned off by Ahriman in a vain attempt to prevent
his escaping from Tartarus. Now here he was, back in
the same accursed world. With the thought, awareness
of everything around him dimmed, and he felt again the
probing, gem-hard eyes of the Persian in his tower.

A harsh, shrill, almost hysterical cry burst on Mac-
Dougall's ears. Startled, he stared at its source, the wild-
eyed Gwyn seated across from him, at Taliesin's right.
The Hunter pointed stiffly at Alan.

"You—you do not belong here! Why have you come?
To torture us? You have not died! This is our place, not
yours. Go! Go!"

Silence greeted the outburst, followed by protesting
voices from both tables. The deep calm tones of Manannan rose above the hubbub.

"Gwyn! Is it not time for you to leave and to go about
your hunting? Only you can bring in the wanderers. Your
dogs and horse are waiting."

Sullenly submissive, Gwyn stood up; glancing neither
to right nor left, he stalked from the room. Conversation
went on as before, no one seeming concerned about the
interruption. The words from Caradoc continued their
relentless flow; Alan closed his mind to them by sheer
force of will.

He caught Taliesin's gaze and sent a mental question,

"*Is there any way we can get out of this without bringing Manannan's wrath down upon us?*"

"*Not immediately, I fear. But when the Druids leave, as I believe they will when they have eaten their fill, I think we can safely plead weariness and go. Manannan seems so engrossed with Nuada that he won't miss us. Let me handle it.*"

Endlessly the time dragged by for MacDougall. He tried to concentrate on appearing to eat without actually doing so. He no longer enjoyed the converted mushrooms, no matter how flavorful. He spoke an occasional word to Idris, listened without appearing to do so to a lengthy reminiscence from Ler, and heard snatches of conversation between Mathonwy and the Bard, or between Nuada and Manannan. Finally the welcome sound of the Druids leaving came to his ears; shortly thereafter, Taliesin asked for the sea god's permission to seek rest. Without causing the slightest ripple, he and the Bard were able to withdraw.

Waiting for them were their escorts; in silence, they were taken to their rooms. With the doors closed behind them, Taliesin began the silent conversation with an amused comment.

"*I overheard some of that most informative speech of your charming dinner companion. I knew him in the olden days when he was called Caradawc of the Strong Arm, a son of the elder faith. Now, of course, he has a different body, not one like the original, and a face, I should say, quite in keeping with his true nature.*"

"Let us forget him," Alan answered. "He is utterly revolting. Better we consider our next step."

After a brief pause the Bard said, "*For me a time of sleep is in order. I am weary. A lot has happened since last I slept.*"

"Very well."

MacDougall stretched out on the bed, but sleep was far away. After all, while he had slumbered on the shore of that distant lake, Taliesin had been imprisoned and awake. He thought of the dinner just past and of its strange ramifications. After a time, he rose and began pacing the floor. Tiring of this, he stared out through the window, watching the landscape flow by. Idly, he examined the substance of the wall. It was glass. Why not, in this strange world? For some reason he felt uneasy and restless; some instinct urged that he spend time at the window. He set himself for a period of watching.

There appeared a progression of views that in time formed a pattern. Close up, the blocklike wall surrounding the castle, as nearly as he could estimate, formed a perfect square. By craning his neck, Alan could see that, inside it, the moat was crossed by two drawbridges. He observed the dark, mirror-smooth ocean, the wharf with its gleaming copper coracle, and the stone quarters of the great white horse, Splendid Mane. These were followed by an expanse of turf, then a stream, arrow-straight, coming out of the darkness. Just before it vanished into what must be an underground conduit, a branch flowed off to a stone-lined pond, the overflow going into the moat. Then came a stone corral with horses grazing; after that was more trackless plain.

Now and then, as a break in the monotony, the beam from the sky flashed on, sometimes in the distance, at other times nearby, holding and circling for long periods, or appearing and disappearing in moments.

Time passed with rotation following rotation, each one, after a while, seeming to take longer and ever longer for its completion. At first, Alan remained at his post because some instinctive feeling impelled it; later his vigilance became an exercise in grim determination.

Finally his vigil was rewarded. The panorama had passed the corral and the turf that followed, when the flashing beam, distant and pointing obliquely to the far left, gave a fleeting glimpse of moving objects. The sight was so brief that he could not be certain; he waited for the completion of that rotation, hoping against hope for a closer flash of light.

It came! Clearly seen, as the beam held, were Gwyn and his hounds, silent now as death; behind them, riding side by side, came the god Beli and King Arawn; at their back were Beli's two hundred gray-cowled Druids and, behind them, a score of Roman soldiers!

"Taliesin! Taliesin!" Alan sent a mental shout. *"Wake up. We've got to get out of here!"*

CHAPTER 9

The Empty City

The calm thought of the Bard came to MacDougall. *"If you've been hunting a way to frighten me to death, seek no more. I never knew a thought could be so loud. What happened?"*

Quickly, Alan described what he had seen. *"And they are close! They are planning to surprise us, and I, for one, don't want to meet Beli and his two hundred Druids on their terms. We must find Nuada in a hurry and get out. If we don't transfer to Tartarus at once, we won't be able to. Join me in the hallway."*

Swiftly, he slipped on his cape, fastened his sword belt, and stepped to the door. It was locked—though there was no lock. Of course; he should have expected it. In moments Taliesin reported the same situation—the door was held shut magically.

"Lord Enki and Lady Inanna," Alan directed a thought toward the armlet. "Can you open the doors? And will you give us your full attention until we are out of this? I fear we have problems."

The Lady Inanna answered, "The doors are freed and the spell countered. But you do indeed have problems. Those Druids are back; already I feel their negation. I shall recall my Lord Enki from Nether Cuthah whence he was summoned to deal with Nergal, the dark lion who has again begun to roar."

Out in the silent corridor, Alan and Taliesin met, each ready for departure. The Bard said softly, "Now I agree we should transfer to Tartarus. I observed things through Nuada's eyes a moment ago without his knowing, and he is with Manannan, already alert to the arrival of Beli and King Arawn. We cannot count on him. I have not the power to take us to the island. Has your armlet?"

Alan shook his head regretfully, meeting Taliesin's gaze. "There are things the armlet cannot do, and this is one of them. But there is another way—Manannan's boat. And there's a rear exit to this castle. Come on!"

Not yet had anyone appeared in the area, attention evidently held by the commotion outside. They passed the spiral stairway which they had ascended when going to their rooms. Alan recalled having seen another when visually following the sea god and Nuada on their tour. They reached it and started down, moving as quietly as possible, then heard the clatter of footsteps on the level below and halted.

"Invisible!" Alan sent the thought.

Instantly each vanished from the other's sight. At the foot of the stairs, a guard ran past, followed in moments by two others, oblivious to their presence, heading toward the growing group at the far end of the corridor. With no one else near, Alan and Taliesin hurried toward the rear wall, now in sight.

Reaching it and about to ask to have it opened, Alan halted abruptly. He felt the Bard's hand on his arm. Through the doorway, he could hear the baying of Gwyn's hounds. Invisibility would mean nothing to the sensitive noses of the canine hunters. Mentally, MacDougall cursed.

"Disconcerting," Taliesin's low voice came calmly out

of the air. "And now what do we do? I follow your lead. The pupil has surpassed the teacher."

The mouth of the sloping corridor leading to the under-sea city lay near at hand. Silently MacDougall directed, *"Down that hallway into Lochlann! We certainly can't stay here, with the danger of the Druids countering our invisibility; but we're not stopped, by any means. In an empty city, there must be many places to hide; given time, we'll find a way out."*

They hastened down the steep slope to its end, a barrier of curving, translucent, sea-green glass with just a sug-gestion of luminosity. It moved slowly to their left. Of course! The castle revolved; Lochlann did not.

Impatiently, they waited for the entrance to appear. As Alan watched the smooth surface move silently past, he thought of the marvel of this endlessly revolving mass of incalculable weight. It had to have a rounded base, mov-ing in a great cup of matching shape and size. What an engineer, Lucifer!

"Alan," Taliesin's quiet voice interrupted. "It might be advisable to find out through Nuada what is happening. What say you?"

"Excellent idea. We should really know."

"Perhaps—" The Bard hesitated. "Perhaps you should join me mentally—to listen. Then both of us will know."

The interchange that followed required only seconds. *"Nuada, am I reaching you?"* Taliesin asked.

"Yes—and where are you? Mathonwy has just reported that you have left your rooms."

"For the moment we are safe. But tell me what is happening."

"Beli and Arawn have entered Caer Pedryvan, as have some of the Druids. More will enter with each revolution. Manannan is speaking with Beli—and you and I are not his concern. His—and Arawn's—anger is directed at MacDougall. His capture is all that matters to them. So, Taliesin, tell me where you are, and all will be well."

The Bard delayed his reply, finally answering, *"We are*

hiding on the roof among the bronze archers. We will be difficult to find." He terminated the connection.

He spoke aloud, a note of regret in his voice. "I was afraid of something like this happening. Nuada and the sea god were entirely too friendly. I have known him for a long time—a vain man, pride his greatest weakness. And in his view you humbled him."

At that moment, both became visible, the Druids evidently countering another spell on general principle. An instant later, an opening appeared before them, the way into the city. As one, they dashed through, then turned to watch the glass base of the castle slowly move over the opening.

MacDougall faced the Bard, then reached out and grasped his hand. "My friend, thank you. I must confess that I have doubted you because of your repeated insistence on my returning to my own world. There are no more doubts. Whatever your motivation, I know it is honest—and I know, too, when you deem the time to be right, that you'll tell me what is in your mind."

The Bard returned the handclasp and, with solemn mien, met his gaze, but with the trace of a twinkle in his eyes. "In the meantime, we have a problem to resolve. You and I—and the armlet."

They turned to see what they faced.

MacDougall had no preconceived ideas as to what they would observe, but certainly not this. They were looking down a long, green glass tube, its bottom flat, its rounded sides merging into a perfectly arched top, about the size of the corridor they had just left. The walls glistened with internal luminosity; the floor was dull and scuffed. At least a city block in length, it sloped downward rather steeply.

"Let's go!" Alan exclaimed. "We want to get out of this tunnel before the opening comes around again." He began jogging briskly down the slope and heard Taliesin at his elbow.

When they reached the end of the passageway, the

Bard had fallen back a dozen strides and was breathing heavily.

"I'm not accustomed to running," he wheezed.

Motionless, catching their breath, they gazed into Lochlann, a city most strange. It was an immense oval dome, with curving walls stretching away on either side and sweeping high above them in a perfect arc. They appeared to be standing at one of the narrower ends; the other was beyond their range of vision. And because everything—walls, domed ceiling, and floor—gave forth a greenish phosphorescence, Lochlann seemed veiled in a sort of ghostly light like that which would come from a million massed fireflies.

Before them lay what once made Lochlann a city—its buildings that had once been the homes of the Fomorians. Alan knew immediately why Manannan had called the place strange. The houses were as distorted as their one-time dwellers.

Involuntarily, he moved among them for a closer look, Taliesin at his side. His first reaction was one of incredulity. Never had he seen an aggregation of structures so completely lacking in organization and uniformity. There were only three points of similarity. All were approximately one storey in height, all were small, and all were formed of the sea-green glass. Otherwise they were indescribable.

There was no order in their shapes, in their positioning, or in their spacing; some were closer together, others far apart. There were no streets. The buildings were solid enough, and all had openings of one sort or another to permit entrance or egress. Otherwise they were as malformed as the Fomorians themselves. And scattered among them were objects that Alan supposed were intended as ornamental images, all as grotesque as the houses. Statuary and structures together, seen in the cold green light, suggested a tortured painting from the mind and brush of a mad surrealist.

It was as if a Dali and a Picasso had been combined

in one, had been challenged to surpass their own wildest creation—and had succeeded.

MacDougall chuckled as he turned to Taliesin. "I never thought of Lucifer as having a sense of humor, but this changes my mind. I can imagine his laughing almost as heartily after completing this creation as Picasso must have done after selling the City of Chicago the monstrosity outside its City Hall. All of which means nothing to you."

The Bard looked doubtful, then said practically, "Where shall we hide?"

Suddenly Alan sobered—and not because of their needing concealment. In his mind had formed a picture of the monstrous Fomorians, taken from their grotes- querie to the beauty of Murias—which only emphasized their own ugliness. Not mirth, but malevolence and bitter malice had prompted such action.

"A place to hide," Alan commented, frowning. "Let's think a bit. Where will they expect us to hide? In some remote spot, as inaccessible as possible. So we'll seek a place out in the open. And since we must get out the way we came in, if we are to use Manannan's coracle, we should stay as close to the exit as possible. It may very well be that this is the only exit." His expression changed, brightened. "I have an idea—but before I propose it, we need to determine how much time we have before the searchers enter Lochlann. You said you observed through Nuada's eyes without his knowing. Can you do it again? I'll try to see what I can through the armlet."

He addressed the serpent-gods. "Lord Enki and Lady Inanna, help me to see Manannan and whatever he's doing."

A mental picture formed—the sea god at the center of a group, among them the god Beli, King Arawn, Nuada, Mathonwy, and Gwyn the Hunter, as well as a score or more Druids. Behind them rose a crenelated parapet with life-sized bronze archers. Beli was speaking, everything about him suggesting fury.

"They certainly are not on the roof!" He glared at Nuada. "Were you deceiving us?"

Vehemently, Nuada answered, "I reported only what Taliesin told me. It is evident that he deliberately lied. I would have to be a fool to attempt another deception."

Manannan interrupted smoothly. "We'll try another way. Gwyn, get your hounds. You, Mathonwy, go with him and lead them to the rooms I have assigned the two to give the animals their scent. We'll find them—unless they've vanished altogether or have gone to the other island."

"With my Druids here," Beli growled, "it would take strong magic indeed for that to have happened."

Alan terminated the vision. "You saw and heard?" he asked the Bard. At the other's nod, he added, "So did I; and we do have some time. But Manannan is doing just what I feared—bringing in those hounds." He scowled blackly. "Hiding won't do much good with them sniffing around. Maybe the armlet has the answer." He closed his eyes.

"Lord Enki and Lady Inanna, we are concerned about Gwyn's hounds. Have you a solution to offer?"

The serpent-god's thought expressed mild disappointment. "Surely the answer is obvious. Recently we controlled thousands of wasps. We could easily control the hounds—but there is an easier solution. We'll simply interfere with their sense of smell. It should be amusing to watch frustrated hounds that can find no scent at all."

Grinning broadly, MacDougall opened his eyes and exclaimed, "The hounds will no longer be a problem. They will have lost their sense of smell. There will be no way they can detect us."

"Good," Taliesin said. "And you said you had an idea?"

"Yes. I think we should take on the shape of two of Beli's Druids, exactly following their dress and even having a swelling or two on very ordinary faces. Hmm. Swellings should change the faces enough to disguise us if we should appear unfamiliar to other Druids. Then we will hide in separate structures, perhaps in the third or fourth rank of houses. When the search begins, we'll emerge and join the others."

"But what if the Druids counter shape-changing? We would return to our normal appearance—"

"Not if we give them several decoy MacDougalls to chase!" The idea had come in flash. "The armlet *can* create illusions—and just imagine the confusion if they catch a glimpse of MacDougall and Taliesin at the far end of the city, being pursued by Druids. Then another somewhere in the central area. Maybe a third—"

The Bard held up his hand for silence, a look of deep concentration on his face. At last he lowered his hand.

"I received a call from Nuada. He is now back in Tartarus, and shocked and angry at having been sent there. He's inclined to blame you, but I assured him you were in no way involved. He had been in the midst of a group of Manannan's Druids, purposely avoiding the other gods because of their anger at our eluding them, as well as Beli's Druids, who are still annoyed about the wasps and the dragon's fire. Then, without warning, he was whisked away to quarters he maintains in Falias. I tried to calm him, telling him he should be grateful to be out of all this, but he's still angry. He's not accustomed to such high-handed treatment."

Alan scowled. "Ahriman transferred him, as sure as you're born. But why?" Abruptly his face brightened. "Regardless of why, it provides a perfect cover for me. I'll appear among the searchers as Nuada—" He stopped short. Was that what Ahriman wanted? Was he conveniently providing the suggestion by lifting the King of the *Tuatha de Danann* out of the action? "On second thought," he concluded, "we'll stay with my first idea—two of Beli's Druids mingling with the rest. Nuada's form would be too conspicuous."

At Alan's word, the Bard assumed an altered shape, slimmer and taller, with a very commonplace face marred by a puffed and discolored cheek, half concealed by the full gray hood of the Druid. Moments later, MacDougall became a second Druid, totally unlike himself. Separating, each entered one of the glass structures to await developments.

Alan glanced at the faintly luminous interior, bare of furnishings except for a narrow bed, an appendage to one wall. In the days of occupancy, he supposed, there must have been other furniture, but certainly nothing that could have made this twisted cubicle inviting. He stood just inside the opening and waited.

After a time of unbroken silence, MacDougall thought, this is silly. I can be watching what's going on. The armlet!

He closed his eyes. At his thought, a mental picture formed, the serpent-god commenting. "I wondered at your lack of curiosity."

The hallway leading down to the door into Lochlann was jammed with people and the red-eared white hounds. Beli and Arawn were nearest to the door; behind them stood some of Beli's Druids and three of the hounds of Gwyn. At the start of the slope where the corridors met, Manannan stood, trying to keep order.

"There is no reason to crowd in," he shouted. "At most, only ten people and three hounds can enter at each opening of the doors. We know the two are in Lochlann; the hounds have traced their spoor thus far. But remember, if you are caught in the doorway, you could be cut in two. So wait where you are. Make way for the Hunter. You, Gwyn, must be among the first to enter in order to control your animals."

The Lochlann opening finally slid into position, and the designated ten, with three of the hounds, rushed through. Visually, Alan followed this group as they started down the tunnel, his attention centered on the hounds. With noses to the floor, they zigzagged about, ranging from side to side, circling and backtracking, quite evidently failing to find the spoor they sought. Finally Gwyn, who had started down the slope, called impatiently to the animals, and they sped eagerly toward the city, their eerie baying filling the passageway.

The others—Beli, Arawn, and the seven Druids—who had halted, waiting for the hounds, now hastened after them. As they entered Lochlann, MacDougall thought, if only I were looking down at the city, I could follow their line of search. Instantly his perspective changed, Lochlann spread out below him. It was disconcerting—and how had Enki known?

The answer came instantly. "You asked for full attention until you were out of this difficulty. You have it."

With a mental "Thank you," MacDougall watched the first group fan out, most of them following Gwyn and the hounds. In moments, the animals' aimless wandering clearly indicated the effectiveness of Enki's treatment. None of the searchers came near the cubicle Alan occupied, but wandered deeper and deeper into the maze.

A second and third group came through the passageway, among them the others of the sea god's retinue, including, surprisingly, Saint Caradoc and Idris the Astrologer. No one approached either Alan or Taliesin; and with each additional searcher moving through, looking into or entering the ugly structures, the chances of their being detected decreased, since, had they been approached, they would simply have joined the hunt. With the Druids' preoccupation with other things, their countering of shape-changing became increasingly unlikely. Finally Alan stepped out and joined the search.

The Bard reported, "All is well. I am out."

And still the Druids came, their very number providing greater concealment. Finally all two hundred appeared to have made their way into Lochlann, the flow from the tunnel ceasing. Fleetingly, MacDougall thought of Manannan's Druids, deciding they had remained on guard in the castle with the soldiers. The men and hounds had spread through the length and breadth of the undersea city. Beli's bellow could be heard above the general noise, his anger and frustration mounting. The sounding of the hounds from widely scattered areas indicated the futility of their search.

Alan and Taliesin had worked their way closer to each other and had managed to remain in the vicinity of the exit without drawing anyone's attention. Now for the distraction, Alan thought; maybe it would provide the cover for their escape.

"Lord Enki, I suggested to Taliesin that glimpses of me could appear throughout the city—but can you do this?"

"Can we do this?" There was indignation in the Lady Inanna's response. "I alone could do this and more—I who have been Neveb-Kau and Uazit, Nintu and Kandalini—"

The Lord Enki's interruption expressed unbelief. "Have you forgotten so soon the mighty golden serpent in the prison of Ninshubur the Messenger? Of course we can. And it is a good idea. But your imagination has not gone far enough. Suppose, while you seem to appear here and there and confusion is at its height, something else happens. A great crack might appear in the top of the glass dome, above which lie the waters of the sea; and those waters would pour down, raining upon the searchers. Of course such an idea would have to originate in the mind of our resourceful Master.

"And having thought of all this, you need but ask and it will be done."

Jubilantly Alan responded, "I ask, I implore, Lord Enki and Lady Inanna, may the illusory MacDougall appear, and may the cataclysm follow." To the Bard he thought excitedly, *"Join me quickly, Taliesin. And when I say the word, follow my lead. Things will be happening."*

Immediately, at the distant end of Lochlann rose a sudden commotion, shouting voices, and chorus of cries echoing from the dome overhead. Mingled with the uproar, eerily sharp in the enclosed space, came the eager baying of the Hounds of Death. From all parts of the city came the clatter of racing sandals and excited cries.

"They've found him!"

Closer rose another shout. "No—there he goes. I just saw him dash around that house! This way—come on!"

Then high above everything came a scream, "The ceiling! The dome has cracked!"

With the cry, there burst forth a ripping sound, frightful to hear, a terrifying noise like the crackle of lightning just before thunder. Then there was the roar of rushing waters. Pouring out of a growing rent in the dome there seemed to come frothing torrents—a cascading flood that had to drive every thought but itself from the minds of those who beheld it.

From scores of throats rose screams, shouts, and wild curses, a chorus of terror that filled the great dome, mingling with the roar of falling torrents to create absolute bedlam.

Taliesin, staring in fascination at the incredible waterfall, turned swiftly as MacDougall clutched his arm.

"*Go invisible—now!*" Alan flashed the thought as he vanished. The Bard was quick to respond and needed no urging as Alan dashed toward the tunnel.

"*It's illusion,*" Alan explained swiftly, "*and they've forgotten all about us and their counterspells. The deception can't last very long—but we have our chance.*"

With all possible speed, they raced through the glass tube, Taliesin only a step behind Alan. Both were gasping when they reached the barrier, and they welcomed the short wait for the opening to appear, drawing deep breaths to recover. When at last they stepped through, Alan glanced back to see several gray-cowled figures entering the tunnel. Hardly pursuers, he thought—rather Druids seeking to escape the flood. What lay ahead was of total importance at the moment.

There was no one in the sloping corridor, but at its end in the intersecting passageway stood four of Manannan's white-robed Druids and two Roman guards. None seemed especially alert, engaged in casual conversation, evidently convinced that their quarry was in Lochlann. Carefully, as soundlessly as possible, the unseen fugitives made their way up the slope. As they reached its end, MacDougall's heart sank. This corridor was crowded with Druids and Beli's guards, especially at the end to Alan's left with its exit to the wharf. The door stood open invitingly, but getting to it undetected presented problems. To expect to make their way in their invisible state through forty or fifty men without detection was absurd. If there was some way to move them—

"Lord Enki and Lady Inanna, I have another problem—"

The serpent-god interrupted. "You have several problems. Manannan, himself a master of illusion, has detected the hoax; and Beli is bellowing for attention. It will not be long before some of the gods and Druids will come pouring back through the tunnel. But I see you need a diversion here. We will provide it."

With the thought, there came a clatter of boots from the floor above and a hearty voice came loudly down both spiral stairways. "Hi! I have just seen him! He's heading for the roof. Hurry!" Again came the clatter of footsteps racing along the corridor overhead.

Instantly, Romans and Druids sprang into action, darting toward the nearest spiral stairway, racing upward. In an unbelievably short time the passageway was clear.

"Let's go while we can." MacDougall sent the thought to the Bard, reaching out and finding a grip on his arm. As they started along the corridor, they heard the footfalls of the first Druids to return from Lochlann; ignoring stealth, they dashed toward the exit. Reaching it, they stepped out onto a wide stone platform, closing the door behind them.

"Lord Enki, it might be prudent to lock the door—your strongest spell."

"I have already done so."

They were looking out over the mirrorlike surface of a dark sea. Overhead shone the faint aurora.

Impatiently they waited while the castle slowly turned,

grateful that, with the sea before them, the drawbridge and wharf must be close.

"Alan." Taliesin spoke aloud. "Even if we succeed in reaching Manannan's coracle, can we make it move? I understand only the sea god can control it."

"You *would* think of that!" Alan exclaimed. "There has to be a way."

At that moment the drawbridge appeared, fortunately still in the lowered position, and they crossed over. As they started down the stone path, MacDougall addressed the serpent-god.

"Lord Enki, how am I to make *Wave Sweeper* move? I believe it is somehow attuned to Manannan alone."

The Lady Inanna answered. "I suppose you expect us to provide the power. You already have the answer if you have the wit to see it."

He already had the answer! What did that mean? Light dawned. He would become Manannan!

Pulse quickening, he visualized the sea god as he had last seen him, wearing a long, dark green cape, kilts to match, white tunic, and gold-mesh boots. He added his crest of blue-white hair, carefully trimmed mustache and beard, strong features, and intensely blue eyes to complete the picture.

"Lord and Lady, will you make the change? I need perfection."

With the thought he felt the transformation, with it visibility returning; and he knew he matched Manannan. Would appearance be enough?

"Taliesin, as you can see, I have become the sea god, to move the coracle. I suggest you remain unseen until we are on our way."

"A perfect match," the Bard began admiringly, to be interrupted by a shout from one of the grooms who cared for Splendid Mane.

"Ho! Whence come you? None are allowed—"

As Alan turned to face him, the groom stopped short.

"Forgive me, my Lord. I did not see you approach. But with all the visitors wandering about—"

MacDougall waved aside the protests. "I understand. And I appreciate your alertness."

He completed the walk down the stone walk, his eyes fixed on the sleek lines of Manannan's boat, gleaming in the light of the castle's slowly passing torches. Eagerly, he stepped aboard and felt the gently rocking deck under his feet. He heard the Bard's faint, "I am with you!"

And now, he thought, the test. With all his thoughts centered on the coracle he cried, "Go!"

Like a sprinter out of the blocks, the copper craft leaped into action, its sickled prow springing high in the water and its deck tilting sharply, sending both men sprawling. In moments, the wharf was left far behind, the shout of the startled groom lost in the silence. Flat on his back, MacDougall burst into triumphant laughter. "It worked! We made it! And if I never see Ochren again, it will be too soon."

Struggling to his feet, he exclaimed, "Slow down, Matilda, slow down! No reason to break speed records now."

Obediently, *Wave Sweeper* slowed to a more comfortable pace, her prow settling into the water, the churning wake behind them shrinking to normal size.

Grinning broadly, Taliesin stood up and found no difficulty in remaining erect as they rode the smooth surface of the tideless sea.

"Wonderful," he said, "but do you have any idea where we are headed?"

Before answering, MacDougall found seats projecting from both port and starboard hull, and sank onto one of them. The Bard seated himself on the other.

"I was hoping," Alan replied, "that you had a built-in sense of direction like that Nuada professes to have."

The Bard shook his head emphatically. "I have no idea where Tartarus lies—if, in fact, it is on this same sea."

"In that case—" Alan left the sentence unfinished, grasping the armlet and closing his eyes. "Lord Enki, we are going—but we have no idea where. Can you help?"

Promptly the answer came. "Visualize Tartarus as being sharply to your right, and so direct *Wave Sweeper*."

Smoothly, the coracle changed to conform with Alan's thought, settling into the new course. "Quite simple," he said, "when you wear the Armlet of the Gods. We're on our way."

For a time, they rode on in silence, reliving their fantastic experience in the glass castle, its grotesque undersea neighbor, Lochlann, and their swift escape. But MacDougall could not remain quiet for long.

He waved exuberantly toward the frothing water sweeping by. "I'm glad Nuada was not with us to transfer us to Tartarus. I wouldn't have missed this ride for anything. It's the first real enjoyment I've had since I entered Ochren."

"It is enjoyable," Taliesin agreed, "but let us not forget that when Manannan learns what has happened, as he will from the groom, he has the means to follow—that enchanted horse of his. And he is the god of the sea."

"True, but I've become something of a fatalist. We'll deal with that when the time comes."

Far behind them they saw a flash, a slanting lance of light from the sky, dimmed by distance, like a last reminder of the land of eternal gloom. Briefly, it swept along the horizon, then vanished.

On they sped interminably under the twilight-gray sky with its weak aurora and over a mirror-calm sea; the only disturbance of the waters came from the swells and foam of their own passing. How many miles they traversed, MacDougall could not guess; but this world of Lucifer's forming was far larger than he had imagined. The serpent-gods had said Ochren and Tartarus were on the same sea, so it was a logical assumption that the lands beyond the other Gates were in the same realm. And all, almost certainly, under the control of Ahriman.

A startled exclamation from the Bard interrupted his thinking. "What is that?" He was staring fixedly over the prow. MacDougall peered into the darkness ahead, realizing that the sky had changed and that there was no trace of the aurora before them. They appeared to be rushing toward a wall of black. Instinctively, he cut the speed of *Wave Sweeper* to a mere crawl.

With the slowing, another phenomenon appeared. Incredibly, the sea had developed a current, the foam of their wake moving alongside the coracle, speeding past the prow, and racing toward the blackness!

Then faintly came a strange yet familiar sound, almost imperceptible at first, but growing steadily louder with the passing moments. MacDougall groped to remember where he had heard a similar roar, like the fancied roar in a conch shell, multiplied a hundredfold. It was the all-pervading roar of a Niagara, muted by distance, as if the sea itself were rushing toward a precipice, plunging into an unseen abyss!

Into MacDougall's mind flashed Manannan's remark to Nuada: "I have been to the very edge of the waters, even to the brink!" Had he been referring to what seemed to lie ahead? But that was absurd—A flat world where one could go to the edge and fall off! Yet that mounting noise toward which they were moving—what else could it be? Whatever the source of the din, it still lay some distance ahead. They would approach with caution.

With eyes fixed on the blackness, MacDougall urged *Wave Sweeper* to a bit more speed. It responded with gradual acceleration, skimming over the water, the arched neck of the figurehead on the prow leaning farther back, the white waves breaking gracefully along port and starboard bows.

"Alan!" Again Taliesin's exclamation burst forth. "Behind us! I believe it is Manannan!"

MacDougall wheeled and stared into the murk. There, far behind them, riding in their wake, came a white figure, its form indefinite in the distance, but unquestionably a speeding object. It had to be the sea god on Splendid Mane. The figure grew larger as he watched, rapidly gaining upon them. Definitely, it was Manannan on his white horse. At their present pace he'd be with them in a very few minutes.

And ahead lay—whatever it was. Could the serpent-gods help?

"Lord Enki, what are we approaching?"

"Apparently the edge of this world, with the sea pouring over into a bottomless abyss and the auroral sky ending. But actually, it is illusion—a barrier that doesn't exist. There is no wall of blackness, no fall of water, but only a continuous calm sea. However, if you believe it is there, you will drop into a vast abyss. Like Beli's phantom soldiers, who were deadly for those who fought them and who believed they were there."

"Whose illusion? Not Manannan's."

"Obviously, the Lord of Light himself, the master creator of illusions. It is a barrier to prevent what you contemplate—travel from island to island."

Whirling about, Alan darted to the entrance of the little cabin, grasping the broad copper upright that formed one side of the doorway. He indicated its counterpart and cried,

"Taliesin, grab that and hang on! The darkness, the current, the waterfall we hear—all are illusions, the creation of Lucifer himself. We have the assurance of the armlet! Believe me, never doubting. We're going through!"

As the Bard followed orders, Alan shouted, "Full speed ahead, Matilda! Give it all you've got!"

Like a cruelly spurred horse, the boat leaped forward, almost standing on end; stinging spray lashed their faces, and the wind whistled shrilly in their ears. MacDougall cast a glance over his shoulder, seeking sight of the pursuer. All he could see was their wake, like giant twin mounds of foam rising higher than their high-riding prow.

Then Manannan, god of the sea, made his presence felt. The wind in moments changed from a comparative zephyr to a howling, shrieking hurricane. It pushed against them like a giant's hand; and under its lash, the waters

ahead became a frothing, leaping tumult. *Wave Sweeper*
bucked and reeled from trough to wave-crest like something alive, fighting for survival.

Spray shot over MacDougall and Taliesin in sheets that
drenched them to the skin. They could only cling with
both hands and feet, heads bowed in a vain attempt to
shield their faces from the worst blasts of this unnatural
storm. If it were not for the steep slant of the deck they
would have been swamped at the very beginning of this
onslaught.

Then came the cold; the wind suddenly cut with icy
whips, and stinging pellets of sleet added to their misery.
Where the spray struck now, it froze; in an unbelievably
short time, both shivering wretches became coated with
glistening armor.

The noise, which was not Manannan's doing, had
become a tremendous, terrifying thing, and the wall of
blackness was rushing toward them with appalling speed.
Never had MacDougall experienced such concentrated
torment. It required all his will to continue their headlong
flight and to shut from his mind any trace of doubt about
the outcome. From somewhere deep in his stubborn Scotch
soul flared a sudden surge of fierce anger. With closed
eyes and clenched jaws, he drove on.

Through the tumult and frozen fury, he sensed Taliesin's tortured thought, *"This is not to be borne. Can your
armlet do nothing?"*

At the same instant came his own bitter thought, *"Win—
come hell or high water!"*

And at that moment, with speed undiminished, *Wave
Sweeper* burst through into a world of light, of calm, of
blessed warmth, where the roar of torrents of water fell
away behind them, receding, lessening, dying. And overhead, glorious in its brilliance, shone the well-remembered
aurora of Tartarus.

"Slow down, Matilda," MacDougall cried in grateful
relief. "We made it."

Instantly, the copper coracle settled to an even keel,

the rush of air becoming a gentle breeze. Stiffly, painfully, Alan released his grip on the stanchion and faced the bow. The wall of darkness, like an endless velvet curtain, extended into the distance to both right and left and merged with the black sky beneath the bright aurora overhead. It seemed utterly foreign to this place, though why the illusion was there was obvious. There were fishing boats in the sea around Tartarus and fishermen might venture this far away from the island.

There was no sign of Manannan.

Alan faced Taliesin as the Bard grumbled, "Such heroics are not appropriate for a man of my mature years. When I was a young man, perhaps—" Their eyes met, and the Bard's ruddy face crinkled in a stiff smile as he opened and closed his hands spasmodically. Suddenly Alan burst into a hearty laugh. Taliesin looked funny, with a ledge of white ice over each eye and the fringe of white hair around his balding head glittering like a crystalline halo under its icy coating.

Indignantly, the Bard frowned, ice flaking from his brows. He ran his fingers through his hair, breaking the frozen crust. Then he laughed in turn.

"You are an amusing picture yourself, Manannan, with ice on your rooster's comb and in your blue whiskers. Well—I can change into dry clothes, and you cannot."

"And what does that mean?" Alan asked curiously.

Taliesin's eyes twinkled. "I think shape-changing will rid me of my wet clothes. And until we reach land, you must remain as the sea god to control this boat. I'll test my theory." In moments the rounded form of the Bard was replaced by the Druid shape he had assumed in Lochlann. He said with satisfaction, "As I hoped, I am comfortably dry and warm."

MacDougall chose to ignore the other's triumphant chuckle, again glancing back the way they had come. The black wall was no longer visible, and there was still no sign of the sea god. "I suppose we've seen the last of Manannan," he said.

Taliesin shook his head. "I would not count on that. Knowing his mastery of illusion, and with his having seen *Wave Sweeper* vanish into the blackness, I have an idea that he will attempt to follow us."

"If that is a possibility, there's no point in our dawdling." To the coracle he added, "More speed, Matilda."

Again the boat responded, the proud figurehead rearing back, the prow riding high, and the wake growing proportionately. Both men slid to seats along the port and starboard sides and hung on. As the sea raced past, Alan wondered where on Tartarus they would be landing. The armlet had merely directed them toward the island; after all, it had a long shore line.

"Where, Lord Enki," MacDougall asked, "on Tartarus are we headed?"

"To Murias. Ochren lies due west of Tartarus."

"Thank you." Good. There were horses in Murias and if, as seemed logical, their destination was the Bard's home in Falias—after a most important stop at Ahriman's tower—they'd need transportation.

"Well, Taliesin, I've just learned that we'll be landing at Murias. Can you think of any reason for entry into the city?"

"We should—borrow—a pair of horses." Dryly, Taliesin added, "I hardly think we'd enjoy visiting Balor."

"Balor?" Alan demanded incredulously. "Surely you can't mean he survived his wound!"

"No, he died; but he's back in a new body. Not a duplicate of his former one—he is now a twisted Fomorian; but he appears like the Balor of old by maintaining a constant shape-change, even to the gold eyepatch." He added casually, "Of course there's no longer any power in his eye."

Crazy world, Alan thought as he stood up, where people didn't stay dead. He looked along the prow across the expanse of rainbow-tinted water with its mirror image of the constantly shifting and changing aurora. And there, where sea and sky met, appeared a gray-green line—land, most certainly, and logically the island Alan had named Tartarus.

"Land ahead," he cried.

"And Manannan aft!" Taliesin responded. "I've been watching, and it must be the sea god."

Turning, MacDougall saw a minute object on the western horizon, growing larger as he watched.

"I didn't think he'd have the courage to do it!" he exclaimed with grudging admiration. "After all, we had authoritative assurance; he didn't. Let's move," he said to the Bard. "Grab the stanchion. We're almost there—and we won't wait for another storm. Matilda—full speed!"

Again *Wave Sweeper* leaped forward, almost standing on end. Despite the shrilling wind and stinging spray, MacDougall pulled himself above the cabin and watched the approaching island. He saw the Hall of the Dead at the tip of the fingerlike islet in the bay grow from a white speck to a long, white building; and as they sped toward it, he cried, "Slow down!"

Smoothly, the coracle drew up beside the little strip of rock and came to a gentle stop, as if it had a mind of its own.

Long before the god of the sea drew near, Alan and the Bard had leaped out on land, clasped hands, and instantly vanished. With invisibility, Alan felt the clammy garments of Manannan leave and knew he was again himself.

Their approach and landing had occurred so rapidly that the several fishermen in two boats about a hundred yards away could hardly have grasped what was happening. There was no one in sight on land.

"I have a plan," Alan said as they strode briskly along the narrow road leading to the causeway, "which I'll explain as it develops." They reached the top of the long ramp—MacDougall's first sight of it, since he had previously traversed it in dense fog. Now the flagstone slope between two mighty stone walls lay clear before them in the auroral light.

As they descended, Alan addressed the serpent-gods. "Lord Enki and Lady Inanna, I need a convincing illusion of two horses and their Norsemen riders who have rushed here from Falias with an important message for the god Balor. The horses should be sweating and lathered, near exhaustion. When they are admitted, one of the riders will tell of his message and request two fresh horses for the rapid return ride to the Mother Goddess, Danu, with Balor's reply. Can this be done?"

"With ease. Consider it accomplished."

With a few swift thoughts MacDougall told the Bard of his plan. Unseen, they would follow the illusory riders into Murias and, with luck, lead out the replacement mounts, invisible of course, when Manannan entered. Alan was counting on the sea god's lack of familiarity with anything on Tartarus delaying his entry—perhaps in talking with the fishermen. Some uncertainty was involved, but there was a good chance of the plan working.

As they approached bottom and the great bronze double door, two horses and riders appeared. One of the Norsemen reached up and pulled a huge bronze ring that sent a single vibrant bell note into Murias. Alan looked over the horses with admiration. Enki had certainly succeeded in creating jaded animals. Glistening with sweat, they were a picture of weariness, heads hanging listlessly, obviously driven to the verge of collapse.

Slowly the double door opened, drawn inward by two gatekeepers. In tandem, the riders entered with the invisible MacDougall and Taliesin behind them. Most convincingly, one of the illusory Norsemen repeated the message Alan had invented. "I have been here before," he concluded, "and I know my way to Balor's quarters." Without further delay, both Norsemen stalked away into the throng of idly walking Fomorians.

MacDougall, turning toward the grooms as they led the exhausted horses into the corral, caught a glimpse of a familiar face in the crowd.

Dalua! Dark Dalua with his burning black eyes. This

was the mad god who laughed without reason and who had trailed him during that last dash for freedom from Tartarus while the armies of Nuada and Balor fought their senseless war. The gaze of the Witless One was fixed intently on the two supposed Norsemen; like a blood-hound on the scent, his cadaverous, black-clad form slid through the crowd in pursuit.

"Taliesin, did you see Dalua?" Alan asked silently. *"I'm glad he's not lingering here. I hope the illusions lead him a merry chase."*

The Bard was more interested in the grooms. *"Alan—they're using the gear from the imaginary horses! Can't you stop them?"*

Agreeing, MacDougall silently protested, "Lord Enki, that will never do! We'd have to maintain the illusion all the way to Falias—or ride bareback."

With the thought, the guard muttered, "Better use fresh blankets and harness. These are soaked with sweat," and proceeded to secure what he needed.

"A close call," Taliesin's thought came to MacDougall. *"I never cease to marvel at the powers of that armlet."*

"Amazing, is it not?" Alan replied. *"Now all we need do is await the arrival of Manannan."*

With the thought came three impatient bell notes, fol-lowed in moments by another. The god of the sea was seeking entrance.

CHAPTER 10

Ahriman

The great doors swung wide, and the god Manannan, astride the giant white horse, Splendid Mane, rode majestically into Murias. As he frowned down at the gatekeepers, he was a picture of regal power, from his crest of blue-white hair and beard, through silver-ornamented dark green cape, white tunic, green kilts, to gold-meshed boots with their strange blue glow.

"I am Manannan, god of the sea," he announced dramatically. "I must see whoever rules this city."

"Manannan!" One of the gatekeepers repeated the name in awed tones; as dawning recognition became certainty, he sank to his knees. "It is indeed Manannan come to Murias!"

The other guard, more stolid, remained erect, but he spoke with deep respect. "Greetings, my Lord. It has been a long time since we left the Old City. Welcome to Murias. The god Balor is ruler here. Shall we summon him?"

"Balor! Balor of the Evil Eye? We did not always see

alike. No—I shall go to him." Looking around he added, "This is hardly a suitable place for us to meet."

Watching, MacDougall saw his expression change from one of curiosity and interest to cold anger and determination. "I come seeking two men—"

"The Norsemen!" The guard was greatly excited. "We just admitted two Norsemen who they said came bearing a message of great importance for Balor and are on the way to him now."

"Norsemen, indeed! They are masters of shape-changing who appear as they wish. They are the two I seek." Quickly, Manannan slid from the saddle. "Quarters at once for Splendid Mane—and guidance to Balor."

"Master, I fear we have no private stalls." The words were hesitant and apologetic. "Unless your horse can share quarters with Balor's Black Fury."

Impatiently Manannan answered, "I suppose that will have to suffice. Show me."

The grooms led the white horse away with the sea god walking at Splendid Mane's side.

During all this the great gate had remained wide open. *"Taliesin,"* MacDougall's thought was incredulous, *"is it possible? Never have I seen such cooperation. They want us to go. Quick, the horses!"*

In moments, the saddled horses vanished and as quickly were led through the exit. At the base of the ramp, the two mounted and began the upward ride. There was little mental exchange except for Taliesin's admiring observation.

"Alan—I stand in awe of your scheming mind. I am more impressed with each demonstration of your ingenuity. Those illusions served not only as a means of our getting mounts, but as decoys for Manannan. He is thoroughly convinced that even now we are hiding in Murias."

Alan spoke aloud. "Thanks for your praise. I am tempted to accept it as something I deserve; but in honesty I must confess that Manannan's interpretation of the hoax was a bonus I did not foresee. I was solely concerned with getting horses."

Without incident, they reached the top of the ramp, still invisible, rode over the stone causeway, and continued up the long, sloping, white gravel road to the forest at its top. Here MacDougall turned off, halting under the trees.

"No further reason to remain invisible," he said with relief. "Invisibility is a great asset, but it has its disadvantages. I think now we should see what is happening in Murias. I'll view things through the armlet and pass the picture to you."

With the reins hooked over convenient branches, they found comfortable seats on clumps of turf, and Alan closed his eyes.

"Lord Enki and Lady Inanna, I should like to observe the movements of Manannan."

There was no verbal response; but instantly MacDougall was a spectator, visually following the sea god through the throngs of Murias. It was evident at once that he had not been forgotten. Fomorians stopped and stared at him as he walked by; paths through the crowds opened spontaneously, greatly speeding his progress to Balor's quarters. His gatekeeper guide remained with him until Balor was sighted; then, in obvious fear, he turned back.

Well before Manannan and Balor met, MacDougall saw the giant figure of the god of the Fomorians. And though Taliesin had told him of Balor's permanent shape-change, sight of the reality was startling. He had seen his death-blow—a sword-thrust deep into that supposedly lethal eye. Balor was almost seven feet tall, broad and massive, with the same craggy features, black hair, and short beard, the gold band slanting over his forehead supporting the hinged eye-patch. He even wore the same green breeches and jacket, gold belt, and two swords.

In a flash, Alan thought, "Lord Enki, what is really there?"

The visual change was startling. Alan now saw a tall,

scrawny man, his upper body twisted, back humped, totally unlike the Balor of old. Balor, domineering, savage, mighty Balor, was an empty shell.

The gods met in the tiled corridor of the second floor of the Hall of Games—where Alan had encountered the hag Morrigu in the guise of Macha of the Red Hair and had almost been deceived.

But the meeting of the two gods swept away his reminiscences. Balor spoke first, his face expressionless. "Manannan—it is indeed you. Word had come through my chief Druid, Semias, that you were here, but he cannot always be relied upon. What brings you to Murias?"

Alan saw the sea god's face grow grim. "I seek one I have reason to believe is hiding here—Alan MacDougall who, it is said, comes from the Other World, and whom I will find. And when I do—"

Balor's face became livid, the cords of his neck standing out like taut wires. "MacDougall here! Are you sure? Never have I hated a being as I hate him!" Their eyes met, and suddenly both gods smiled grimly; as one, they swung out right hands, striking in a resounding clap.

"Not always have we been allies," Balor began.

Manannan's laugh interrupted. "As both know, there was a day in the Olden Time when we were at each other's throats. Now we meet, bound together by one common purpose—the slow, tortured death of that insufferable MacDougall."

"If, as you say, he is in Murias, invisible or in any other guise, sooner or later he will be caught. Word will pass to every Fomorian to be on watch for anything—*anything*—suspicious. If, unseen, he so much as touches any of them, he will be seized. And my Druids will be questing everywhere, seeking with all their sensitivity for this alien. He will be caught—oh, he will be caught. And when he is—" Balor left the threat unfinished.

Manannan chuckled unpleasantly. "I have just come from another island—Ochren, where MacDougall meddled unbelievably with the affairs of Beli, Arawn, and me, the three rulers. He insulted us and defied us. You remember Beli and you may recall Arawn. They will join us. Both hate MacDougall as we do. I will bring them here in my *Wave Sweeper*—which *he* dared to use! Or perhaps they can be brought by other means. They, too, will contribute to the entertainment when he is captured."

Alan was grateful indeed that he was watching at long range. The goal of these four evil gods, his enemies, intent on his slow death, was not something he cared to contemplate.

As the two gods approached Balor's apartment, Balor raised a question about the other island.

As they settled into oversized chairs, Manannan spoke on another subject. "During my short stay in Murias, I have seen the great overcrowding that seems to exist among the Fomorians. Are you aware that Lochlann, the city whence these people came, lies empty and waiting? Perhaps some of them could be returned, relieving your congestion and making use of all that space. Something to think about—"

MacDougall opened his eyes and stood up.

"I believe we've seen enough. Neither of us is interested in Manannan's favorite subject, his regaining subjects for his rule—nor in whatever he may have to say about Ochren. You observed what I saw?"

"Clearly," the Bard answered, shaking his head. "It is evident that you have four deadly enemies." Amusedly, he added, "Perhaps you noticed that they didn't even mention me. Not that I object to the neglect."

MacDougall shrugged. "Nothing I can do about it, except try to avoid them." He added dolefully but with a mocking half-smile, "And I really meant no harm." He swung into the saddle. "On to the golden tower of Ahriman."

The horses so generously supplied by Murias were fine animals, and their progress eastward was rapid. MacDougall enjoyed the ride through pungent pine forests and over undulating country, beneath the kaleidoscopic wonder of the Tartarian sky. In contrast with the gloom and dolor of Ochren, it was a fantastic spectacle. Then, for no evident reason, he thought of the austere beauty of the Scottish Highlands, with wisps of downy clouds in a deep blue sky, the rugged hills and tumbling burns, with gemlike lochs, and with the song of birds—and he knew where his preference lay.

After miles of steady riding, Taliesin spoke. "Alan, the tower you refer to—as you know, it could not be seen by Danu and Dagda, so certainly I will not be able to see it. Even for me to go close, since the area is forbidden, would be most uncomfortable. Is it your thought that I wait some distance away so that, after you leave the tower, we may ride on together to Falias—or shall I keep going?"

"You wait, by all means. If I am welcome, I hope to be your guest. I have no plans, since I don't know why I am back in this world. I'll simply have to await developments." Vehemently, he added, "Damn such a setup!"

"Of course you are welcome." Taliesin smiled slyly. "Until you decide to go home."

Finally they reached the place where it seemed to MacDougall they should turn off and head southeast. They left the road to cross a wide expanse of turf, followed by a dense thicket of close-growing trees through which they had to lead the horses. Beyond this, they came to another meadow; and Taliesin said uncertainly, "This feels like a Forbidden Area—not strongly so, but—"

"And there lies the tower!" MacDougall exclaimed triumphantly, pointing southward. A hundred yards away, a shimmering golden cone rose from the lush pasture of the pallid green grass of Tartarus. Perfect in its symmetry, it pierced the black sky, its tip hidden by curtains, streamers, and dancing veils of multicolored aurora. No windows, no lines of any sort marred its geometrical perfection.

"Can you see—?" He turned to the Bard.

"Taliesin!" he exclaimed, startled. Either the Bard had suddenly become invisible or he was gone. "Taliesin!" he called more loudly, but there was no response. His horse stood docilely waiting, but of the Bard there was no trace. Grimly MacDougall stared at the tower. Ahriman!

"*Alan,*" Taliesin's thought came clearly into Mac-Dougall's mind. "*Am I getting through to you? I am back in Falias, in my own quarters. Quite sudden, the trip, and surprising, to say the least.*"

"*Yes, my friend, you are getting through,*" Alan replied. "*It seems the beneficent Ahriman suddenly decided to save you the tedium of the long ride. Or he decided you were in the way. Well—it means I won't have your company for the rest of the trip to Falias. You'll see me when I get there. I'm on my way to beard the lion in his den. Wish me luck.*"

As a fervent, "*You have it,*" came from the Bard, Alan severed the line of communication.

He had one more concern before he entered the tower— the horses. It seemed cruel to fasten them to a tree with all this grass available. Could they be controlled mentally as Enki had suggested? Why not try? There was little likelihood of their leaving the pasture, even if mental control didn't work. Removing the bits from their mouths, he hooked the reins over the saddle horns. Then, while talking soothingly to the animals and stroking their graceful necks, he tried to impress upon them that they should stay where they were. He hoped it would work.

He turned, then, to fix the area in his mind, in case the horses wandered. When he left the tower he did not want, as after that other visit, to head south toward the Desert of Gloom. He noticed in the nearer forest, almost in alignment with the tower, a single tree, taller than the rest, that could serve as a landmark. Quickly, he surveyed the woods to right and left, but saw no other tree as tall. He turned and headed toward the golden cone.

As he approached it, the gleaming gold held his fascinated gaze; but his thoughts were not of the tower, but rather of the man within—Ahriman. He could almost see the gem-hard eyes of turquoise blue and the mirthless smile. He felt momentary doubt. Who was he, to confront so powerful an entity? A man—if Ahriman were mere man—who controlled not only Tartarus and Ochren, but almost certainly those unknown lands beyond the other Gates, with all their ancient gods and peoples. Ahriman was master of magicians, sorcerers, warlocks, and wizards, perhaps second only to the Supreme Lord of Evil, Lucifer or Satan himself.

Yet what of Lord Enki, who considered Ahriman an upstart, a latecomer in the Luciferean history, and who even questioned his claim to the name Ahriman? It was reassuring in a way to know that, at least, Alan was not dealing with omnipotence. For certainly Ahriman did not control the serpent-gods.

Alan drew close to the tower, marveling at its strangely contradictory combination of the metallic and the translucent. From inside, one could look out through the wall. He walked more slowly. What if his plan did not work?

His Scots stubbornness asserted itself. It *had* to work! Once before, he had gone through that wall, though assisted by Ahriman. He'd do it again and without help. With set jaw and muscles tensed, he walked into the wall.

And through it!

He ignored a passing dizziness and an indescribable *twisting*, as a deep voice exclaimed, "I wondered if you would have the courage to make the venture. I approve. You have progressed most satisfactorily. The Master is always pleased with the favorable progress of a prize student, especially when he is the *only* student. Welcome! I expected you."

Alan saw Ahriman a yard away, broad of shoulder, a head taller than himself, clad in blue, sharp against gold-colored draperies.

"Smug, aren't you?" he answered angrily, his annoyance overcoming the apprehension he had felt. "Of course you expected me, since you seem to watch every move I make. Proud of the student who doesn't even want your tutelage! *Why*—tell me *why* I've had this role thrust upon me!"

Ahriman's expression remained unchanged, his incredibly blue eyes meeting Alan's and a faint, fixed smile on his too-red lips. "I admire your costume," he said casually. "'The Man in Black' made identification easy. I find it somewhat similar to the garments I wore during our first visit, without the gold ornamentation, of course. I confess to a weakness, an inordinate fondness for decorative gold."

He assumed an apologetic air. "This blue ensemble, though tailored to my precise specifications, is somewhat disappointing because the gold threads in the design are less evident than I expected they would be." With open palms held out at his sides he invited inspection of a turquoise-blue cape, high-collared vesture, full-cut trousers gathered at the ankles, and pointed sandals, tip-tilted, all of glistening silk with ornate gold ornamentation. "I like the color," he added, "because it matches my eyes. What do you think?"

MacDougall had listened to the Persian with amazement. Could this be real? Could he be hearing what he thought he heard? Realization came as he saw Ahriman's smile broaden, and Alan laughed. It was an act, a clever distraction.

"What do I think? For a moment I thought you had lost your mind. Now—"

"Now," Ahriman interrupted smoothly, "since you've relaxed, we shall ascend to more comfortable quarters for our conversation. You will recall the room surrounded by the aurora. Your hand, please."

An instant later they were in the gold room where they had held their earlier discussion. As before, Alan's interest was seized by the magnificent view of the aurora, seen through the now-transparent substance of the tower wall. He crossed to the side and gazed in fascination at the dancing streamers, waves, and fountains of restless radiance, never enduring, always changing, tinted a sunset gold. At length, reluctantly, he seated himself in a thickly upholstered chair, gold colored, as were the rugs and all the furnishings. Ahriman was already seated, waiting.

"Before we enter into discussion," he said, "refreshments are in order." As though by command, a small table appeared between them. On it were two delicate crystal wine goblets and a matching—decanter, Alan thought would be the word, though unlike any he had ever seen— all exquisitely carved, apparently of rock crystal. The design was Oriental and bizarre; but neither word fitted the red-purple wine that Ahriman poured. Delectable, Alan thought as he rolled it on his tongue.

"There is nothing illusory about the wine or the service," the Persian said casually; then after a pause he began, "So you are angry because of my deception."

"And why shouldn't I be?" MacDougall forced a scowl. This was not the way he had planned the conversation. "Somehow you've gained a hold on me and you use any means at hand to accomplish your ends. Even dreams— the dream of Arawn's Seer and one of Beli's Druids."

Ahriman smiled faintly. "It is quite amazing how dreams sometimes approximate the truth. I have heard it said that coming events cast their shadows before them—in dreams."

"Deception—always deception and trickery!" Alan exclaimed.

Ahriman arched his thin black brows in mock surprise. "Surely you should not consider it unusual that an agent, an emissary of Lucifer would practice to deceive, to use a quaint phrase. And you forget the Scroll. You are the object of a prophecy made by the Lord of Light; and it is unthinkable that his declarations should fall short of fulfillment."

MacDougall felt a sudden chill. There it was again— that damned Scroll!

"Just what is this prophecy?" he demanded. "And why should I be part of it? I thought it merely dealt with the gods returning with—someone—to the Other World, and in a few hours becoming ghosts, their bodies disintegrating. Lucifer's jest! Now there seems to be more. It appears that Taliesin did not reveal everything."

"Why not ask him?"

"I have already done so, but he refuses to answer. I think this whole idea is silly. You are attempting to fit me into a mold—that's why you brought me back—and I want no part of it . . . And why *me* in the first place? Just because I happened to be there—the wrong place at the right time?"

Ahriman studied MacDougall quizzically. "Evidently it hasn't occurred to you that you may possibly be an avatar, a reincarnation, of an early King of Britain, and quite likely in direct line of descent—that you were born to be what you will become."

"And what will I become? King of Tartarus? Or of all the lands under the aurora?" Alan snorted derisively. "This is ridiculous. If I were of royal blood, you may be sure I would know it."

"So?" Ahriman's smile widened. "There are those, if I recall the expression, who were born on the wrong side of the blanket. And who knows what kind of pact may have been entered into in the centuries long gone? Or what promises made?"

"Nonsense!" MacDougall exclaimed impatiently, though he felt a sudden chill. "I certainly can't be involved in any hypothetical something that happened thousands of years ago."

"No?" Again the Persian arched his brows. "The sins of the fathers—you know the rest. And there were promises made to Abraham and David which many believed were fulfilled in a baby born in Bethlehem—"

"Let's not be absurd!" Alan interrupted angrily. "And what does all this have to do with my excursion through the dark world of Ochren?"

"It was necessary that you master the powers of your armlet to fit you for the future; and practicing under what we may call combat conditions seemed the best way to accomplish this. I believe you will agree that the method worked. You have learned well. Beside that, there were certain individuals it was necessary for you to meet. And they, as it happened, were dwellers in Ochren."

Incredulously MacDougall exclaimed, "People I had to meet? All I succeeded in doing was to make enemies of the rulers. I didn't miss one. And who among them——" He broke off. "Part of the mysterious prophecy, I suppose." He changed the subject. "Has it occurred to you that mastering the powers of the armlet could be classified as a hazardous occupation?"

"Thus far, you have succeeded in escaping injury, and I believe your good fortune will continue. At most, you were subject to a bit of discomfort."

MacDougall, sipping his delightful wine, stared into the fantastic auroral display beyond the wall while he dredged his memory for more of the questions he had planned to ask. At length he said, "You called yourself the master, with me the student—so shall we call this research? I have been storing a number of questions in anticipation of this session."

Ahriman nodded without comment.

"A question about your name. According to my reading back in the Other World, the name Ahriman is the equivalent of Lucifer or Satan. Yet you claim to be a lieutenant of your Master."

Ahriman appeared amused. "If you will recall my words, I said you may *call* me Ahriman. With equal accuracy I could have had you call me many other names—Typhon, Apollyon, Iblis, Osiris, Pluto—for during the millennia I have been legion."

An odd term, Alan thought, but to him it still sounded like Lucifer.

"According to legend, Lucifer created this land for the Daughters of Lilith, forming the Four Cities, cities of beauty, as their dwelling places. Why did he create the other islands?"

"He foresaw the need—as he foresees everything. Nothing is concealed from the Master's sight—not in space, not in time. Certainly you do not think the Lord of Light has only this small realm to require his attention. Here are mere thousands of his—wards. His followers and subjects are beyond numbering. This small world is only a minute corner of his creation."

"Sounds to me," Alan commented, "as if you are claiming for Lucifer powers of foreknowledge, omniscience, and creativity that I thought were attributes of Almighty God."

"I suggest you change your thinking; though I concede that you have been thinking in diverse areas."

"Much has happened to raise questions," Alan continued. "For example, in that beautifully staged—though imaginary—scene with the Bard and the Roman soldiers inside the Gate to Ochren, how did you produce the light from the sky at that precise moment?"

Ahriman chuckled. "Shall we call that amazing good fortune, or the wildest coincidence? It was just the touch I needed, but, of course, one could hardly depend upon so unpredictable an element as that beam from the sky. That it came just when I needed it was most gratifying."

"In short, you won't tell me. Then I suppose you also profess ignorance concerning the source of those beams."

The Persian shrugged. "Surely you must have arrived at a conclusion of your own—you with the advantage of the knowledge the armlet gained through the centuries."

"I see only one possible solution—the beam from the serpent's mouth in Findias, reflected from some sort of device or devices permanently in position over Findias and Ochren—perhaps two reflectors, one constantly rotating or wobbling."

"A most ingenious idea, quite worthy of you," Ahriman said with admiration. "Who knows—that might well be the solution."

"In plain words, you aren't telling me." Suddenly Alan snapped his fingers. "Of course! It is obvious. Anyone who can cut off the aurora at will—as happened during my departure from Tartarus, as you know—must certainly have the power to control the sword of light from the serpent's mouth, as well as the beam from the sky over Ochren. Am I correct?"

"As I said, an ingenious solution."

Alan shook his head impatiently. "It doesn't matter. I was just curious. But tell me this—why did you remove Nuada from *Caer Pedryvan*? It really seemed pointless, unless for some obscure reason you wanted me to take on his appearance. And why remove Taliesin from the scene just minutes ago?"

"Nuada complicated the situation in Lochlann. He shouldn't really have been there in the first place. As for the Bard, he seemed a bit weary, so I sent him home. Any more questions?"

"Yes—many more, obviously: questions about those ghastly torture rooms in King Arawn's castle; about that dreadful cloud of souls under Ochren, and about Manannan and his almost-deserted domain. Many questions, but one specific wish. It appears certain that you have a miniature version of Ochren in this tower, as you have of Tartarus. Now that I've left the dark island and never plan to return, may I see it?"

Ahriman stood up and bowed. "There will be no difficulty in complying with that request. Indeed, I had planned to show you the model—though, since much of it is below the surface, you will receive only a partial view." He held out his hand. "Shall we go?"

No matter how often it happened, MacDougall never ceased to marvel at the instantaneous transfer from one place to another. As Ahriman grasped his hand, the golden room vanished, and they were standing on a narrow catwalk overlooking a perfect model of Ochren. Because he had seen a similar replica of Tartarus during his earlier visit, MacDougall had anticipated seeing a startling, gemlike miniature, but the actuality surpassed every expectation. Grasping the golden rail before him, he gazed down in fascination.

This was not the gloom-shrouded Ochren he had

recently traversed from tip to tip; it was the island brilliantly illuminated by floodlights beneath the catwalk, brightly accenting every minute detail—lighting necessary, Alan thought, to enable the manipulator, Ahriman, better to see what he was doing.

The scene filled the entire circular room. The blue-green of water, like glistening jade, provided the border of an island, long and slender. The land was flat; no hill or valley, no peak or chasm, broke the level plain. The gray-green turf, characteristic of the darkened island, covered all the open space like a carpet of finest fibre. The coastline was smooth, with a narrow beach surrounding it, suggesting a uniform fringe around a gray-green rug, all wrought in stone by some skilled gem carver.

This illusion of an immense jewel was strengthened by the three castles—the gloomy masonry mass of that of King Arawn at the lower tip, *Dinas Affaraon*, the castle of Beli, about the middle, and Manannan's glass castle, sea-green and glistening, square and revolving *Caer Pedryvan*, with its round central tower, at the upper end. In minute detail, roads, surrounding rock walls, barracks, gemlike moats, and even incredibly tiny bronze guards in their niches were there. Like sapphire-blue ribbons, the four streams flowed from the oval lake, with the white Hall of the Dead beyond it. These completed the picture.

Ahriman's deep voice interrupted MacDougall's fascinated inspection. "And this is how you remember it."

The floodlights dimmed, and the perpetual dusk closed over Ochren. Tiny yellow-red gas torches awakened to timid life. Even the gloom and the funereal air of hopelessness and evil seemed to cloak the scene.

The floodlights flashed on again, and Ahriman said, "Since you saw the working of my viewing—and meddling—over Tartarus, we shall forgo that part of the demonstration." He waved toward the narrow ramp and the lenslike platform suspended over the center of the model. "The operation is the same."

"I suppose," Alan commented, "despite the dark in the

underground world—the prison of Ochren, Annwn the Abyss, Lochlann—your lenses and forceps can still be used?"

"Yes—with some difficulty and greater mental involvement—but with success, you may be sure."

MacDougall hesitated. "One more request. Before I entered Ochren I opened the Four Gates in the stone tower. Two lands I have explored. I had an interesting but limited view of the others. With all your references to my fated future, I should like to see your models of three and four."

The Persian's face became expressionless. "I think you will agree that for mortals to foresee the future is not really desirable. Such foreknowledge would inevitably influence one's actions and decisions, though that future might already be predetermined. I have not said these lands lie in your future, but I think to grant what you request would be unwise. Let us say, 'Sufficient unto the day is the evil thereof.'"

He reached out and grasped Alan's hand—and they were standing on ground level in the room of the golden draperies. With a note of dismissal he said, "I trust I have been helpful—and we shall meet again."

MacDougall suddenly found himself facing the wall; he reached it in two quick strides and passed through it to feel the thick turf underfoot and see the aurora dancing overhead. As before, on his departure from the golden tower, he felt a strong urge to get away from Ahriman with all possible speed, but he refused to yield to the impulse. With forced calm, he scanned the surrounding woodland for his tall landmark. He sighted it and walked unhurriedly across the pasture.

Helpful! The Persian had seemed to be answering his questions, but the interview had made him no wiser. In fact, Ahriman seemed to have raised more questions than he answered. For instance, there was the matter of Alan's ancestry. A kingly line, indeed! It was nonsense, of course, but a startling thought intruded. Malcolm—his brother

Malcolm—was now one of the Little People, the Sidhe! He had never really thought about it and, if it were not for his own fantastic experience, he wouldn't believe it now. But it was a fact; and there must be something very strange in their ancestry. There had to be.

But a kingly line? He knew of only one ancient king, though obviously there had to be scores during all the centuries. King Arthur! Really the tale was absurd—a king with his Knights of the Round Table, invented by writers in the twelfth or thirteenth century. He'd have to remember to ask Taliesin about Arthur. Anyway, to suggest that he was a descendant of some royal indiscretion— even a reincarnation—was just plain silly.

More disturbing was the mystery surrounding the Scroll. Somehow he'd have to persuade the Bard to tell him the rest of the prophecy; though, no matter what it predicted, there was no reason to apply it to himself.

One thing positive had come out of the visit—if he, in Ahriman's view, was to fulfill an ancient prophecy, he'd have the Persian's protection. Ahriman would have to enable him to survive. But there could be endless complications! Why, oh why couldn't life be simpler, as it was in the normal world, where he could control his own destiny! He considered the thought, then grimaced. Who said he controlled his own destiny back in his home world? A good question.

He thought of what he had seen through the other two Gateways back in the ancient *broch*. It seemed clear that Ahriman expected him to enter both lands and didn't want him to know in advance what he faced. Instead, the Persian had quoted the Bible and talked about the prophecies made to Abraham and King David—

Alan stopped short. The horses—there was only one in sight, grazing close to the edge of the forest. There was no place the other could have gone except into the woods, unless it had run away. And that was unlikely. Well, the loss hardly mattered; he needed only one mount.

As he approached the remaining animal, he glanced

curiously into the thicket; the growth was unusually heavy, with big trees crowded together. About twenty feet away, he saw the missing horse, a big bay mare. She was held awkwardly by her reins, snagged over the broken end of a heavy branch. Apparently curiosity had been her undoing. He certainly couldn't leave her thus.

She saw MacDougall moving toward her and tried to wrench free. "Easy, gal," he said softly, then halted to listen. He thought he had heard a faint sound coming from the undergrowth. Then, in a numbing flare of light, he felt something crash down upon his head. Blackness blotted out the world.

CHAPTER 11

The World of the Trolls

Through sharply throbbing, pain-filled darkness came voices. Voices? Impossible, Alan MacDougall thought dully. No voice could penetrate that piercing ringing in his ears. He sought weakly to hear, to sense the words trying to register on his consciousness. They were faint and far away, barely realized.

"*I tell you, he is not here!*" That was Manannan, the sea god from Ochren. "*According to what these gate-keepers say, he and Taliesin never really went into the city. When those two horses vanished, they were on them. And that was when I first arrived here. We must be on their trail immediately.*"

"You must be right." The second thought was Balor's. "*My Druids and the Fomorians have been searching in every nook, but have found nothing. And Dalua—he saw the two Norsemen who said they had a message for me.*

He followed them—and lost them—unbelievable for the Dark One. I think now they never existed, but were illusion. Even their horses vanished." Through the throbbing, Alan could sense Balor's wrath. *"We shall set out at once. We'll change a group of Fomorians into a pack of wolves and send them roving through the hills. Perhaps Dalua, too, will search—though there is no knowing his mind. He is his own law. But that cursed MacDougall will be found!"*

Voices, actual men's voices, quarrelsome, angry, and loud, blared agonizingly through waves of pain as full consciousness returned to Alan MacDougall. For the moment the ghostly thoughts he had sensed were forgotten, blocked out by the throbbing that radiated from the back of his head, spiraling outward. He seemed to be spinning in concert. He heard a groan and dully realized it was his own, then felt something cold touch his throat. The voices stopped as he opened his eyes and tried to sit up—to fall back as a sharp point pricked the skin just above his Adam's apple.

An oddly familiar voice rasped. "Don't move! Don't do anything if you want to live. I would enjoy leaning on this sword."

With difficulty, Alan focused his gaze on the face hovering over his and recognized Erus! Erus the Druid of Gorias, who, in that stupid war going on during his escape from Tartarus, had played the traitor, had joined Balor's Fomorians, and had lost favor with both sides. But this was not the debonair, polished, bejeweled Erus he had known; except for the long black cape over the shoulders, Erus' clothes were disheveled; he had a bristling beard, and his hair was unkempt.

The Druid trembled with barely controlled fury, a wild light in his pale eyes. "You—*you* are responsible for all my trouble! And you'll help me out of it—or die. Taliesin and Danu and her *Tuatha de Danann* all seem to value you—and they will pay. Any move on your part—invisibility, anything—and I strike." The ranting went on but MacDougall blocked it out.

Despite the thumping headache, he forced his mind to work. His greatest danger was a slip of that sword, and that could happen at any moment. The Druid was mad to think he could hold the blade in position indefinitely.

"Lord Enki and Lady Inanna, are you there? Can you freeze that sword arm?"

The serpent-god answered derisively. "Of course we are here! Where else would we be? We may wander afield now and then in more interesting endeavors, but we are always only a thought away. And quell your fears. I have frozen Erus and all of his band of Outcasts. Once more I have rescued you from the consequences of your carelessness. You should always be alert to possible danger."

Damn, Alan thought; must I be reminded!

He became aware that silence had fallen over the forest. Erus crouched motionless as a wax figure, lips parted in mid-speech. With utmost care MacDougall moved, shrinking away from the menacing sword point and rolling clear. He tried to sit up; felt a sharp pain in the small of his back and a million needle-pricks in his numbed hands, only then becoming aware that his wrists were tightly bound behind him. So were his ankles, he learned as he continued his efforts to rise. It was the second time he'd been bound like this in Tartarus, and both times by Druids. Finally he managed to sit up, the added effort sending new waves of pain through his head. It was then, strangely, that he realized it was his cape that Erus had on. He looked around.

All about him were men, a few sitting, most standing, all facing the center of action. This was not a clearing, but rather a slightly less overgrown stretch of woodland. Stiffly, he turned to look behind him and saw others; there were at least twenty in all—Norsemen and Ch'in and even one Troll, but no Fomorians. Most certainly this was a band of Outcasts, with dirty, badly worn clothes, roughly cut long hair, bushy bangs, and whiskers hiding most of their faces.

And horses—he became aware of horses in a sort of natural clearing beyond the farthest Outcast. Their number was difficult to estimate—perhaps a dozen including, he was sure, the pair he and Taliesin had been riding. His eyes narrowed speculatively. The Outcasts—Erus' doing—had tricked him with a decoy horse, luring him into an ambush. There'd be an accounting. The Troll caught his eye. He was withdrawn from the others, seated with his back against a tree, as if detached from whatever was happening. He was under four feet in height, Alan estimated, somewhat taller than the other Trolls he had seen in Findias, but with the characteristically large nose and ears. He differed, too, in that, instead of the brown hair and whiskers of the male Trolls as Alan remembered them, his hair, a great mass, was snowy white.

On a hunch Alan directed a thought to Lord Enki. "Free the Troll. I think I can get his help."

Lord Enki's answer expressed faint amusement. "Your wish is my command."

As Alan watched, the Troll moved his head slightly, surprise showing only in a widening of his eyes. He glanced sharply at Erus, at the motionless Outcasts, and at the stiffly poised sword, then smiled and nodded slowly. He spoke in a deep and pleasant voice.

"I was certain he could not hold you. Erus has been talking about who you are and what happened, and he should have known that your powers were too great for him. Your wish?"

"That you release my wrists. Open the knots to save the cord for the Druid." The Troll was smart, Alan thought, quick to understand; Alan was secretly pleased with the vindication of his judgment.

As the little man set to work on his bonds, MacDougall said, "What is your name, and why are you here, an Outcast?"

"I am Einurr Gurulfin. I was branded an Outcast by Arias, the Gray Druid of Findias. I was important among my people, and Arias accused me of planning a revolt against him. Entirely untrue, as he knew. We are not a violent people."

"Did you know," Alan asked, "that Arias died in a duel with Nuada?"

Einurr's face expressed momentary excitement; then he shook his head. "I could not go back with this brand on my face. It would be a disgrace."

With his wrists free, Alan rubbed them briskly to restore circulation. Gingerly, he felt the back of his head, touching an egg-sized lump, but there was no blood, thanks, probably, to his thick hair. The Troll set to work immediately on the cords about his ankles.

"You said, Einurr, that you were branded. You mean an actual branding mark?"

The troll swept back the long white hair over his forehead to reveal in its center the red image of a coiled serpent. "So are marked the Outcasts from Findias, though there be few of us thus treated. Those from Gorias, the Ch'in, bear a sword grasped in a hand, and those from Falias a many-pointed star. I have never seen a Fomorian Outcast. I have heard that offenders are mercilessly slain."

"But," Alan objected, "are there not Outcasts without a mark?"

"Indeed there are—and they are those who have committed a crime, or offended a Druid—and fled to the forests without waiting for judgment. They sometimes can slip back undetected." Bitterly, he added, "Those with brands never evade discovery. Someone always reports them to the Druids, to win favor. Even hair worn over a forehead is a suspicious sign."

"Maybe something can be done about those brands," Alan said. "And, though there must be a new Druid in Findias, he must be made to show justice or be held responsible. The Druids are not gods."

MacDougall stood up and surveyed the situation. The

Outcasts were as unmoving as stone. With difficulty, he pried his sword from Erus' clutch and slid it into its scabbard. He returned his cape to his own shoulders. Then, after asking Lord Enki to restore some flexibility to the Druid, with careful efficiency, he tied the Druid's hands behind his back, pushed him to the ground, face up, and tightly tied his ankles. As nearly as he could remember, he placed Erus where he himself had lain so short a time before, drew his sword, and held it poised over his exposed throat. A bit theatrical, he thought, but it should prove quite impressive.

"And now, Lord Enki, restore them."

Impressive, indeed! To the Outcasts, unaware that they had lost minutes out of their unending lives, it appeared that before their eyes the Druid and his victim had magically exchanged places.

To Erus the exchange was devastating. He screamed piercingly, a long-drawn, fading cry that ended when all his breath was gone. It was followed by a succession of gasps, mingled with, "You devil—you devil—why didn't I kill you? Why? Why?"

"But you didn't. Now why shouldn't I kill you?" Alan lifted the sword a foot away from the Druid but held it in readiness. "Tell me, why should I let you live?"

"Because," the Druid babbled, "if it had not been for me, the others would have stripped you bare—*and* killed you. I stopped them. We—we were arguing about it when you awakened. And—and I didn't really plan to kill you. It—it was just a threat to frighten you."

"You mean," Alan demanded, his sword darting to within an inch of Erus' throat, "like this?"

Came another wild scream, checked as Alan drew back his blade and circled the area with his eyes, his gaze missing none of the watchers.

"Who hit me?" he asked coldly.

Almost as one accusing fingers pointed toward the Druid. One of the Ch'in added helpfully, "We saw you coming and placed your horses into position to get you into the woods. He insisted on the privilege of striking the blow." Several raised affirming voices, and Erus groaned.

Ignoring him, MacDougall said, "Come in closer and sit. I promise you no harm, if you make no attempt to escape—quite the opposite. But I warn you, don't try to run or attack. You can't win."

Reluctantly they came, fearing the consequences of disobedience.

"I have some questions which may seem strange. First, are there in Gorias and Falias stores of clothing where people who have need can replace worn garments, as there are food dispensaries?"

"There are," answered an especially ragged Norseman. "But if we appeared there, we would be seized at once."

"I understand," Alan continued. "Now—how many of you are branded?"

The helpful Oriental answered, "All of us." He thrust aside his bangs, exposing the red sword.

Alan looked at the others as, one by one, they exposed their marks. While making a show of examining a few more closely, he addressed the serpent-gods. "Lord Enki and Lady Inanna, can these brands be removed?"

The goddess replied, "I thought you had forgotten me. And, yes; what magic has put on magic can take off."

"Thank you. Now, one by one, as I indicate, remove each individual mark. A second question. Can you for a limited time—time enough for these Outcasts to get back to their cities and replace their clothing—give them the appearance of normal Norsemen and Ch'in?"

"All of this is elementary," Lord Enki answered impatiently. "Why make it so complicated? Get on with the dispersal."

Again MacDougall addressed this now-attentive audience. "Not that it matters, but why are there no unbranded Outcasts among you?" He thought he knew the answer.

After an awkward silence the ragged Norseman said,

"When we find such, they are fair game. They can return. We can't."

After a long pause Alan said sententiously. "I have decided. Most of you have offended no more grievously than many others in your cities. You will be freed. Let the Ch'in step forward."

At his words hope suddenly appeared on the Outcasts' faces. They had seen the result of his powers. Now the Orientals presented themselves; one by one, Alan moved his hand slowly past their faces. As he did so, the brands faded and were gone. He waved both hands over the group, and instantly, as at the touch of a magician's wand, they were in normal dress for Gorias, worn garments but not too badly worn. And their long hair appeared braided in acceptable style.

"That is the best I could do with your hair," Mac-Dougall said apologetically. "You will have to have it attended to. In moments, you will be permitted to go. Share the horses fairly, riding two aboard where needed but leaving my pair. Remember that! You will have time enough to get to your city and get what clothing you need. Do not delay, or your old rags will return—though the brand is gone forever. The rest is up to you."

As smoothly and with the same showmanship, he disposed of the twelve Norsemen, amid their expressions of gratitude.

"Now back to the horses." With MacDougall at their heels, the transformed Outcasts hastened to the open area. There were fifteen horses, including the two recent acquisitions. Under Alan's watchful eyes, the men made a more or less amiable division of the available thirteen and swiftly rode away. MacDougall, the Troll, and Erus remained.

MacDougall returned to the Troll. "Your garments are not too badly worn, so I need merely remove the branding mark." With the words the red serpent was gone. "You cannot see it, but your forehead is clear, and it will remain so." He added thoughtfully, "I believe I shall go with you back to Findias, if you do not object. I should like to see more of your people and your city and learn more about the sword of light from the serpent's mouth."

Einurr Gurulfin beamed with genuine pleasure. "You will be our honored guest as long as you wish to stay among us. You will enjoy the best that Trollheim has to offer. My people—"

A shrill bleat from Erus, still bound and apparently ignored, interrupted the Troll.

"What about me?"

"What *about* you?" MacDougall responded.

"You can't just leave me here! I'd starve to death."

MacDougall shrugged. "Don't you see—that would really be a blessing. And you wouldn't starve; thirst would kill you much more quickly. You would probably be given a new body, not like this one, and you could go anywhere in Tartarus without being recognized. An excellent idea."

"No!" the Druid shouted. "You can't do that. I didn't mean any harm—"

"I agree," Alan said resignedly. "I can't do that, though you would not hesitate to do worse to me, were our positions reversed. I'll give you more than you deserve. I will free you of your bonds—no more. You will have to walk, since Einurr and I will need the remaining horses. Where you go, what you do, is entirely up to you. You know the island as I never shall. You carry no brand. I assume you still have the powers of a Druid. You are no better off now than when you ambushed me—and no worse."

Erus began to plead, almost hysterically, desisting in moments as he saw MacDougall's grim expression. Drawing his pocket knife, Alan severed the Druid's bonds and lifted him to his feet.

"Start walking," he directed coldly. "I suggest in future you stay out of my affairs. Next time you might get hurt."

Casting a single venomous glance at MacDougall, Erus walked stiffly westward through the thicket. Alan watched him go until he was lost from sight, then turned and looked questioningly at the Troll. "And what, friend Einurr, do you think of my highhanded justice?"

"I have nothing but admiration. And your powers are greater than I have ever seen."

"I have had good teachers," Alan answered dryly, "and training under most difficult conditions—as well as assistance unparalleled."

Abruptly, in a sudden flood of weariness MacDougall sank to a seat on the ground, leaning back against a broad tree trunk. He smiled at the Troll, faintly apologetic, and pressed his hands against his temples.

"I still have an atrocious headache and suddenly I feel very tired. With the insane time of this world, I have no idea how long it has been since I ate and slept, but I know a lot has happened since my last meal."

Rather diffidently the Troll crossed to Alan's side. "I can do nothing about your hunger—but we Trolls have abilities of another kind. With your permission—"

Gently he placed large, cool hands on MacDougall's head, one on the crown, the other on his forehead. The effect was startling—as if there flowed from Einurr a soothing, healing current that washed away the pain, throbbing, and tenderness. The hands moved down the sides of Alan's neck and across his shoulders, resting there, kneading gently—and his weariness seemed to evaporate.

As the Troll removed his fingers he asked, "Has that helped?"

"Einurr, that is amazing!" MacDougall beamed. "Thank you, my friend. I feel rested and the pain is gone. My head is clear—"

He broke off, suddenly stiffening, and leaped erect. Out of nowhere had come a jarring recollection of Manannan and Balor in conversation just before setting out to find him—an interchange that, like all Alan's earlier involuntary eavesdropping, involved his subconscious overhearing of the gods of this place while he was not fully awake. Their words came back to him—and most pertinent was Balor's reference to changing Fomorians into wolves and sending them into the hills. Once before, he had been pursued by that wolf pack. And he had forgotten!

"Einurr! We must leave this spot, and at once! We should head overland, avoiding roads. I had known but had forgotten that two of the gods, Balor and Manannan, have by now set out from Murias to find me and destroy me. Can you serve as guide? I think they expect me to go to Falias, to the home of Taliesin, so Findias would be a desirable destination. I despise this running, especially since I have overcome both of them before and do not fear them. But I grow weary of confrontation."

Einurr Gurulfin moved quickly toward the horses. "There are entrances to Findias—the Findias underground—that are known only to my people. One of these lies in the hills south of Gorias, the one I should prefer, leading into several tunnels we have dug to our metal mines. There you will see what none of your race has ever beheld. And of course I know the way, all directly overland."

"Let's go!" MacDougall exclaimed.

Leading the horses out of the woods, they mounted and rode briskly across the meadow, with the Troll setting the pace and leading. Straight as the flight of a homing pigeon they went, following Einurr's instinctive sense of direction. They had not gone far when they heard the first distant, mournful chorus—the howling of Balor's wolves.

Unconsciously, Alan had been awaiting this sign of pursuit; and though it was far away, and though he knew it came from shape-changed Fomorians, it sent the suggestion of a chill up his spine. It brought back recollections of that other flight when, in dense fog, he had been beset by questing wolves, the madly laughing dark god Dalua, and the flapping of the giant bat wings of a transformed Morrigu, bloodthirsty goddess. He banished the thought. This time, he believed, there would only be the wolf pack.

The sound had come as they approached a second stretch of woodland, with wide spaces between the trees, permitting continued riding, but slowing their pace greatly. For mile on mile, the forest persisted, after a time sloping gently downward.

Again and again they heard the eerie wolf cry, but it never came close, rising to their north. Not yet had their scent been picked up.

After seemingly endless riding, they left the woods to cross a white gravel road, the one leading from Falias to Findias, Alan thought. The country became more rugged, the grassy stretches undulating, with jagged masses of rock rising from the pastures and the way growing steadily steeper.

The sound of pursuit had became steadily fainter, finally ceasing altogether; but MacDougall knew, if he remained on Tartarus, sooner or later he'd have to face Manannan and Balor. Let the confrontation come!

At the base of a steep slope on a smooth expanse of turf, the Troll halted. "I fear we have gone as far as we can on horseback. On the other side of this hill lies the entrance to Trollheim; and here is a good place to leave the horses."

"Trollheim?" MacDougall repeated. "I believe I heard you use the name once before."

"Our name for the city we have built under Findias."

Why not? Alan thought. Home of the Trolls; and they no longer lived in Findias.

Both dismounted, removed the animals' gear, and piled it on a convenient rock. There was plenty of grazing on dew-laden grass; and in time, both saddles and horses would be found. They began their climb.

Reaching the top, they stood on a flat expanse of gray basalt overlooking a deep, narrow valley. Einurr spread his arms wide in a sweeping gesture, his white-crowned head thrown back, his face seeming to glow.

"Is it not beautiful? To the north we can see the five hills of Gorias with its strange houses. And there, across the valley, are our spring and the waterfall. Is it not worth the climb?"

For the first time, MacDougall really looked at his surroundings; as often had happened before in Tartarus, he was moved to marvel at the beauty of what he saw. Fallen angel though Lucifer was, Alan thought, if this were his creation, it revealed surpassing skill as an artist whose palette was rock and sky and water.

On every side, in rugged splendor, rose crags and slopes as brilliant as jewels—rock masses of banded green malachite merging into the purples and lavenders of incredibly large amethyst crystals, formed, it seemed, in the tortured heart of a vast geode, their massive, five-sided fingers pointing needle-sharp tips in every possible direction. Other scarps of the rock sentinels were blue masses of brightest turquoise, deepening gradually to night-blue azurite, rising to buttresses of snowy white, slashed through with layers of gleaming gold. In the mad mélange of color, there appeared even the red of ruby darkening to deepest garnet. All intermingled and repeated on every side.

And the waterfall! From the facing wall, leaping out of a great fissure, foamed an arm of crystal water, bounding over broken rocks to fall lazily in a lacy, slumberous waterfall that became thin as a veil of smoke in its long descent to the floor of the valley below. Near the base, it struck an outcrop that funneled it into a channel, which fed it in turn into a wide, deep basin. From it came a soft and sleepy roar, somehow tranquil and unreal.

Above all of this unnatural splendor, as if vying for a cosmic beauty prize, the aurora leaped and danced, a shimmering curtain of multicolored light, brilliant against its backdrop of Stygian black.

Stretched below MacDougall lay the round, level, grassy floor of the valley. At its far end was the silvery glint of a little lake.

The spectacle was beyond adequate description.

"There it is!" The exultant voice of Einurr broke the spell as he pointed toward a dark spot on the plain near the lake. "Don't you see it? The entrance to Trollheim."

Eagerly, the Troll started down the slope. Almost reluctantly, Alan followed, still enthralled by the fantastic view. By the time they reached their destination, a longer hike than it appeared through the clear air, his thoughts had returned to his purpose—the visit to the city of the Trolls and investigation of that strange beam of light.

Side by side, Alan MacDougall and Einurr Gurulfin looked down into the round, ten-foot-wide opening in the plain. Grass grew up to the very edge; and a flight of steps at their feet extended into the depths. Alan became aware of a strange odor rising from below, an unlikely blending of burning fish oil and pine resin, or so it seemed. As they started down, the Troll leading the way, MacDougall saw that the stairs were designed for smaller feet and shorter legs—for Trolls, not men.

The stairway ended in the very center of a domed chamber about thirty feet wide, hollowed out of the solid rock. In the north wall were five openings, each leading into a tunnel, sloping sharply downward. The opposite end narrowed into a single tunnel, also sharply pitched; tunnels and room alike were dimly lighted by peculiar copper lamps, suspended high on the walls, oddly like watering pots with burning wicks projecting from the spouts.

"Here where the tunnels meet," Einurr explained, "we built the room close to the surface for air to enter and to give us a way out. It is known only to us. There are others like it farther south."

A deep rumbling sound came from one of the tunnels. Moments later, Alan felt a faint vibration in the rock underfoot, suggesting the approach of a miniature subway train. The rumble became more of a clatter, increasing in volume; in one of the shadowed tunnels, he saw a moving light, wavering, flickering, and drawing steadily nearer.

A Troll appeared, leather harness strapped to his shoulders, a potlike metal helmet on his head, and a copper lamp rising like a crest above his forehead. Behind him came a four-wheeled metal cart about six feet long and four feet wide. Harnessed to its sides were two Trolls and, just visible above the rear, the tops of four heads, pushers evidently.

The cart reached the bottom of the slope and almost came to a halt. The leader gave voice to a loud, shrill, "Hai!" In unison, from the others came an answering "Hai!" and all seven bent their backs to the task. Slowly, inch by inch, the cart moved up the slope and at last rested on the level center of the room. The Trolls halted, panting, and straightened up.

"A fine effort, my strong ones, a fine effort!" Einurr Gurulfin exclaimed. "I am proud of you."

The leader, broad, powerful, and unusually hairy, peered at Einurr from under heavy brows, then suddenly shouted, "Einurr! It is Einurr Gurulfin come back! Joy! Joy! Einurr has returned."

Slipping their harness, the front three crowded around the white-haired Troll, joined immediately by the four pushers, all leaping and shouting in their delight. Alan stepped to one side, watching, happy to have had a part in restoring Einurr to his people. He glanced at the cargo weighing down the cart—dark, gray, metallic chunks. He lifted one, unusually heavy, and saw a bright gash in one surface, a silvery glint evidently caused by a pickaxe. Silver! By all the gods of Tartarus, almost pure silver! Little wonder the Trolls had struggled to push it up the incline.

He heard sounds of another cart approaching through the lone tunnel in the southern wall, this quite definitely more of a clatter than a rumble. The other Trolls paid no attention to the new arrival, nor, momentarily, to MacDougall. An empty cart with its crew of seven came rapidly up the slope, stopping near its counterpart.

Immediately the newcomers joined the first group, crying as they had done, "Einurr! Einurr has come home!"

The white-haired Troll finally called a halt to his boisterous welcome, raising both hands high and calling,

"Quiet." Silence fell instantly, all paying respectful attention.

"My friends," he continued, "you must meet my deliverer, Alan MacDougall. You have heard of him. He has come from the Other World, and he is a friend of the Hill-people. When he speaks, I speak. What is his will is mine. Now to your tasks." He caught the eyes of the new arrivals and held up a delaying hand. "Hold."

Promptly the crew with the load of silver started out, vanishing with a rumble into the single tunnel. Tight quarters, Alan thought as he watched them go, if they met an empty coming the other way. The other crew waited.

Einurr turned to Alan. "Do you wish to see our miners at work?"

Eagerly Alan assented. A rare opportunity, something to remember.

"Which tunnel?" Einurr asked the crew leader.

"Number three, the gold," came the answer.

"Good! We ride with you." Following the Troll's example, Alan climbed into the cart and sat cross-legged on the floor. Instantly they started, gaining momentum as they coasted down the incline and clattered on through the passageway. The noise made conversation difficult, but MacDougall wanted answers. He leaned close to Gurulfin's ear. "Are you, perchance, ruler of the Trolls?"

The other smiled and nodded. "If my people had a King, I would be that King. I ruled a long time before Arias the Druid became jealous. At my behest, we moved underground. Through my leading, we built these tunnels. For only when the Hill-people are busy are they happy . . . The Hill-people—so were we called in the Olden Times when our homes were under the hills."

Alan watched the stone wall moving by, studying the strata of rock. Never had he seen the like, a veritable hodgepodge of minerals, many of the layers standing on end. Igneous rock butting against what was clearly sedimentary, followed by alternating layers of granites and basalts, and great masses of obsidian. It was a geologist's nightmare.

"But why tunnel where you did? What reason for all this incredible labor?" And it must have been unimaginable labor without explosives.

Einurr shrugged. "What matter labor, where there is no time? And where, if bodies wear out, new ones replace them? Why? We tunneled where we knew the metal masses were."

"But how could you know where they were? And why five tunnels?"

Einurr chuckled. "We are Trolls. It has often been said, 'We follow our noses.' We *know* where the metals lie and what they are. And why five tunnels? There are five hills in Gorias. Deep under one lies gold, under another silver, a third iron, a fourth copper, and a fifth tin. These masses are so vast that it would take an eternity to exhaust them. They are not altogether pure metal, but fine enough to make mining and smelting easy. And there is something in the iron that gives it hardness and temper without our adding anything."

Incredulous, Alan had nothing to say, his thoughts dwelling on all he had seen and heard.

The cart, which had been staying close to the center of the tunnel, now veered to one side to avoid a lone Troll with a lamp on his helmet, walking and pulling what appeared to be a copper tank on wheels, about a foot wide and a yard long. Alan glanced back to see him stop at one of the lamps, which he removed from its place, though he could not see what followed.

Observing Alan's backward glance, Einurr explained, "He is one of those who keep the lamps filled with oil. We burn a mixture of fish oil and oil from evergreen trees. It gives more light and burns more slowly than fish oil alone." He paused, then pointed ahead. "We approach the gold mine."

Fascinated, MacDougall watched as the tunnel ended in what the dim light revealed as a great cavern, hollowed out of solid rock; it was all of sixty or seventy feet high, its walls pitted with holes in which flickered the firefly lights of the lamps on the miners' helmets. Those walls were of white rock, probably quartz or calcite, shot through with bands and nuggets and great masses of gleaming gold! Never, Alan thought, was there a gold deposit to match this. The pounding of hammer on drill or chisel or wedge echoed and re-echoed through the hollow.

The cart came to a halt on the level floor beside another, almost filled with the precious metal, with its crew busily carrying nuggets and masses from the base of the walls where it had been dropped by the miners.

The two passengers scrambled out, and the leader of their crew shouted exuberantly, "Hai! We bring Einurr Gurulfin. He has come home!"

Immediately all work stopped. Amid joyful cries of "Einurr!" miners who were perched in crevices high on the wall slid down ropes anchored to outcroppings of gold. In moments, every Troll in the mine gathered around the ruler, and the effusive welcome was repeated. Again Alan was introduced; and again activities returned to normal at Einurr's command.

Finally, with the waiting cart filled and with Mac-Dougall and Gurulfin perched on the golden treasure, they began their return journey to Trollheim. At the hill leading to the entrance, the two passengers, over the crew's objection, helped to push, adding little to the fantastic strength of the short but massive Hill-people.

They passed several openings in the tunnel roof which admitted air and light and diluted the ever-present and most unlikely odor of pine-scented fish oil. They also passed several empty carts being drawn back to the five tunnels, just managing to squeeze by. After a time, the rock walls were replaced by clay, and Alan knew the city of the Trolls could not be far away. They must be under the Desert of Gloom.

Here they came upon the first of the smelters and forges, when the load of gold moved from the main tunnel down a branching passageway. They halted before a huge bin, a space hollowed out of the clay, roughly the volume of a three-room cottage. Here the Trolls began unloading their cargo, adding to an already breath-taking mound of gleaming yellow metal, and warm farewells followed.

On foot now, Einurr and Alan made their way to another room which advertised its presence before they reached it, heat, floods of light, and the reek of hot metal filling the air. As they entered, Einurr was recognized; but at the first cry, he called out, "On with your work. We shall talk later."

Dominating the room was a great iron pot or crucible with a wide lip around its top, circled by a heavy collar, with massive rods projecting from opposite sides. These, resting on metal supports, ended in two great wheels with projecting spokes. High above and surrounding the crucible was a sturdy platform, aswarm with Trolls, some controlling jets of gas flames trained on the contents of the pot and others pumping great bellows that forced streams of air into pipes that merged with the nozzles of the gas jets. Still other workers wielded long-handled scoops that skimmed the dross from the molten mass. Above all this, like a great inverted cone, the ceiling, blackened by the soot of centuries, opened into a wide chimney, bearing fumes out into the upper air.

There came a hoarse "Hai!" from overhead. As one, the gas flames shortened. Trolls stopped pumping bellows, and out of the shadows came a stream of little men. Methodically, each stepped into a vat of water, immersing himself, then, dripping wet, grasped a long-handled ladle from a rack and approached the crucible. Four grasped the wheels, while two others clutched projecting rods at the bottom of the pot. Slowly, the great vessel tilted and sent a heavy, glowing golden stream into a waiting ladle. As the Troll stepped clear and crossed to soot-blackened ceramic molds, another took his place. Then another— until the crucible was empty.

As Einurr led MacDougall away, Alan asked wonderingly, "How long does this go on?"

"It never stops. We work continuously, group following group."

"But what do you cast?"

"Very shortly, you shall see. But first, the other shops."

Not far away, off the same corridor, Einurr halted at a second storage bin and smelter, very like that which processed gold; silver was the product of this operation. Beyond this, Alan was shown copper being processed, next tin, and then copper and tin in alloy to produce bronze. Near the latter were several shops where the fine bronze vessels were turned out; all handcraft was of the highest skill.

Finally, they came to the iron works—steel, rather, since what they mined, as Alan learned, must be a natural alloy of iron and probably nickel, with possible traces of manganese and chrome, perhaps matching the iron-nickel meteorites that fell out of space. The weapons that came out of these shops were of finest quality, in large part due to the workmen's skill, mastered over centuries. Here they found the blackened, sweat-begrimed battlers against refractory metal, exposed to the searing heat of the open furnace, the showers of fiery sparks, and the clouds of steam rising from metal plunged into vats of water—all that went on in the production of steel. In the blacksmith's shops, they were nearly deafened by the ring and clangor of sledge on steel.

It was in one of these shops that Alan met his biggest surprise—two men stripped to the waist, one a veritable giant, with great rolling muscles in arms and chest and back, wielding a huge sledgehammer as if it were feather-light, while the other, wearing thick gloves, held to anvil a smoking, eight-foot-long lance. With a final blow, the giant cried, "Now!" He stepped back as the smaller man plunged the weapon into a deep vat of water.

They looked up in surprise as the usual cry arose. "Einurr Gurulfin! Einurr has returned!" The Trolls crowded around, while the two men stood to one side, smiling their appreciation, but looking curiously at MacDougall.

After restoring order, Einurr introduced Alan, saying as before that he was friend of the Trolls and that his wish and his word were also Einurr's. Then he presented the waiting giant and his companion.

"Here are Gobniu the Smith, who, with his companion Credne, master bronze-worker, made Nuada's invincible sword. They are of Danu's family, gods of the *Tuatha de Danann*. They spend more time here than anywhere else. Almost, they have become one with the Hill-people. Perhaps you have heard of one another."

The two looked curiously at MacDougall, obviously interested. The Smith spoke first, his booming voice in harmony with his massive form. "We have indeed heard of the son of Dougall and of the turmoil he created while guest of the Bard of Bards. We concern ourselves little with the affairs of the island; but anyone who is enemy of Balor and his Fomor is friend of ours. Not so, Credne?"

Absently, the bronze-worker removed his gloves, then nodded, quietly commenting, "Nuada, who often joins us here, told of your slaying Morrigu and Balor, though he could not tell how. If King Einurr calls you friend, that is enough for me."

As if searching his memory for an elusive thought, Alan frowned and pursed his lips. "As I recall it—though I cannot be certain—" He halted, groping, while he studied the two in uncertain light. "Did you not play an important part in the Battle of Moytura? You were the armorers, were you not, keeping the *Tuatha de Danann* in weapons?" He remembered this from his reading in the British mythology.

Pleased and surprised that MacDougall should know of their exploits, the two burst into reminiscences about the conflict with the Fomorians, fought fourteen centuries in the past. Alan seemed to be listening, thinking the while that he had never seen a more unlikely pair.

Gobniu, taller than MacDougall by an inch or two, was

a mountain of a man, a mass of muscle; he had curly
brown hair and beard, and was swarthy and heavy fea-
tured. Credne, on the other hand, was six inches shorter
than Alan, strong and lithe, sharp of chin and nose; his
red hair was quite thin, except at the temples, and he had
a straggling red beard. His hands, Alan noticed, were
broad and spatulate, the hands of a craftsman.

Einurr ended the conversation. "Both of us have done
much since the last sleep; and both are hungry. There will
be a gathering, and we shall see you there."

As they retraced their steps to the main corridor, Alan
asked, "With all the fumes of these fires pouring into the
upper air from the metal works, how does it happen that
there seems to be no sign of them on the surface?"

"We are under the Black Plain to the east of Findias;
in the darkness and still air, the vapors move upward and
disappear into the sky."

They had reached the main tunnel, and Alan became
aware of the first general change. The oil lamps had been
replaced by gas torches. Then they came to the first door
Alan had seen underground, a massive bronze barrier,
tightly closed.

"You asked what we cast. Here," Einurr said proudly,
"is something I want you to see."

At his touch, the door opened, revealing, dimly seen
in the light of a few scattered torches, an incredible spectacle. Under a ceiling of medium height, stretching back
and back at right angle to the tunnel, carefully stacked
on the clay floor, were thousands upon thousands of gold
ingots, piled higher than Alan's head, carefully criss-
crossed, with narrow aisles between. By earthly stan-
dards, Alan thought, it was a treasure beyond calculating.
But here it was worth nothing. A sudden, arresting idea
followed. On earth, except for jewelry and some limited
use in industry and in electronics, it should be worth little
more, in terms of real wealth.

Alan almost burst out with an incredulous "Why?"
Instead, he said politely, "Most impressive." And to him-

self he added, most impressive—and utterly futile. Which was worse—nothing to do as in the other cities—or endless labor to accomplish nothing?

"And this," Einurr boasted, "is only one of our storage rooms. We have similar stores of silver, copper, and tin. The iron we store as weapons, and the bronze as finished vessels." He changed the subject.

"You must be hungry and tired. You spoke of investigating the brazen serpent with its sword of light. Can that wait until after you have eaten and slept? Or shall we go there now?"

At the reminder, MacDougall realized that he felt starved and exhausted. A lot had happened. It had been a long day.

"Let the mystery remain a mystery for the present. A leisurely study later will be more rewarding. Right now, some food and a bed sound far more interesting."

The city itself began as a widening of the tunnel, quickly spreading to become a rough counterpart of circular Findias overhead. Alan recalled the trapdoors in the floors of the beehive dwellings; the ceilings of these rooms were the floors of those above. The houses of Trollheim, like those of Findias, formed a succession of concentric circles in groups of five, with spaces between the clusters.

They began to pass more and more of the busy Trolls, the women balancing large buckets on their heads, the males carrying bundles of newly made garments or vessels holding fish or fruit. One bore a great basket of freshly baked and aromatic barley loaves. Troll after Troll recognized Einurr, but a simple gesture with his open hand prevented their stopping. To each he said, "After a sleep— in the Circle."

Unexpectedly, one of the Trolls stopped short at sight of MacDougall, the nostrils of his unusually large nose flaring, his bearded face growing livid with rage. He seemed about to choke with fury.

"You!" he rasped. "You! Why are you here? What new deviltry do you plan?" His glare shifted to Einurr Gurulfin and his eyes widened in unbelief. He bared his teeth as a beast might. "Gurulfin! You here too! An Outcast!"

He darted forward and swept the Troll King's hair aside to bare his forehead; then, with a cry of frustration, he whirled and sprinted between two houses, to vanish down a curving street.

Alan looked wonderingly at Gurulfin, now staring in blank amazement. "What was that all about?" he asked.

The Troll ruler shook his head. "I am as puzzled as you. I am sure I never saw him before."

Vainly, MacDougall searched his memory. "I'm certain I've never seen him—I've seen so few Trolls—but I definitely never harmed any of your people. So the whole thing makes no sense."

In silence, they resumed their walk. After a time, they halted before a doorway into one of the dwellings, and Einurr called, "Ornah!"

A broad female Troll appeared in the opening and cried excitedly, "King Einurr—you are here! Knorri will be so pleased."

"Ornah," Einurr continued, "I hoped I would find you. I chose you for your fine cooking. We have a guest. He needs a meal and a bed. I suggest he sleep in the house above and that you prepare for him one of your delicious meals."

The Troll wife beamed. "At once. At once. Yes, yes. Ulva told me of your visit before. Come. This way."

As Alan turned to thank Einurr, the Troll King said, "I believe you will be more comfortable in a bed above. Ours are very hard. Sleep as long as you wish. Ornah will know when you awaken and will serve you. I have tasks which must yet be done."

At Ornah's motion, MacDougall passed through the white-coated, clay-walled, two-room dwelling, climbed a steep, built-in ladder, and pushed through a trapdoor into a softly lighted room. Glowing walls revealed a low, broad bed, two contour chairs, and a small table, bringing vividly to mind his visit ages ago to an identical room. He remembered a breakfast which had been drugged by the Gray Druid, Arias, the incident that in due course had led to the latter's violent death.

Alan cast aside his cape, dropped into one of the chairs, drew off his boots, and stretched his legs out before him. It was good to relax! Gingerly, he touched the lump on his head, smaller now but still tender, his thoughts on Erus. He wondered how the Druid had fared at the hands of Balor and Manannan, assuming they had met.

There came a tap on the trapdoor. At his "Come," it was pushed up by Ornah, who carried a huge bronze jug of hot water, a large bronze basin, and a rough towel—a welcome sight indeed. Quickly, Alan stripped to his waist, hunted a bar of motel soap he remembered having tucked into a pocket, and luxuriated in hot water and foam. By the time he finished, another tap announced his dinner—a savory soup, a broiled fresh fish, a cold sauce made of dried fruit, and the inevitable barley loaves.

Having eaten and enjoyed all of it, MacDougall tapped for Ornah, gave her the dishes, and ordered fresh water to complete his bath. While this was on its way, he hunted through the neighboring rooms. Surely somewhere there must be a Necessary Room. He found it at the end of the row. Evidently when Findias was prepared for the Trolls, the planner envisioned sharing.

When at last MacDougall slid under the single coverlet, he was eager for slumber. He thought of reaching Taliesin, but decided that later would do. He yawned enormously and closed heavy eyelids. A confused mixture of images scampered through his mind, blurring into nothingness; then faintly, in the remote distance, he sensed the voices of Danu and Dagda. He thought he heard mention of Balor and Manannan, then even more faintly the names Beli and Arawn. Dreaming, he told himself, as sleep erased the world.

CHAPTER 12

The Gathering of the Gods

They came from everywhere, the Trolls converging on the center of the underground city. Alan MacDougall halted at the edge of what evidently was his destination, the Circle. It also appeared to be the destination of all the Trolls in Trollheim; they came pouring in from every crossway, a chattering, noisy throng, like a holiday crowd en route to a circus. He felt a tug at his elbow.

"We should move closer, Master." It was his guide, Knorri, the spouse of Ornah, whose dinner and breakfast he had enjoyed. "You are to be with King Einurr."

"In a few moments, Knorri," Alan said quietly. In fascination, he glanced around the Circle, already crowded with Trolls. Well named, it was a wide, level area, rimmed by massive stone monoliths, regularly spaced at about twenty-foot intervals, suggesting a reconstructed Stonehenge. They supported a dully gleaming domed ceiling of fluted steel, ending in a central pillar—no, not really a pillar, but a five-foot-thick cylinder wrought, it seemed, of translucent blue crystal, glowing with a strong internal light that cast an unearthly radiance over the entire Circle. It was definitely not a mere pillar.

Yet, MacDougall suddenly realized, that cylinder must lead into the base of the great brass serpent, from the mouth of which sprang the laserlike beam, the Sword of Light! It must be supporting that great weight. And he had hoped to investigate the mystery! The very idea was absurd. Whatever its secret, it lay somewhere deep in the heart of Tartarus.

"Master, please." Knorri was insistent and anxious. "Better we move."

With eyes fixed on the radiant blue cylinder, Alan followed his guide. A path opened before them, leading to the column of light. Now he saw Gobniu and Credne silhouetted against the lambency; with them was Einurr, whose mound of fluffy white hair picked up the glow, to give him a veritable blue halo. They stood near a flight of steps that led to a circular platform, like a flat collar encircling the cylinder. Evidently they had been awaiting Alan's arrival; at his approach, Einurr waved and mounted the steps, followed by the others. The three men ranged themselves behind Einurr as he raised his hands for silence.

An expectant hush fell over the mass of Trolls.

"As you see," Einurr began in a strong voice that carried through all the area, "I have returned." Cries of pleasure rose here and there from the more enthusiastic. "We must thank our friend Alan the son of Dougall for my return. He is the master of all master magicians." He bared his forehead. "He has removed my mark of disgrace. And he tells me the new Druid of Findias will be made to treat us fairly or will have to answer to him."

A ringing shout swept through the crowd. Gurulfin walked around the platform to face the audience on the opposite side. "Do you hear me?"

Cries of "Yes, yes! We hear!" rose from everywhere.

"A new day has dawned for Trollheim. We will obey the Druid—but only if he deserves to be obeyed—"

MacDougall listened with mounting amazement. Where had Einurr gotten the idea that he would guarantee future fair treatment? What could he have said to create that impression? He tried to remember—and it came to him. Back there in the forest, he had made reference to the new Druid being accountable, indicating that Druids were not gods. Mentally he berated himself.

The Troll King continued, "So we have freedom such as we have never known. With Arias the Druid gone—"

He was interrupted by a shout from the edge of the Circle, a shrill voice that rose above his own.

"You see! There he is! I told you! Gurulfin himself—the Outcast. And that is the troublemaker, MacDougall."

A second voice followed, angry, indignant; and sudden commotion erupted among the Trolls.

"Make way! Make way for Maelcen the Druid. Who is responsible for this assemblage? Why was I not consulted?"

The Trolls fell to right and left as a mass of men ploughed through them, stalking toward the platform. Alan caught a glimpse of a Troll scampering just ahead of the group—the one with the big nose who had confronted them on their entry into Trollheim; behind him came an unusually fat, white-robed Druid. And behind—it couldn't be!

Side by side, all eyes glaring at MacDougall, came Balor, Beli, Arawn, and Manannan! Questions tumbled pell-mell through Alan's mind. Balor and Manannan, yes. But Beli and Arawn! How could they have come? Had there been time in this time-mad world for Manannan to ride *Wave Sweeper* to Ochren and return with the two? Or had the sea god mentally communicated with Beli and summoned the pair to Tartarus, transferred by Beli's god-power? The last was more logical.

Questions, only seconds in duration, ended as action exploded. Beli thundered, "Seize him!"

They charged toward the platform through the mass

of Trolls, sweeping aside all in their path. Instinctively, without conscious effort, MacDougall became invisible, even as he darted around the cylinder to put its mass between him and his enemies. He heard a violent curse in Arawn's voice, then Manannan's triumphant cry. "Erus *said* he was here!"

Bedlam followed. Trolls were trying to move out of the way with no place to move to. Shrill cries came from the Troll women. Then Gobniu's ponderous voice was raised in growing anger, "Who are you? What is going on here? Balor—get rid of that stupid mask. That body died. Be yourself!"

Through it all, MacDougall tried to bring order to his chaotic thoughts. Erus the Druid had said Alan was here? Of course! The Druid heard Alan talking with Einurr about visiting Findias. He must have encountered the gods in their search and had used his information to try to gain favor.

Above all this confusion of thought flared mounting fury. He'd had enough from these four!

Unseen, he darted around the cylinder. Balor had reached the platform and was almost at the top of the steps, looking angrily at the Smith, when Alan swung a rock-hard fist, well aimed and well timed, not at the visible Balor form, but at the jaw of the twisted Fomorian it masked. The god sagged and fell backward off the steps, his head and shoulders striking the floor, where he lay motionless. It was not cricket—but neither was four against one.

Arawn, a few steps back, stopped short and looked down in unbelief at the unfamiliar face in Balor's clothes, his magically maintained appearance vanishing with loss of consciousness. Comprehending, the King of Ochren whipped out his sword and brandished it wildly before him, his gaze darting fearfully about, seeking the unseen assailant. Alan drew his own weapon, looking for an opening to strike, but knew abruptly he couldn't do it. It was not his nature to attack from ambush; it had even gone against the grain for him to slug Balor.

With a glance, he surveyed the scene. Only seconds had elapsed. Beli was watching Arawn's antics; Manannan had his attention fixed on Einurr and Credne. Gobniu glanced uncertainly from one to the other, obviously puzzled. It was time for action.

"Gobniu, get Beli—the red-headed bull," Alan cried. "He's your size."

With a roar, the Smith leaped high into the air, his great arms spread wide, and landed full upon the startled god. They struck the floor together, arms and hands grappling, rolling, legs entwined, and magic forgotten in sheer animal combat.

Arawn turned toward the struggle; and at that instant, MacDougall leaped to the floor, regaining visibility, his own sword swinging. The King of Ochren responded instinctively, and their weapons clashed. Alan had hoped the aging monarch was not a skilled swordsman—and so, fortunately, it proved to be. Had it been otherwise, there would have been a quick end to the duel. Yet, though not skilled, Arawn was a better swordsman than Alan. For minutes, it required all MacDougall's agility and foot speed to avoid Arawn's blade. But the King had the misfortune to back into a Troll and stumble over his prone form— and before he could rise, Alan swung his sword mightily, striking the top of the balding head with the flat of his blade. The King of Ochren collapsed and did not stir.

MacDougall looked hastily around. Beli and Gobnui still lay on the floor, almost motionless. The Smith had somehow gotten his mighty arms around Beli's chest, his hands locked behind Beli's back, and he simply squeezed. The red-bearded god was gasping desperately for breath, a look of agony on his face, now almost as red as his hair. Beads of sweat rolled and dripped from Gobniu's forehead, nose, and whiskers; but nothing could unlock that grip. Inexorably it tightened. Only the extent of Beli's endurance was in question.

Manannan—what of the sea god? He alone had tried to resort to magic, but he was not doing well. He faced two opponents, grim-faced, rigid, meeting his eyes and countering every spell—the god Credne and Einurr Gurulfin. Apparently some Trolls, too, had powers; and perhaps Manannan had depended too long on his Druids.

Even as he looked at them, a great wall of blue water started to rise at one end of the Circle, instantly leaping up in a frothing comber and sweeping down on screaming Trolls—as suddenly to slump and disappear.

At last Alan thought of the serpent-gods, forgotten in the fury of conflict. "Lord Enki and Lady Inanna, can you terminate this stalemate between Manannan and the Credne-Einurr pair?" He added apologetically, "I forgot about you and tried things the hard way."

There was delight in Inanna's response. "It was fascinating to watch—primitive man at his worst."

Lord Enki added, "Manannan has felt the need of sleep."

Indeed, at that moment the sea god slipped to the floor, eyes closed, and curled up in deepest slumber. What an anticlimax, Alan thought.

He turned at a sudden sound. It was the loud thump of Beli's head striking the hard-packed clay. Slowly, Gobniu the Smith climbed erect and stretched mightily. A broad grin wreathed his face as he flexed strained muscles.

"I don't know what that was all about, but it was more fun than I've had in a long time. He was tough—but I think he'll live."

Quiet had returned to the Circle. The Troll over whom Arawn had fallen, apparently unhurt, had managed to crawl from beneath the unconscious King. At one side stood a rigid unwilling spectator with no place to go, the new Druid named Maelcen. Behind him, held firmly by three sturdy Trolls, cringed the one with the big nose, no longer loud of voice.

"You!" Alan pointed stiffly at the Druid. "You saw

what happened here. I have promised fair treatment to
the Trolls. That includes King Einurr. *Especially* King
Einurr! Gobniu and Credne will be here to see that justice
is done. I am leaving Findias and Trollheim. But I can
return."

He pointed a boot toward the four recumbent figures
on the floor. "They will be leaving in moments—but if
they come back looking for me, be sure to tell them I
have gone to Falias, where they can find me—if they
have not learned their lesson. Unless Einurr wishes to
speak to you—" He looked questioningly at the Troll
King, who shook his head. "You may go now."

Wordlessly, his face pale, the Druid walked through
the silent Trolls, trying hard to maintain some semblance
of dignity.

"And you!" MacDougall addressed the cringing Troll.
"I have decided now who you are. Your appearance has
changed somewhat—an improvement, I should say. You
were Arias the Druid, famous swordsman who tried to
best an invincible blade wielded by Nuada. You are Arias,
returned as a Troll and as sweet tempered as before you
died!" He bowed to Einurr. "I leave him to the justice of
the Trolls."

Gurulfin frowned. "He will be well cared for. It is not
generally known, but we have a place reserved for such
as he."

During all of this, the assembled Trolls had been regaining their courage, slowly drawing closer, but still very
quiet. They had experienced more excitement in a very
short time than perhaps in all their previous existence in
Tartarus and now had more to wonder at and more to talk
about, with a new hero, Alan MacDougall.

Alan closed his eyes and crossed his arms, gripping
the armlet. "Lord Enki and Lady Inanna, again I have a
problem. I think its solution lies within your powers. I
wish to place these four on their horses outside Findias
and on their way to Murias. Can you possibly place them
under some kind of mental spell—a confusion, a semi-

sleeping state, a sort of stupor—that will permit their riding, but without their knowing what is actually happening? Perhaps to remain so until they are well on their way. Have I made my idea clear? Can this be done?"

The answer was delayed, but Enki finally replied. "The mental state can be induced—but I assume you will attend to getting them on their horses."

"Of course."

Alan opened his eyes and met the awed gaze of Einurr Gurulfin. He noticed that silence, an expectant waiting, held all in a circle around. He supposed his pose had appeared a bit theatrical. He repressed a grin and spoke casually.

"Einurr, I have been considering what we should do with these four. Can you have them carried to their horses? They will not awaken. Get them outside Findias and into their saddles. Then they will awaken and ride away."

The wonder on the Troll King's face grew as Mac-Dougall spoke, which was not surprising; his positive assertions sounded incredible. Abruptly, Gurulfin made a slight gesture, then began issuing orders, calling out the names of Trolls who were to carry the inert intruders.

"Hold!" Gobniu's voice broke in. "I can carry two of these myself." Stooping, he slipped one arm around Balor and the other under Arawn; as if burdened by two sagging sacks of grain, he stalked away. Moments later twelve Trolls, six per god, followed with Manannan and Beli.

As the throng closed around them, some following, MacDougall turned to Credne, a silent watcher.

"My friend, I need your help. You are one of the *Tuatha de Danann*, the family of Danu. You have an ability I lack. I should like to be transported to the home of Taliesin in Falias. He is expecting me and I am long overdue. May I ask this?"

Credne looked surprised. "I expected no such limitations after what I have seen—" He halted, then began again. "It has been so long since I practiced such travel, haste being of no importance; but I suppose I still have the ability." He frowned, seemingly in deep thought. "So very long—but we can try."

MacDougall put an arm around Einurr's shoulders and squeezed. "I am glad we met, my friend. I trust all will be well with you and your people. Give my thanks to Gobniu for his help. I leave now."

"I cannot find words—" The Troll King's voice broke and he turned away.

Credne placed his hands on Alan's shoulders, his jaw set, his eyes closed. "Now," he said softly. Again Alan felt the breathless, heart-checking sensation of instant transfer, then felt an unfamiliar drop, a sharp impact as his feet landed jarringly on a solid surface.

Incredulous, he stared around. He had landed in pale green turf on the crest of a hill. To his left, in the distance rose the crystalline spires of Falias, bright against the aurora. There was no sign of Credne.

Well, Alan thought philosophically, he wasn't certain—and I came this far. But where is the god?

Out of nothingness appeared the Bronze-Master to land a yard away. He shook his head, obviously embarrassed. "I am sorry, my friend. Lack of practice. Let us try again."

This time they made it, appearing together in the dwelling of the Bard of Bards.

Taliesin, seated in his favorite chair, looked up in mild astonishment. "Welcome, Alan!" he said warmly. "And Credne! This *is* a surprise." Putting his book on the little table at his elbow, he got to his feet. "I have been expecting a visit from you, Alan—though not without some warning. But you do unexpected things—bringing the Bronze-Master, for example."

"I will not stay," Credne said hastily. "I but gave the son of Dougall transportation. And that not too successfully." And he vanished.

"An unusual god," the Bard said as he motioned toward the same chair MacDougall had used during his original visit to Falias.

"I should have communicated, I know," Alan apologized, "but I have been very busy—as you will learn."

Taliesin looked keenly at his guest. "You appear to have passed through whatever you experienced with no visible scars, something I have come to expect." He picked up the book, *Mythology of the British Islands*, which Alan had given him. "I believe I have begun to decipher these strange hieroglyphics of the Other World. I remember having seen parchment manuscripts with similar characters which the priests of the new religion carried when they came to Alba and Erin. But the language was different. Perhaps you can help me with my studies. But that will come later. After a bit of brandy you must tell me what delayed you."

There followed a period of casual conversation before Taliesin insisted on MacDougall's telling about his experiences after they separated.

Alan began with his visit to the golden tower and his meeting with Ahriman. Intentionally, he passed over much of what they discussed, deferring details for later consideration. The ambush by the Druid Erus and the Outcasts, his subconscious overhearing of Manannan and Balor, and his subsequent freeing of the Outcasts received full attention, especially his discovery of the Troll King, and the departure of Erus.

"It seems evident," he commented, "that the Druid encountered Balor and Manannan during their search for me. I made the mistake of telling Einurr Gurulfin in Erus' hearing of my wish to visit his people, and he must have remembered and told the gods. You'll see shortly why I think so."

MacDougall continued with his description of the Trolls' mining and metalworking operations, and the Bard was fascinated. Several times he shook his head in unbelief. "When you think of their labor—the mountains of rock and clay they have moved—it is beyond imagining."

Finally Alan told of the assemblage in the Circle around the crystal pillar, referring to its evident relationship to the brazen serpent. Again Taliesin was impressed. "I believe I have heard references to it," he commented, "but I've never actually seen it. I must pay a visit to Trollheim and meet this Einurr Gurulfin."

Alan concluded his narrative with the end of the meeting, his inadvertent guarantee of future justice for the Troll King and his subjects, and the arrival of Arias as a Troll with the new Druid of Findias, and with Balor, Arawn, Beli and Manannan. By the time he had described that most unconventional conflict, the Bard was laughing aloud. Alan joined in the mirth, though at the time it had not seemed funny.

Sobering, the Bard said, "We are certain to hear more from the three from Ochren. Knowing them as we do, I foresee problems."

Ruefully, MacDougall agreed. "And again I seem to have stirred up trouble. I should have stayed in my own world."

This time of conversation with the Bard was the first of many. They enjoyed sessions poring over the two books, the *Mythology* and the Bible. Gradually, Taliesin learned the secret of the alphabet, the formation of words, their pronunciation and meaning. His mind was amazingly keen, and his memory was phenomenal. He began to master the intricacies of the English language. Meals came and meals went; sleep followed sleep—but in a world where time was a variable, where events or their lack determined the rate of time's passing, there was no way to measure the length of Alan's stay.

MacDougall felt little concern about this. He only knew he was enjoying the period of tranquility, a great change from the hectic stay in Ochren and the not exactly peaceful happenings since his return to Tartarus. Several sleeps after his arrival, Alan brought up the subject of his visit to the golden tower.

"I had many questions to ask Ahriman," he began. "And he seemed to be telling me a great deal while we talked; though I knew no more after I left than when I arrived. I asked about his name, which is that of the Persian god of evil, and which would be the same as Lucifer or Satan. He evaded and offered a half-dozen other names which he said he could have used. All had the same significance.

"I asked about the creation of the other three islands—since, unlike Tartarus, they certainly were not created for the Daughters of Lilith—and he said Lucifer foresaw the need. He made claims about his infinite foreknowledge and omniscience—equality with the Creator."

Taliesin listened without comment, so Alan continued, finally getting to the matter that weighed most heavily on his mind.

"Several times Ahriman spoke about the prophecy of the Scroll. He even suggested that I might be a throwback, a reincarnation of one of the ancient Kings, and by descent, of the royal line—possibly through an illegitimate off-spring. Thus I could be part of a pact entered into many centuries ago. Can you shed any light on any of this—since you have read all of the Scroll?"

The Bard of Bards was deeply troubled, his face betraying his uncertainty and concern. He stared at the floor with narrowed eyes, his jaw set firmly. Suddenly his expression brightened, as if he saw a solution to his problem. He looked up, meeting MacDougall's gaze.

"Trust me, Alan. I have an excellent reason for not telling you all of the prophecy at this time. However, there is a way to clear up the question of your ancestry—and if you are not of the royal line, you cannot be the fulfillment of the prophecy of the Scroll. Then I can freely tell you what I have read."

"Great!" MacDougall exclaimed. "But how can this matter of my forebears be cleared up? By what miracle?"

"There is in the Great Temple, which also houses the School for Druids, the ancient *Lia Fail*, the Stone of Fal. When one of royal descent sits upon it, it cries out. I have never heard the sound, though many in jest have tried the seat."

Alan peered quizzically at the Bard. "You are serious? But according to my reading—indeed, in this very book on Britain's myths—there is the story of the Stone of Fal, also called the Stone of Scone, now part of the Coronation Chair in Westminster Abbey, a name which means nothing to you, but a place where all the Kings of Britain are crowned. There are some who claim that the actual Stone rested for centuries on Tara Hill, but now is a marker on a tomb."

Taliesin shrugged. "Both obviously false, since the original stone rests where it began—in Falias. You must try that seat."

"But—what if the stone cries out?" The question came reluctantly from Alan, almost as an afterthought.

"When you have made the test, we shall decide."

Several times after this interchange, the Bard suggested a visit to the School for Druids, but each time MacDougall found an excuse, avoiding what might be a crisis. He berated himself for his reluctance, but none the less delayed. And then the idyllic period ended.

Alan received the first inkling of change during one of his preslumber times of unsought eavesdropping on the *Tuatha de Danann*. The first voice to register through his drowsiness was that of Nuada.

"I have just been in conference with three visitors from Ochren. Beli, my father in the Olden Times, was spokesman. He proposed a general meeting of the powers of our island to discuss a request on which I am inclined to look with favor."

Danu the Mother Goddess said mildly, *"It might perhaps be wiser for you to withhold your own view until we have heard the proposal."*

"True," Nuada agreed. *"Before I repeat their request I think I should mention the time I spent on Ochren in company with Taliesin and MacDougall, who, as you must be aware, is now guest of the Bard. While there I was entertained by Manannan, god of the sea, who spoke of the empty city of Lochlann where the Fomorians lived*

before they were moved to Murias. He and Arawn were the other two in conference."

A new voice exclaimed, *"You have told us again and again of all your Ochren adventures; we recall them vividly."*

"At least, Diancecht—" Nuada made no effort to conceal his annoyance. *"—I have something to talk about."* Diancecht was the physician of the *Tuatha de Danann.*

"The suggestion, please." Alan recognized the voice of Dagda.

"It is simply that we send half of the Fomorians back to Ochren to live in Lochlann. I favor the idea for several reasons. First and of greatest importance, it would greatly reduce the number of troublemakers in our own land. I am really surprised that Balor agrees with Manannan, but he does."

"But what about replacements for the slain?" Danu objected. *"Have they reserves, as Murias has?"*

"I believe they are counting on normal bodies for replacements, since, at most, there are only a few thousand Romans on all of Ochren. But that would have to be discussed."

"And what do you propose?" Dagda asked.

"Simply that we call a general gathering of all the gods and Druids in the Great Hall of the Temple, there to meet with the visitors from Ochren—ten of them, I understand. The others were brought here on Manannan's boat, Wave Sweeper."

"I approve," Danu said. *"It should be an interesting meeting. There can be no harm in discussing."*

On sudden impulse, which afterward made no sense at all, MacDougall did something he had never before thought of doing. He made his contribution to the discussion.

"This is MacDougall. Your conversations come to me unsought. May I say a word? To send anyone, even a Fomorian, to Ochren is unthinkable. As for the empty city, it is a nightmare. You, Nuada, never entered Loch-

lann, so you have no idea what it is really like. I know whereof I speak. I have been there. The only sensible thing for you to do is to have no conversation whatever with the visitors from Ochren."

"MacDougall!" Nuada was furious. *"How dare you listen to a private conversation? You are never happy unless you are meddling in matters of no concern to you. You brought a war to the island, then left. You opened the way for Manannan and others to come here. Had it not been for you, we would not know that Ochren exists. And now you have the audacity to tell us how to deal with issues we would not face, were it not for you. Why don't you return to the Other World—and stay there?"*

Danu's quiet thought followed. *"I think there is merit in MacDougall's suggestion. Ochren sounds like a dreadful place; and trouble can only follow interference in the plans of the Lord of Light. Logically, he had a purpose in moving the Fomorians to our island."*

"An interesting thought," Dagda commented. *"But if MacDougall, too, appears to be part of Lucifer's plan, the changes he has brought about may also have been destined. I think—"*

What Dagda thought, Alan was never to learn, for in mid-sentence the discussion was gone. In annoyance he sat up. Just when things were getting interesting he'd lost them—and suddenly, he realized why. He was wide awake; and his eavesdropping only happened when he was half-asleep.

At breakfast he told Taliesin what he had overheard, including his own contribution. The Bard agreed with Alan's view, but expressed regret that he had interfered. "The meeting will probably be held—in part because you advised against it."

Several sleeps later, without the Bard having received any official word about the conference, he said to MacDougall, "I have learned by means of my own that the meeting is about to begin. I have not been invited, which is most unusual; the reason, I think, is the fact that you are my guest. Well—they can do without my sage wisdom. But I can think of no better time than this for us to visit the Stone of Fal. With most or all of the Druids and gods present at the Temple, there will be a lot of activity. The building will be open, and, with all assembled in the Great Hall, we can visit the Stone, while we're invisible, without our being noticed."

When they finally started toward the Temple, Mac-Dougall had become eager for the test. At last he'd be getting some information, for most assuredly there was not a chance in ten thousand that the Stone would cry out. There was no way he could be in the royal line.

They set out on horseback with two guards, their course taking them through a section of Falias never traversed by MacDougall. This was not surprising since he had really seen very little of the City of the North. As always, he marveled at the beauty of the crystalline structures reflecting the ever-changing aurora. He and Taliesin rode side by side, with guarding horsemen behind them, moving at a leisurely pace, for the distance was not great. In a very short time, Taliesin pointed out a magnificent building at what must be the center of the city.

Larger than any of its neighbors, it rose sheerly into the aurora, suggesting a mass of quartz crystals tinted an icy green and standing on end, carefully controlled in their growth to fit precise dimensions. These graduated toward a central peak on which was mounted a great multi-pointed star. The glittering star, water-white, rested upon six scimitarlike blades of crystal, sweeping up and up with perfection of form and grace to meet in a point that created what seemed to be a completely inadequate support. Star, blades, and the building as a whole flashed in the auroral light like a tremendous gem.

They approached what most nearly resembled a great circular mall, an expanse of flat, white flagstones completely surrounding the Temple. Streets like the spokes of a wheel ended at the rim. Small marble buildings, delicately carved, Oriental appearing, and uniformly spaced, formed a circle about twenty feet inside the perimeter of the circle.

From streets on every side came Druids, their white robes immaculate. They had one common destination, the wide white steps leading into the Temple. There was no conversation among them, but an air of solemnity; bowed heads and their slow pace suggested reverence, if that were possible in Tartarus.

"Here we wait," Taliesin said quietly; then, turning, he said to one of the Norse guards, "Thorsen, care for the horses. You saw the field at the last turn. Wait there for our return."

As the horses were led away, the Bard sent a thought to MacDougall, *We are not being observed. Invisibility— now!* As one they vanished.

"I deem it wise for us to wait here until all have entered the Temple," Taliesin said softly. "Although we cannot be seen, we could be heard, if we entered a crowd, or perhaps touched, or someone might feel the moving air of our passing. There is no reason for haste. Here, except for a possible tardy Druid, none will come close. The buildings around the circle are not occupied. They are not needed, and there is something about the Temple, indeed the area, that the Norse find disturbing."

Alan could appreciate their feeling. He was aware of a subtle atmosphere completely out of harmony with the beauty on every hand, an aura of ancient evil. To him, it seemed as if malevolent eyes were watching. He tried to ignore the uncomfortable sensation.

"These small white buildings—what was their purpose in the days of Lilith?"

"They housed the chosen attendants of the Temple, Daughters of Lilith."

"Like vestal virgins," Alan suggested facetiously.

The Bard grunted. "Hardly virgins."

Gradually the flow of Druids mounting the white steps dwindled; and finally, all appeared to have entered.

"Now we go," Taliesin said. "Your hand. And from now on only mental communication."

As they crossed the white expanse to the great stairway, Alan involuntarily looked upward. It was an awesome spectacle, this sight of the sheer crystalline walls reaching into the aurora. He knew it was Lucifer's creation. Inexplicably, there flashed into his mind a picture of the ghastly living, whispering cloud in the black depths of Annwn—also created by the hand of Lucifer. Allan shut out the thought.

Walking as quietly as possible, they passed through the great arched doorway. They entered a long corridor of translucent crystal, high and vaulted, rising to a peak twenty or thirty feet above their heads. This led to another great and ornate doorway, and beyond it lay the Great Hall.

Taliesin and MacDougall halted, standing side by side, and Alan caught his breath. He had considered himself beyond superlatives—but this must be the most dazzling of all the creations in this fantastic world.

A silent symphony in crystal, it suggested a vast cathedral, its sheer, gleaming walls thrusting up in a great circle to merge into a ceiling of glittering planes, mounting gradually toward its center to form a five-faceted point. Dimly seen through that brilliant expanse, like the muted fire of an immense diamond, shone the rose, violet, saffron, and blue of the aurora. This, Alan knew, was the inside of that cluster of mighty quartz crystals!

All of this he saw at a glance, and a glance was all he could venture, his eyes being caught and held immediately by the wall he faced. There, on a level with the entrance, rose an object whose brightness must outshine anything else in Tartarus.

The figure rested on a base of palest gold, fashioned in the form of an immense cupped hand, holding a trinity of five-sided crystals, each terminating at its upper end in a perfect, tapered point. The enormous central crystal, all of five feet in diameter, rose halfway to the ceiling.

On either side jutted the other two, breadth and height identical, as if the shortness of the supporting objects were to magnify the importance of the central upright. And with brightness almost blinding, the trio sent forth a slowly pulsing light that shed its radiance throughout the greater chamber.

A symbol, most certainly, MacDougall told himself, of Lucifer, the Lord of Light, to give him the title most used by the dwellers in Tartarus. But why the tri-form? An imitation of the Biblical Trinity? Or—suddenly the thought struck him—an enormous phallic symbol!

With the thought, Alan felt the short hairs rising at the nape of his neck. Despite the undeniable beauty of the place, he dreaded entering. This had been—perhaps still was—the place of worship of Satan.

He tore his gaze away from the almost-hypnotic light and, with the Bard, hands clasped, began moving along a downward sloping aisle. The floor seemed to be of white marble, with tier upon tier of long, backless seats following the circular contour of the chamber. There were two other aisles, each ending, a quick glance revealed, in doorways like the one they had just passed through.

After a few steps Taliesin halted, mentally saying, *"No reason for our going any closer to the Druids. We must cross to the next aisle. We reach the Room of the Stone through that corridor."*

"What's the rush?" Alan asked a bit impatiently. Now that the test was at hand, he had lost some of his interest in their objective and felt a reluctance to learn the answer. *"Let's watch the proceedings. It could be interesting."*

"I think the delay is a mistake," the Bard replied, *"but as you wish."*

Stealthily, they moved between two curving rows of seats to the aisle they would have to ascend. Below them, under that awesome, pulsating form, lay a level area in the center of which were seated ten familiar figures, facing the mounting rows of seats—the visitors from Ochren.

The gods and Druids of Tartarus occupied the first

several rows of seats, the gods in the first row. Nuada, standing, was speaking. He had adopted an oratorical air, and his words echoed metallically through the chamber.

"It is interesting to learn, after all these centuries, that another island exists in this world of the Lord of Light. This may well mark a new era in the society of both lands." He continued, referring to the possibility of other islands to be visited, speaking about the mutual advantages of peaceful coexistence, extolling the virtues of the Land of the Four Cities and its never-dying light; in short, enjoying to the full a rare opportunity to take advantage of his Kingly position.

MacDougall, only half hearing, studied the visitors. All were clad in their finest, looking as regal as possible. The big three, of course, were there—Arawn, Beli, and Manannan. Their faces were impassive, telling nothing of what they really thought about this meeting and its setting.

The King of Ochren had brought Pryderi, his jailer, evidently leaving Pwyll at home to guard the prison. Seated beside Beli was a Druid, gray cowled, probably the chief of his corps of two hundred. Manannan's staff had arrived in full force—Gwyn the Hunter; Ler, the sea god's father; Mathonwy, in charge of Manannan's Druids; Idris the Astrologer; even Caradoc, that revolting, onetime saint. After all, why shouldn't Manannan bring whom he chose? He owned the boat!

Eventually Nuada arrived at the introduction of the visitors; and after each had spoken briefly about himself, Manannan presented his request concerning the Fomorians. He spoke at length about the empty city under the sea, built for the Fomorians, extolling its advantages, and of crowded conditions he had seen in Murias—on and on to MacDougall's complete boredom. Alan didn't really care what happened to the Fomorians, though he thought it unfair that they should not have a voice in their own fate.

He concentrated on the listeners, the gods of Tartarus. Both Danu and Dagda seemed to be having difficulty in maintaining an air of interest. He looked in vain for one who might be Morrigu in a new body; if she had not yet returned, it was small loss. He saw Credne and Gobniu, the giant obviously bored. He looked for Dalua, the Dark and Witless One; not surprisingly, the antisocial god was not there.

But Balor was there, seeming none the worse for his experience in Trollheim. That was the sham form the god maintained. As he studied the grim face, Alan became somewhat puzzled. It was somehow different, as if it had undergone a subtle change. It bore a look that seemed strangely triumphant, as if Balor were gloating over something. He sent a thought to the serpent-god. "Lord Enki, may I see Balor as he really is?"

Instantly, the old Balor vanished—but instead of the twisted Fomorian, Alan saw a handsome, square-jawed, black-bearded Norseman, a man fully as big and powerful as the original god! It can't be, Alan thought. Another sham? He sent a thought to Taliesin.

"Look at Balor—as he really is. How can this be?"

He saw the Bard glance at the god of the Fomorians. He showed no surprise.

"I expected this to happen when Balor returned as he did. It has been done before, though rarely. He must have waited at the edge of the Forbidden Zone here in Falias, watching the new replacements. When he saw one with a body that pleased him, he gambled. His spirit left his Fomorian form and entered that of the Norseman. A battle must have taken place, and Balor evidently won, displacing the soul newly embodied. I said he gambled. Had the spirit of the Norseman been stronger, that of Balor would have been left to wander bodiless—for the Fomorian Balor-body might well have died when he left it. He took the risk—and won."

"And the Norseman?"

The Bard looked at Alan and gave a slight shrug. *"Perhaps he has joined that cloud of disembodied souls eternally wandering in Annwn. It is only a guess."*

MacDougall stared at Balor with intensified distaste, thinking savagely, I should have cut your throat when I had the chance!

He gave casual attention to the speaker—now Beli, presenting a proposal concerning some of the Trolls.

He was saying, "We lack skilled workmen, and I understand the Trolls are gifted metalworkers. Practically all of our men are Roman soldiers, and, though capable enough in rough construction, fine work is beyond them. If we might have the Trolls' services for a period, it would facilitate the construction of the fleet which we will need to transport the Fomorians to Ochren."

As the import of this sank in, MacDougall felt utter disgust. What an idiotic idea—for the Tartarians. Give us help to build a fleet to bring the Fomorians to Ochren—and to be used later by predatory Romans to invade Tartarus!

How did the sea god plan to get the Fomorians or the Trolls through that wall of blackness or past the thundering waterfall? True, they were illusion, but nevertheless devastatingly real; and what of those who might think of the barrier as reality? Reluctantly, he conceded the passengers could be placed under a magical stupor. Manannan had succeeded with those before him, perhaps by using blindfolds. Anyway, it was not his problem.

He turned his attention to the Druids, seeking to find those he knew. Some, of course, had their backs to him, so identification would be well-nigh impossible. Quickly, he found ancient Moirfhius, Druid of Falias, and Caermarthen, who had worn the armlet before he was slain by Malcolm. He saw Semias, Druid of Murias, his sunken eyes in restless motion, never still, glancing about as if in constant fear. He felt a sharp pang of guilt as he always did at thought of the Druid. He remembered the utter horror on the face of the man when he had crouched on the roof of the Hall of the Dead, a Forbidden Area, which had evidently driven him mad with terror. And Alan had placed him there.

Beli concluded his speech, and Nuada stood up.

"I believe our backs may well need a rest. We will delay the discussion of our visitors' proposals for a period to allow us to consider all that is involved. At the head of the center aisle, you will find a room where refreshments await us. We will return when I give the word."

With alacrity, everyone arose, many stretching and all moving toward the aisle. A hubbub of conversation broke out immediately, the influence of that gleaming crystalline figure seemingly dispelled.

"Let's make the test," Alan said softly, "then get out of here."

Jarringly, with the last word, there burst in Mac-Dougall's ears a wild laugh, high-pitched and strange. Once heard, it could never be forgotten—the mad laughter of Dalua the Witless One! He, too, must have been invisible. Alan's instinct had been right; there had been eyes watching—Dalua's eyes.

There came a shrill cry, thrice repeated. "MacDougall! MacDougall is here!"

At the same instant, Alan realized that he was no longer invisible, the spell countered, and that he stood revealed to all in the Great Hall.

"Lord Enki! Let me see Dalua."

Just behind him, he saw the dark god. Without conscious thought, he slashed out with stiffened arm and hand, catching the other just under the chin with a vicious blow. With a single, strangled cough, Dalua dropped to the floor and lay there, writhing and gasping, clutching his throat.

All this had happened in fleeting seconds; again invisible, MacDougall darted up the aisle with a thought to the Bard. *"Where to? The Stone of Fal?"*

Taliesin was at his heels. *"The second door on the right."*

As he ran, Alan could hear a mob racing up the slope, an angry rumble rising above the clatter of sandals. He glanced back, to see Beli, Balor, Manannan, and Arawn in the lead. He felt like a hunted creature and had to quell an impulse to turn and face them all. Darting through the second doorway into a sort of classroom, he saw another at the rear and dashed through it, then halted. Sounds of pursuit were passing by, continuing along the corridor.

"The next room to the left," came the Bard's thought. *"Move quietly. They won't look for us here, since there is no exit."*

This room was their destination, a chamber about thirty feet square. The doorway, though an arch like all the others, was small, lacking the ornate decoration of most. And except for the Stone of Fal itself, the room was empty. Side by side, visible again by common consent, the two entered. The sounds of pursuit had dimmed.

Before them lay the Stone. Curiously, Alan examined it, a deep brown block, a cube not quite waist high. It had the appearance of an iron meteorite, but the perfection of its form suggested tooling or, barring that, an enormous cubic crystal. Only the apparent fusion of its edges prevented perfection.

There was a time when Alan would have scoffed at the whole idea of a stone that could identify a king. Not now. Stranger things than this existed in this strange land.

"Sit," Taliesin said quietly. "We have little time."

Alan forced a chuckle. "We'll soon know if great-great-grandpa, five times removed, was a bastard." In spite of himself, he felt his pulse quicken. More clearly, he heard the sounds of commotion and angry voices, the frustrated hunters returning.

"Sit," the Bard repeated.

With a gesture of resignation, Alan MacDougall sat.

Through the room and out through the other room and hallway rose an indescribable sound. Like a mingled cry and shophar blast, rising and falling in eerie cadence, it echoed and re-echoed in mounting volume until it seemed that it must fill all of the vast crystalline temple with its unearthly voice.

MacDougall sat as one frozen, unable to move, unbelieving, his thoughts whirling. At last, penetrating the inexplicable paralysis, he heard distant crowd noises and tried to stand up. He was held as if by a powerful magnet that resisted his every effort to rise. With undiminished fervor, the strange wail continued.

The sound of running feet and alarmed cries grew louder, drew close, guided by the cry of the Stone of Fal. He heard Taliesin's voice at his ear, low and incredulous, somehow reaching him through the din.

"The royal line!"

The wailing ended as the first of the gods entered the room. Alan struggled erect. They came like a flood, the gods and Druids, quickly filling the small chamber, crowding around MacDougall and Taliesin. Together, a foot away, stood Beli, Balor, Manannan and Arawn, grim faced, a weight of hatred, almost tangible, almost physical, emanating from them—yet held by an involuntary restraint of wonder. All knew the story of the Stone. Beside Arawn, pushing through the crowd, Alan saw pallid Dalua, eyes glaring, massaging his throat. From every side came cries, demanding to know what had happened.

Loudly, the Bard called for silence, then explained, "It is foretold in Lucifer's Scroll that the Chosen One who shall come will be in the line of Kings. I brought MacDougall to make the test. He sat on the Stone and it cried out."

Suddenly, Alan felt a sharp blow between his shoulder blades, like an over-forceful clap on the back. But there came with it instantly a lance of pain, a tightness that caught at his throat, and a gasping cough.

Someone cried out shrilly, shocked, "He's been stabbed! MacDougall has been stabbed! There's a knife—in his back!"

A gray mist seemed to rise before him as he spun around. He blinked, squeezed his eyes shut, trying to clear his sight, and stared into the face of Semias the Druid. It was a face bearing a gloating, triumphant, savage leer.

Alan felt weakness surge like a wave through all his body; his knees gave way, seeming to crumble. Faintly through a darkening veil, dim with distance, he heard a voice shout, "Diancecht! Where is Diancecht?"

Another name, another thought rose to consciousness. "Lord Enki—the Gate—to the Other World." But Enki—Enki could not lift him! He tried with all his strength to picture the smallest stone in his graduated rock marker—then saw sharply a face, the sober, hard-eyed visage of Ahriman, sternly disapproving. It vanished, and there was only unbroken blackness and a stillness like that of death.

CHAPTER 13

Elspeth

The sound of voices, dimly heard on the edge of con-
sciousness, was the first clear impression to come to Alan
MacDougall. He made no attempt to distinguish words,
trying to remember where he was and how he came to be
there, but without success. He was aware of soft comfort,
of warm coverlets over him, of sunlight forming a pattern
of shadows on a flowered wall, and of a faint breeze,
laden with the scent of mint and roses, of heather and
barnyard. It was a comfortable sort of aroma. His eye
was caught by the white curtains over the open window
as they billowed out like cheeks full of air, only to part
in the middle and fall back to await the next puff of breeze.

Now he heard other sounds coming from outside—
bird calls, near and far, the lowing of cattle, and the hissing
of quarrelsome geese. Through the closed doorway could
be heard voices, growing louder and recognizable. The
Camerons!

He groped for comprehension. His brain started func-
tioning. There had been the morning of departure after a

night spent in this very room—he recalled it clearly—
the walk down the road, the hike up the hillside, the entry
into the oak forest, the tower, Cinel Loarn and the *Shee*,
and his opening the four Gates.

Overwhelmingly into his mind poured a flood of images,
dark and somber, a phantasmagoria, a disordered mon-
tage of scenes from Ochren. Almost, it drove him back
into that well of darkness out of which he had climbed to
hear voices and see sights of his own sane world. Somehow, his thoughts centered on that fantastic ride in *Wave
Sweeper*; and again he saw the temple of crystal with its
brilliantly glowing image.

The Stone of Fal! The eerie sound throbbed again in
his ears. Then he saw the gloating face of Semias and felt
again the blow on his back. It all came back—his des-
perate but futile effort to reach the Gate and the face of
Ahriman, a disapproving Ahriman who had not planned
this and who had not foreseen the workings of a demented
mind. Ahriman must have brought him through the Gate.

He lay without stirring, forcing calm upon his mind.
It was the song of a thrush, bursting with the joy of living,
that brought him back to equanimity and peace.

But how—*how* had he reached the Cameron farm from
the room in the tower?

The clear, high treble of David Cameron reached his
consciousness. "But if I don't see him, I can't tell if he's
awake. An' a' the day I'll be wonderin'. Ye can't tell me
he'll stay that way. I'll no' believe it." He sounded close
to tears. "It can not be!"

"Aye—then just a look." That was the deep voice of
Duncan Cameron.

There came faint sounds on the stairway and the hushed
opening of the door. Then the brightly staring eyes of the
brown-haired lad looked into Alan's own.

"Good morning, David." MacDougall's voice sounded
strange and weak in his own ears. "It's a wonderful morning. But I'm hungry. What must a man do around here to
get breakfast?"

An instant of stunned silence was followed by a wild whoop and the headlong flight of childish feet down a carpeted stairway.

"He's a' richt! He's a' richt! Alan's awake an' wants breakfast. An' I want to gi' it to him!"

Amid joyous cries, there came a rush for the stairway, David first and Elspeth at his heels. Then came Norah and finally Duncan Cameron, clumping along on his plaster cast. All crowded around MacDougall's bed, trying to be restrained as became staid Scots, but hardly succeeding.

MacDougall had eyes only for Elspeth. As he saw her smiling face and saw the joy in her steady gray eyes, he remembered dimly the times when those same gray eyes had hovered anxiously over him.

The high, reedy voice of Norah returned sanity to the visit. "Dinna ye see the puir mon i' starved. Porridge an' eggs an' a glass o' milk is wha' he needs. As for ye, Elspeth an' Dyvid, ye'll be late for schule." She started the exodus from the room.

At that point Alan asked, "How did I get here?"

Norah had already started down the stairs, but all stopped where they were. It appeared he had asked the dreaded question. Alan saw David's face light up, expressing an eagerness to speak, quickly repressed by a warning glance from his father.

Cameron finally answered. "There came a knock on oor door. 'Twas late eve, almost dark. An' there ye lay, nigh to death." He added stubbornly, "How ye reached there wi' a' that loss o' blood we canna say. We carried ye to bed wi' prayer, then Elspeth drove for Doctor Maclean. An' if it hadna been for Elspeth—"

A loud sniff came from the stairway. "An' I didna do a thing. Nothing I did was guid enoch for her—"

"Please, father," the girl interrupted. "Alan must be tired. We should let him rest. And he needs his breakfast."

"Aye. An' we dare not forget to gi' praise to th' Lord.

He was a great help to Alan i' his battle." They descended quietly to the floor below.

Recovery followed steadily for Alan MacDougall, though the return of his strength seemed incredibly slow to him. Bit by bit he learned some of the details regarding the days of his illness. Norah, caring for him while Elspeth was at school, emphasized his near approach to death. Duncan Cameron extolled the virtues of the "good Doctor M'lean, th' best in a' the Heelands," his hands guided by the good Lord. But little David, alone with him in his room one afternoon after school, gave him the information he sought.

"David," Alan asked casually, "when the Little Men, the *Shee*, brought me here, did you actually see them?" This had to be the answer, Alan had decided—they or Ahriman.

The lad looked startled and burst out excitedly, "Aye, that I did! I saw them. The geese were a'makin' a gaggle o' noise an' I went oot to see wha' ailed them. An' there were the Little Men at the door. An' then they were gone. I was no' to tell ya—an' I didna. Ye told me."

There were some awkward moments when Norah commented on his strange black suit, and asked about his blood-stained cape. This led to blunt questions about his wound and assailant, which he evaded by vaguely hinting at a blow from ambush and indicating he had no clear memory of the incident.

Duncan Cameron apologized for their having opened the trunk of his car and his suitcase where they had found his pajamas and other garments. But since he had left the keys, they thought he would not object.

Alan could see there were other questions they wanted to ask; but he decided the least said the better.

From walking about in his room, MacDougall progressed to journeys outside in the welcome sunshine. He had begun light exercises after he had gained the doctor's approval. And then there were leisurely walks with Elspeth about the countryside, during which Alan learned more and more about the strong and lovely Scotswoman, mature beyond her years. His growing knowledge convinced him of what he instinctively had known—no other woman he had ever met appealed to all of him as she did.

They spoke little about Alan's illness during these walks, seeming to avoid the subject by mutual consent. But once when he had referred with impatience to the slowness of his return to strength, she said,

"You were terribly ill, Alan. You had lost an awful lot of blood. You had to have an immediate transfusion. It was fortunate that you carry a card showing your blood type."

"I learned that long ago during my years in the wilderness," Alan responded. Puzzled, he added, "A transfusion here? Odd that there should be a supply."

"A direct transfusion," she said, then hastily changed the subject. "Your fever caused the biggest problem. It was so hard to break."

"Hold everything!" Alan exclaimed. "Who gave me blood? Who knew his own type?"

Elspeth looked embarrassed. "I shouldn't have mentioned it. I happened to know—and it was no problem. But your delirium—" Again she checked herself. "Another slip!"

They had been walking along the rough stone wall that bordered Cameron's fields. Alan took the girl's hand in his and drew her to a seat beside him on the wall. He looked deep into her eyes, retaining hold of her hand.

"Tell me, Elspeth, did I talk much?"

"A very great deal—though mostly to me."

"What did you hear?"

"Far more than I could ever retell—but only as much as you want me to know."

"And what do you believe? That I was suffering a fever-induced nightmare—or that I am demented? Or that I have undergone an adventure beyond any ever given to man to experience?"

She took his hand in both of hers and, with deepest

earnestness, she said, "Remember—I have seen the armlet. I tried to remove it, thinking it might be causing you
discomfort. Those gem eyes looked into mine—and that
is what I mean. Alive. And I not only have seen the Sidhe,
but I have spoken with Cinel Loarn, who appeared to me
in the meadow to learn how you were faring. And, Alan,
I am a Scot!"

Slowly MacDougall's grasp tightened, his breath quickening as he stared unseeingly across the gently rippling
field of grain. His mind was in turmoil. He knew what he
wanted to say, what he wanted to do, but the hard reality
of the band of gold about his upper right arm demanded
silence.

"Elspeth," he said finally, "you know, as I do, that I
must return to that Other World." With difficulty he kept
his voice steady as he released her hand. "I believe you
have heard enough to understand that, all unsought, I am
part of something that has me trapped. It's a game I have
to play to the end."

"But it's not fair!" she protested indignantly. "You
almost died. Next time it could be—worse. Is there no
other way?"

His answer was long delayed. He thought of the armlet
clinging with unchanging strength, of Ahriman in his golden
tower, of the Stone of Fal and its pronouncement, and of
the Scroll with its prediction.

"I see no other way," he said at last, "but come what
may, I shall return."

ABOUT THE AUTHOR

Lloyd Arthur Eshbach was born on a farm in southeastern Pennsylvania on June 20, 1910. He still lives in Pennsylvania and has spent most of his years in the same area. He began reading science fiction and fantasy in 1919 with the fanciful tales of Edgar Rice Burroughs, A. Merritt, and their contemporaries in the pages of the Munsey magazines. He wrote his first salable SF story in 1929 and in the 1930s became a "big-name" writer. He began publishing SF books as Fantasy Press in 1947. Although he was not the first specialist publisher in the field, he was the first to present a full line of science fiction titles. His own writing, always a spare-time effort, included, in addition to SF, tales of fantasy and the supernatural, mystery stories, adventures, romances, and juveniles, some published under pseudonyms. With his entry into publishing, his writing became quite sporadic, and his last story appeared in 1957.

After the failure of his publishing venture—a fate met by all of the SF specialist houses—he became an advertising copywriter, a religious publisher, advertising manager of a major religious publishing house, and a publisher's sales representative.

In 1978, in retirement, Eshbach began writing again, his first effort being *Over My Shoulder: Reflections on a Science Fiction Era*, a memoir of his life in SF, concentrating on the history of the fan hardback book publishers of the 1930s, 40s, and 50s. This was issued in a limited edition in 1983. He completed E. E. "Doc" Smith's last novel, *Subspace Encounter*, left unfinished at Doc's death in 1965, which was also published in 1983. *The Armlet of the Gods* is the second in a four-novel fantasy, the first volume of which was *The Land Beyond the Gate*.